Facing Truth

THE ROSE TRILOGY

Facing Truth

THE ROSE TRILOGY

JODIE LOUISE VAIL

ACKNOWLEDGMENTS

After writing for more than 10 years, it's safe to say that this book has been a long-time coming. And yet, I praise God for the inspiration to write such stories.

Through this journey, there have been many people who have stood by me. I wanted to take a moment to acknowledge these wonderful humans.

My parents, Mama and Papa Bear, who have had many random and unusual conversations with me. There aren't many people in my life who can understand my weird dances as words or phrases.

My sister, who would only have to say 'yes', and I would often remember the word I was looking for. She has inspired some of these strong characters.

My best friend, Naomi, who, still to this day, will always inspire me. I couldn't write about friendship without knowing what it truly meant. Thank you.

My sweet husband, Jesse. Oh, how I love you. I'm so thankful to have you championing me through this.

Thank you to everyone else who supported me.

We did it.

CHAPTER
One

"Rose!" A voice squeals from behind me.

My heart jumps in my chest. I turn to see who it is, and I'm greeted by a familiar face. A dainty, confident girl waves at me from across the corridor with gleaming emerald eyes. She takes a moment to glance back at her male admirers to wave flirtatiously. There's a smile spreading on my lips as she begins her catwalk; her hips swinging side to side. She always did it when she knew people were watching.

Tutting loudly at her, I shake my head disapprovingly. She flutters her eyes at me, a picture of innocence. Mindlessly, she flicks her hair; the long black mane she possessed was rather suited to her name.

"Ebony!" I say with a pointed look.

Her raised eyebrows don't fool me. I knew exactly what she was doing and so did she. Poking her gently in the ribs, Ebony bursts into giggles and throws her arms around me.

"How are you?" she asks as we part.

I shrug, "I'm okay, I guess."

In all honesty, I didn't want to talk about me. I'd been feeling weird since the beginning of half term. Secretly, I'd hoped returning to college would help me feel a sense of normality again. Ha! College, normality, who would've thunk it?

"I love the new outfit. You actually added some colour!" I tease.

Hoping it'll take the focus off me; I gesture to her pale blue, sleeveless turtleneck. She beams at me and tells of her shopping trip over the holidays. We link arms as I slam my locker door shut. We saunter together along the busy hallway, catching up on our recent endeavours.

"How was your half-term?"

People dash by as we walk further into the college. I give a brief overview of my holiday and skip the unusual happenings and experiences. My topics remain around my mum, revision and driving lessons. I wasn't ready to talk, and even if I was, I doubted Ebony would believe me.

"Oh, same. Apart from driving with your mum, obviously," Ebony agrees.

I can't help the little laugh that escapes my lips.

"What?" she gasps and turns to me, feigning disbelief.

"You liar!" I laugh, "You spent all your time with your *oh-so-lovely* admirers… One in particular," I add mockingly with a wink.

Adam, that was the one she liked. He was definitely the *pretty boy* of the bunch, with his blonde hair, blue eyes, and big, muscular arms. Well, I didn't blame her. He could be rather decent when he wanted to be. However, catching him when he wasn't saying something flirtatious was rather like seeing a rainbow.

Although, that's what Ebony liked; the tease. Playing coy was a sport to her, knowing that nothing would ever really come from it. She didn't want anything serious. Just a bit of harmless fun.

"I didn't!" Ebony frowns.

She walks off in a playful sulk. As she gets further away, I wait for her to stop and throw sorrowful glances at me. When she doesn't turn, I call after her and hurry to catch up.

"Hey! I'm only playing."

Ebony sticks her tongue out at me and pretends to reluctantly link arms again.

"So…" I say after a long pause. "*Did* you revise?"

"No, of course not," she replies.

We both erupt with laughter that fills the emptying hallway and even catches a teacher's attention.

"You sound like two old women when you cackle like that!"

A deep, mocking voice pauses long enough for us to find who the insult came from. Ebony spots him first and we both throw teasing glares at the tall, olive-skinned boy with a grin pasted on his face. His black canvas bag is crushed between him and the blue lockers he's leaning on. For a second, his hazel-forest eyes wash over me and then flicker to Ebony. The boy strides towards us and I reach out to hug him with my free arm. It's slightly uncomfortable with Ebony's eyes on me. Her disdain is clear as I continue to interact with the 'enemy'…

My other best friend.

"Hey Shark-Finn," I smile, using his nickname.

We had chosen it when we were little, and it had stuck for many years since. He even had a nickname for me. Subtly, I glance over at Ebony who's staring out the window, ignoring Finn. This was a reoccurring behaviour in response to Finn's presence. I could never tell if it was a joke or not.

"Hello Rosebud," he grabs my attention again.

There's a short pause as his gaze flickers between Ebony and me. He can feel the awkward tension build around us and tries to defuse it, unsuccessfully.

"Aw, come on, are you still not talking to me?" Finn says with a laugh, "I thought you and I had something special…"

Finn playfully goes to poke her on the arm, but she grabs him before he can make contact.

"Don't you dare," she snaps and presses her nails into his skin.

A warm rose tinge fills his cheeks as Finn retracts his hand from her grasp and apologises. I can't help feeling sorry for him. Her response was way out of line, even if she didn't like him.

"Was that really necessary, Ebony?" I ask, trying to defend Finn.

"Yes," she says sharply.

I lightly pinch her on the elbow which makes her squeak and scowl at me.

"What was that for?"

"You know what. Stop it, okay?" I say with a warning.

This rivalry had been going on since we started college last year. I was the common denominator which was supposed to 'glue us together', but apparently it didn't work like that. Finn thought Ebony was a self-obsessed flirt and Ebony thought he was a, and I quote, "loser". Neither of them had got to know each other properly and that's why they probably never realised how similar they actually were.

I had known Finn since I was little; my parents were neighbours with his parents, so we used to play a lot in our garden. He moved away when his parents split up and we saw each other less. Whereas I met Ebony when she got kicked out of private school and joined in year eight. We immediately clicked. Now, six years later, we all go to the same college, yet they refuse to acknowledge one another. I had tried to smooth things over between them at the beginning, but it was to no avail. I never really understood it; they got along with me so easily, but I guess that was about as far as it goes where similarities were concerned.

"Anyways, I'll see you at lunch!" Finn smiles again, reminding me of our plans.

Agreeing, I wave goodbye as he strides down the corridor and wait until he is out of sight to scold Ebony.

"Really?" I mutter.

"You pinched me!" Ebony snaps.

"I'm sorry Ebs, but you need to get over whatever this is with Finn."

I sigh as we continue towards our first lesson. She exhales deeply, composes herself and grumbles under her breath. Amused, I stare at her expectantly.

"Yes?"

"He's an idiot," she states defiantly.

"I'm pretty sure he would say the same thing about you!" I tease.

"Rude."

We're both giggling again by the time we enter the English classroom. Thankfully, we're slightly early for class and take our place at the back of the room in the corner. Light danced through the windows filling the room with a vision of late spring. Potted plants near our corner look greener as the kaleidoscope of vibrant flowers is in full bloom.

A cool breeze washes over my skin as Ebony and I wait patiently for the other students to filter in. My eyes glaze over as Ebony starts to talk to another friend about her half-term. I listen half-heartedly; my eyes fixed on the whitewashed walls with my head in the clouds. When our teacher finally walks in, I snap out of it and tap the girls' arms to quieten them.

"Ah!"

I gasp as a sharp pain shoots up my hand. Pins and needles quickly follow, and I try to shake it out. My pulse is increasing as the shocks fire up and down my forearm.

Not again, fear whispers.

It's happening again.

My palms begin to sweat, and I can't concentrate on what the teacher is saying. I'd hoped it wouldn't happen here, but I was wrong. It had found me, and it was getting worse. With my mind racing, I try to make a decision on what I should do. It was obvious I was panicking as my lungs were tightening with each passing second. I needed to get some air…

Ebony's sudden touch stuns me into hearing her.

"Rose?" another voice calls loudly, "I said, Rose O'Donnell!"

Hastily, I snatch my hand away from the heat of Ebony's hands. The shock immediately calms so I flash her a sheepish smile.

"Did you hear a word I said to you, Rose?" Miriam, our teacher, asks irritably.

Embarrassed, I respond with an apologetic 'no' and she rolls her eyes.

"What's wrong with you?" she sighs, her tone lacking any sense of sympathy.

"I…" I try to answer, but I get distracted.

"Are you okay?" Ebony whispers.

"I-I-I need a few minutes," I stutter, "I'm… not feeling well…"

With a long exhale, Miriam nods and allows me to leave. She waves me off as if to hurry me away.

"Only come back when you're feeling up to it," she says.

As I stand up, Miriam continues calling the register and asking questions. Ebony's eyes are burning the back of my head. I know she wants to ask questions, but I can't bring myself to look at her. She whispers my name and I ignore it, pick up my bag and walk out.

Trying to steady my breathing is nearly impossible with every step I take. A teacher passes by and asks if I'm okay. I nod but they suggest I go to the First Aid room. If only they knew that I had already seen a doctor. Mum took me last week and they told me it was just anxiety.

It's just anxiety, you're okay…

Nausea rises, my hands trembling in front of me as cloudy confusion fills my mind. Before anyone else can stop me, I break into a sprint to the stairwells. I knew nobody would be there during lesson time so I could have some peace and quiet. The only way I could stop myself from getting worse was to breathe evenly and call Mum. Battling against me was a headache that pulsated in my temples, making it hard to concentrate. I needed to rationalise the whole situation and focus on my breathing.

In, two, three, four…

I count in my head as I take a seat on the cold, solid, concrete steps. There's a lot of dust around and I can feel it tickling the back of my throat.

Out, two, three…

"Hello?"

A voice echoes through the darkness, making me snap open my eyes. I hadn't realised I'd closed them until now.

Looking around, I see a face appear from the double doors at the bottom of the stairs. Concern is plastered on his face as he searches for something. When they find me, his expression softens, and he appears to be somewhat relieved.

"You had me worried," he says with a twang in his voice. I can't place his accent, but it's melodious and soothing as he continues to talk, "I thought you were going to be sick and I was going to say, you're going the wrong way."

The boy's smile falters once he gets closer.

"Oh, I didn't realise you were crying. I'm sorry, are you okay?"

Surprised, I touch my cheeks and sure enough, there are warm liquid rivers trailing down my face. I'd been panicking so much on the inside that I hadn't noticed the outward effects.

The thing was these shocks had been overwhelming me all week. I knew they weren't normal and now they were causing me anxiety. I guess maybe the doctor was right, I did have anxiety. He was wrong that it was what was causing it though. The anxiety was only a side effect of something bigger.

"It's okay," the singsong voice interrupts my train of thought.

He says something else, but I don't catch it.

"What?" I ask, dazed.

"I said, my name's Jasper," he smiles, offering a hand.

Looking at Jasper's hand, I hesitate. I notice his dark attire. He's wearing a leather jacket, a grey V-neck shirt and black jeans. Something seems familiar, but I can't recall where I've seen him before.

"You're supposed to shake it," Jasper says with a chuckle, "I won't bite you, I'm just trying to be friendly."

Forcing myself to focus, I immediately apologise and introduce myself. I'm unsure how to get out of the handshake, so I take it and hope for the best. To my surprise, there's no shock.

"So, Rose," Jasper says, taking a seat on one of the steps below me, "Why are you crying here all on your own? Has something happened?"

Shaking my head, I come up with a vague excuse to satisfy his question.

"It's not been a great week," I say, "I'm okay though. I was going to call my mum actually…"

My attempt to reassure him obviously fails as the frown on his face doesn't change.

"You know it's only Monday, right?" he states as his lips begin to curl into a grin, "Surely it can't be that bad. You have six more days to go before you can say it's a bad week."

His eyes light up as he tries to make me laugh, but I can't. The reality was, I had no idea how I was going to make it through the week.

"If you want me to leave you alone so you can call your mum, I can," Jasper says, already moving to get up.

"No," I blurt.

He had come to find me so I, at least, owed him a conversation.

"I appreciate your kindness," I force a smile, "It's just a really bad day for me, that's all. I promise it's really not you."

Nodding, Jasper's eyes glaze over in thought as he considers whether to ask more questions. In the prolonged silence, I study his angular face and realise where I've seen him before.

"You're Jasper King," I announce loudly, clearly startling him.

Overlooking the awkward moment, I explain my thought process: firstly, recognising his face, then, realising he's in my Biology class and finally, remembering his name from the register. I only stop talking when I notice the amusement on his face lighting up.

"What?"

"Nothing," he smirks, "I knew I'd seen you before too…"

His tone is low and playful. A blush sneaks in as he smiles at me. He's sweet, but I had only just gotten over someone who I'd been hopelessly chasing for years. Alas, that was another story for another time.

"Rose?" Jasper nudges me gently, "I thought I'd lost you again for a minute."

His smile is pearly and gleaming as he looks up at me. From this angle, I could see he was actually very attractive; his juniper green eyes, darkened ash-blond hair and sun-kissed skin were hard to ignore.

"Sorry," I smile self-consciously, "You've really caught me on the worse day, haven't you?"

My laugh is feeble as I try to make a joke.

"It's okay," he reassures me, "I'm just here to keep you company. If I can help, then great. If not, then let's just talk..." he pauses, "Well, I can talk, and you can keep getting lost in your own thoughts, hey?" Jasper winks and his smile widens.

Someone is coming.

The thought catches me off-guard; urgent and quiet. Before I can question it, an abrupt bang of a door grabs our attention. Both of our heads snap up to see who was intruding on us.

A couple of gossiping voices fill the stairwell and I exhale softly. I don't recognise either of them which suggests they're the year below us. Their footsteps tap on the concrete as they descend, giving us a countdown to their prominent arrival. One of the girls with long, toffee-blonde hair sees Jasper and giggles, before whispering something to her friend. They both cast lingering stares at Jasper as they scurry by and continue their countdown to the main hall.

"Anyway," Jasper says, unfazed, his eyes still on me, "I think we have Biology next, don't we?" He pauses to check his black, leather watch. "Shall we go together?" he continues, "Saves you having to talk to anyone on the way and we can get a quiet seat at the back if you're up to it?"

Nodding, I smile back. Jasper had been very kind to me and had made me wonder why we hadn't spoken before. His presence made me curious, and I liked that about him. I wanted to know more. My mind drifts to Ebony and how I left her so abruptly. She would be worrying all day if I didn't go and tell her I was okay.

"Can we see my friend first?" I ask, "It's just that I didn't really explain when I left the lesson earlier and I need her to know I'm alright."

Jasper raises his eyebrows and leans in towards me, "But are you okay?" his knowing look suggests he doesn't believe I am.

"Sure," I flash a smile, grabbing my books and bag from beside me.

We both stand up in unison and I join Jasper on his step. He's a few inches taller than me which is impressive when you're already tall.

"What?" he asks, mirroring my expression.

"Nothing," I reply, "Let's go!"

Leading the way, I skip down the stairs and check that he's following me. My anxiety has dwindled and I'm able to think clearly again. Jasper says something to me about doors, but I'm too busy planning what I want to say to Ebony. She's going to ask a lot of questions, so I need some good, but vague, answers.

Students busy themselves in the hallways as we pass through towards the English room. I look over to see where Jasper has gone and notice he's fallen behind me. Gently, he touches my elbow to let me know he's still there when he catches up. My confidence is fading as I get closer to the English room. Ebony's slender frame filters out of the classroom with a less-than-impressed face, until she sees me.

"Rose!" she says, making a beeline towards me.

Stretching her arms out, she wraps them around me and squeezes.

"Are you okay? What happened?"

Brushing off her concern, I tell her the same thing I told Jasper. She doesn't seem convinced but doesn't push for more. Instead, she spots the unfamiliar male presence beside me. I quickly introduce them, and it appears they recognise each other from last year.

"We did Art together," Ebony explains, "Did you drop it in the end?"

She looks at him with a tight-lipped smile. Only people who have known her for a long time would recognise that this meant she was uncomfortable.

"No," Jasper says, unaware of her growing discomfort, "I quite enjoyed it, so I decided to drop another class instead. I'm far more creative than I am academic."

"Cool," Ebony replies.

Her short response is enough to tell me that the conversation is over. I'm not sure why she's acting this way with him. I know I upset her earlier and maybe she was a little hurt that I hadn't told her what was going on.

Before we go, Ebony grabs my arm.

"Hey, call me when you get home, okay?" she says, meaningfully.

Her eyes flicker to Jasper and I can see she's expecting an explanation about him as well.

"Okay," I nod before leaving.

"TODAY WE WILL BE REVISING ALL EIGHT TOPICS..."

A loud voice booms through the classroom door and we know we're late.

Checking one of the clocks along the corridor, I see it's around four minutes past the time we're supposed to be there. I hold my breath and hope Fabian, our teacher, won't be too funny with us. Jasper opens the door first and we both creep into the back and head towards the seats near the window.

"Miss O'Donnell, Mr King," Fabian growls, "So nice to see you decided to show up."

"Sorry I'm late," I apologise quickly, but Jasper shakes his head.

"She wasn't very well so you're lucky she turned up at all," Jasper retorts and Fabian seems slightly taken aback.

"And what's your excuse?" Fabian says, narrowing his eyes at the boy who stood between us. "Too busy saving the damsel in distress, huh?"

He smirks, proud of his comeback, and there is a rumble of laughter from the class. The embarrassment is flushing pink on my cheeks as I avoid all eye contact.

"Hey!" Fabian snaps, making everybody jump including me. He then continues, "Come on, sit down. We can talk about it after class."

Following Jasper, we find our seats by the window and sit down. A few students mutter to each other, and I hear one commend Jasper for defending me. My cheeks are burning red by this point. In my peripheral, I can see Jasper pretending not to hear anything as he slides off his jacket. He scans the room, his eyes sparkling with confidence.

"Right," Fabian smiles, "have we done our revision over the holidays?" he asks, and everyone moans. "Clearly not, let's start with page one, shall we?" he tuts and starts writing up some notes on the board for us to copy down.

"Thank you," I whisper, leaning towards Jasper, "You didn't have to say anything though. We were late."

"Yeah," Jasper shrugs as he replies, "But Fabian is always mean to students because they're a minute or two late. He needs to lighten up or back off a bit. Nobody realises that we are all struggling with something so getting yelled at isn't going to help anyone," he turns to me and whispers, "You need to stand up for yourself more. Show them who you are, Rose."

Flattered, I try to hide the small smile that takes hold of my lips. My gaze drops to the tabletop as I fidget with my pen, unsure how to respond. Thick, copper-brown hair falls across my face, creating a barrier between me and his perfect smile. Jasper was extremely sweet and appeared genuinely concerned for me. He's almost too sweet, but I liked it.

After a while, I feel someone's gaze on the back of my head. I scan around the room to see who it belongs to. The room is full today of students and it's hard to work out who is watching me. I notice a girl along the back row with almond eyes and wavy hair framing her oval, pale face. She seems mildly unnerved by my presence and I realise I've never seen her here before. We both make eye contact for a split second which seems to upset her more. Jasper notices my distraction and follows my gaze. There's a snigger under his breath as he seemingly knows the girl. He mutters her name, but it isn't familiar to me.

"She's an ex of mine," he says, "She gets jealous very easily, so don't pay her any attention. It's pathetic really."

Despite not knowing her, I can't help feeling somewhat sympathetic towards the girl. Her expression suggested she was pained by my existence or maybe it was my close proximity to Jasper. Either way, I could feel her unease from across the room and I'm sure others could feel it, too.

"What happened?" I find myself asking and Jasper seems surprised.

"It's a long story," he whispers, "but, in short, she cheated on me with a guy from here, Adam."

"Really?" I ask and Jasper nods, solemnly.

Shaking my head, I can't quite believe it. It never made sense why people couldn't stick to one person at a time – some of us couldn't even get one interested. Jasper's gaze is fixed on me as I suddenly realise, I've started talking to myself out loud. He seems entertained by my monologue of thoughts.

"What?" I ask after he doesn't stop staring.

"Nothing," Jasper replies cryptically.

There's a brief moment where I want to ask him again, but Fabian calls our attention to the whiteboard. He explains a couple of units which other students are struggling with before letting us return to our revision. Thankfully, I'm familiar with most of the topics as Mum made sure I revised throughout half term. However, Jasper hasn't read anything. His knowledge is shocking which meant I spend my time teaching him rather than revising. In between topics, Jasper asks about my family and friends, especially Ebony. He seems to have quite the interest in her.

Of course, he does. I think to myself, *she's gorgeous.*

"Right then, you miserable lot," Fabian says with an awful cockney accent, "Time for lunch."

The room erupts with a buzz as students pack their bags and talk to their peers. It doesn't take long for the room to clear until Jasper and I are the only ones left. Fabian approaches us with an unreadable expression which makes me tense up. I hated being in trouble.

"Rose?" Fabian addresses me first which catches me off-guard, "Could Mr King and I have a minute to talk? I will see you next lesson," he says sternly, and I nod quickly, "Don't be late next time!" he adds.

As I turn to leave, I notice Jasper's fallen gaze and wonder if I should wait for him outside. I'm grateful Fabian has let me go with only a warning, but he must know Jasper was only sticking up for me. Hopefully, Fabian will let him off with a slightly stronger-worded warning. I'm almost out the door when Jasper glances at me and winks. His smirk says it all.

Maybe he really was fearless.

CHAPTER Two

G rinning to myself, I almost don't see the student in front of me before narrowly dodging them. I'm about to turn the other way when I recognise a boy with curly, chestnut hair. A relieved smile spreads across my lips as I say his name.

"Finn."

"Hello, you," his voice softens as he pulls me into a hug, "I heard you weren't very well today?" he says with a questioning look.

This takes me by surprise as I know this meant he's spoken to Ebony. She must be really worried to say something to Finn.

"I'm fine," I insist, "I just had a wobbly earlier."

Shrugging, Finn accepts the white lie and continues down the hall with me. I'd almost forgotten we had made plans for lunch today.

By the time we get to the cafeteria, we can see it's too busy. Finn turns to me, thinking the same thing, and we both head outside towards the car park. We find his red Volvo and I slip in the front passenger seat as he jumps behind the wheel. He puts the keys into the ignition, but then stops and turns to me.

"Rose?"

Finn seems to hesitate as he finds his words.

"Yes?" I reply.

There's a long pause which makes me feel nervous. He's not usually this quiet.

"What is it?"

"Nothing," he sighs.

Finn shakes his head and turns the key. I'm about to ask another question when he interrupts me with his own.

"Where would you like to go?" he says.

I shrug, there are not many places to go. I guess it'll have to be the usual.

"Annie's Diner?" he says with a smile, "Of course…" he chuckles as we reverse and pull away.

My eyes don't leave the busy road as Finn drives. He's eight months older than me so he's been driving for a long time. I'm still a baby. I turned seventeen last August and I had only just passed my theory test. Mum tried teaching me in her car which was eventful, to say the least.

"You seem quiet?"

Finn's calming voice pulls me out of my deep thoughts. He nudges my arm with his elbow to make me look at him.

"What's wrong?" he probes.

"Nothing, I was just thinking," I smile back.

Finn frowns and searches my eyes to see if he can read me. Usually, he's extremely good at working me out, mainly because I end up telling him everything. This time, I'm not letting up, so he gives up and changes the subject.

"So, how are you feeling about exams? Ready?"

Finn glances over at me but keeps his eyes mostly fixed on the road ahead. It's busy today because of the lunchtime rush.

"No… well… kind of. I'm not sure. I think I am…"

Finn chuckles to himself and I furrow my brows at him.

"What?"

I don't know what's so funny.

"You! You always have to worry about everything, don't you? You're going to ace these exams because you're awesome. You know your stuff so have a little faith in yourself," Finn reassures me.

He's right, I didn't need to worry so much. Even if I wasn't being very transparent at the moment, Finn knew when I was stressed. He also knew when I needed that little bit of encouragement. It was all part of the responsibilities of being childhood best friends.

"I know, I know," I say putting my hands up in surrender. "I just want everything to be perfect, y'know? I want to finish with good grades."

"And you will," Finn says, leaning over and grabbing my hand, "I promise…"

We look at each other for only a moment. I withhold the sigh as I get lost in his hazel-forest eyes. The remnants of butterflies were threatening to return. My hand begins to throb under his touch and pins and needles swell at the tips of my fingers. I want to let go, but I know he'll ask more questions. The ache is almost unbearable when he finally lets my hand go.

"So, what do you want for lunch?" Finn says, spotting the bright, blue lights of Annie's Diner on the horizon. "Chicken nuggets?" he winks, teasing me.

We had been enough times for him to know my order and that I always had the same thing. I liked their BBQ burgers and fries. It was my favourite.

When we get to the order station, Finn tells them what we want. I get a cream soda with my meal which disgusts Finn. He can understand why I like it, but I swear it's the best drink I've ever tasted.

"Thank you," Finn says to the lady before pulling away to wait in the queue.

"We're going to be late back," I state, realising how long the wait was, and Finn shrugs. "I guess we are *always* late to Adrian's class."

It's true, we always manage to be late. If I had to do an exam on being on time, I think I would fail. My timekeeping is… *interesting.*

"Then again, Adrian is never on time anyway," Finn laughs.

Once the food arrives, Finn drives us to our usual quiet spot that's a few minutes away and parks up. We had tried eating whilst driving before and it ended with a lot of drink and sauce over our laps. Finn opens the windows to let the cool breeze in. The sunlight streams through and warms the leather on our seats. Rays of light dance on my skin as we eat in a comfortable silence.

"Shall we head back?" he asks.

"Sure," I smile.

Gathering the rubbish, Finn opens his door and takes it to the bin. When he returns, there's a thoughtful look in his eye. I ask him what's up and he shrugs.

"If there was something wrong, you'd tell me, right?" he asks.

"Of course," I reply automatically.

UNABLE TO SHAKE AN UNSETTLING FEELING FOR THE REST OF THE DAY, I try to enjoy the lessons we have left. It's a double class of Acting which means I'm with Finn. This is both comforting and more unsettling. I feel as though I should tell him about the shocks and anxiety, but it seems irrelevant now. Until I work out more about what it was, I don't want to raise any alarm. He probably wouldn't believe me anyway…

"That was perfect you two, well done. I'm impressed!"

Adrian, our teacher, winks at us and throws us a thumbs-up. He gives his notes on our performance before addressing the whole class.

We've just finished doing our stage combat session which was based around dance and music. Finn wanted us to couple up and do a piece which was based on domestic violence. It seemed like a great idea at the start. However, my confidence wobbled once I got in front of the class.

"Okay listen up, you've all done a great job today…" Adrian praises the class. We were the last ones to perform before the lesson ended. "Have a great afternoon, I'll see you all on Thursday," Adrian finishes, and everybody gets up and quickly exits.

Before I can leave, Finn grabs my hand to ask me something. A shock explodes up my arm and it's enough to make me cry aloud, even Adrian seems startled. I try to brush it off, but Finn doesn't let me go. My arm is roasting under his grip and the sensation grows intensely.

"Finn!" I yell, snatching my hand away.

Surprise flashes across his olive-skinned face and confusion quickly follows. He opens his mouth to say something, but I interrupt him with a short apology and leave, embarrassed. I can sense him following me and up my pace, swerving through the flurry of students who are also finishing their day.

A couple of students bump into me by accident. I recognise the girl with wavy hair from Biology and a smile half-heartedly. Her glare makes me think of Jasper and how I left him with Fabian. I wondered if he was okay or whether I would see him again.

Pushing on, I'm almost at the main stairs. Finn is getting lost in the flow of students, so I take it steady on the steps. I weave my way through a couple of boys who are mocking each other loudly and one grabs my arm.

"Look at you," I hear him say, "I think you should come to our party don't you think?"

The boy and his friends start snickering and I rip my arm away from his grasp.

"Aw, did we scare you?" Another boy asks and presses his hand onto my shoulder.

There's an intense shock that runs down my spine and I'm barely able to hold it together. The boys are sniggering as I try to ignore the pain, humiliation, and spiralling anxiety.

"Rose?" a familiar melody rings in my ear and I feel an arm snake around my shoulders. "Come on, I'll take you outside," he says.

I exhale. *Jasper.*

Swiftly, he guides me through the crowds and politely, yet firmly, asks people to move out of the way. I'm shaking under Jasper's hold and I'm sure he can sense it. Tears have escaped down my cheeks again, so I hide my face, embarrassed. Finn must be far behind us because I can't see him when I glance back.

"This way," he whispers.

Jasper gently pulls me to the right as we exit through the main college doors. He finds a quiet spot near the flowerbeds and shields me from the flow of students.

"Glad I found you," Jasper says, his gaze bright and attentive.

"Thanks," I reply, but you can hear the strain in my voice.

Usually, I hated crying in front of strangers. Yet, this was the second time Jasper had found me unable to control my emotions. It wasn't a good first impression.

"I'm sorry," I say.

Nervously, I swallow the lump wedged in my throat and force a smile. Jasper calmingly tells me to breathe, counting each breath aloud. I exhale forcefully and look around as students pass by. It felt good to have fresh oxygen in my lungs.

"Better?" he asks, his arms folded across his chest.

Grateful for his kindness, I begin to say thank you when something catches my eye behind Jasper's head. The familiar, tall boy approaches us with a bewildered smile. His searching eyes study Jasper and then land on me.

"Rosebud?" Finn's voice is full of concern, yet there's an edge of caution in his expression. I think that's because Jasper's here.

"I'm sorry," I sigh, "I didn't mean to yell at you and explode like that. I'm just having a bad day…"

"You seemed fine earlier," Finn states, his tone bordering defensive.

My shoulders droop in defeat. Tears threaten again but I fiercely hold them off. I didn't know how to explain everything without sounding like I had lost my mind. Yet, the more I hid it, the worse it became, and the harder it was to hide. I didn't know much longer I could keep it in.

And this is only day one.

"Hey," Finn says, pulling me into a warm, secure hug. "It's okay," he repeats.

After a minute or two, I remember Jasper and step back from Finn, reassuring him that I was fine. I wipe the one escapee tear with my hand and begin the introductions. Jasper offers his hand and Finn takes it, grins, and shakes. Finn jokingly calls me his soul mate, but Jasper doesn't quite understand.

"Anyways," Finn continues, completely unaware, "I really want to stay, but I have to get back to something…" he glances at me to check, and I nod.

"Don't worry," Jasper interrupts the silent conversation, "I'll look after her."

"Yeah, I was going to call Mum anyway," I say, taking my phone out of my pocket as if to prove it.

"Okay," Finn nods, pulling me into him and kissing me on the forehead. "Right, I'll see you later, okay?"

Smiling, I wave as he strides off toward the car park and disappears out of view. He always kisses my forehead, the same way my dad used to when I was upset. It was his way of comforting me when he couldn't do anything else. Somehow, it really worked this time, and I felt my head clear of all anxiety.

"Your boyfriend really cares about you," Jasper says suddenly, snapping me back into reality.

"Oh," I shake my head and try to explain, "No, Finn isn't my boyfriend. He's a… a close friend of mine. We've known each other for years."

"I see," Jasper nods, "Then, let me give you my number. I'm sure you have space for another guy in your life," he says as he gets his phone out.

Trying not to blush, I agree to exchange numbers and swap phones.

"Don't worry, I'm not looking to replace him, I'm just hoping for another close position."

Once we've put our details in each other's phones, we switch back and I see he's put a cute monkey emoji next to his name. I giggle and finally meet his gaze. He's beaming at his phone and typing something. A second later, a message pops up on my screen.

Jasper: Hi! Is this the pretty lady I've been thinking about all day?

His flattery is making my cheeks hurt from smiling. It's not fair that on my worst day, I finally meet a guy who wants my attention. I mean, why is he being so flirty? I never get this kind of attention.

"What is it?" Jasper asks.

"I mean you're sweet, but I barely know you…"

"I know," Jasper cuts in, understanding my response, "But I want to get to know you better. Is that okay?"

"I think I can allow it," I reply.

Abruptly, my phone starts ringing, and I look down to see who's calling me. It's Mum and I realise she must be waiting for me to tell her to come and pick me up. It was already ten minutes later than when I usually call her. Jasper sees the name on the screen and mouths something to me that I don't understand. It's followed by a smile, so I mirror his expression. With a nod, he walks away and waves goodbye. I'm beaming when I bring the phone up to my ear.

"Hello darling," I hear her chime.

"Hey Mum, are you okay to pick me up now?" I sigh once Jasper has gone.

"Sure, I'll be there soon."

SUNLIGHT IS WARMING MY BARE SHOULDERS AS I WAIT FOR MY MUM to arrive. Most of the students have gone home or got into their cars. A couple of students walk by, and I watch as they laugh with their friends. It makes me think of Ebony and Finn and how I wished our friendship could be.

Today felt like the longest day and I was exhausted. There were too many confusing events to process. Mum's advice would be to sleep on it. She said everything felt better in the morning. I could almost hear her soothing, sweet voice in my head calling to me...

Oh, wait...

"Rose!" her voice shouts across some commotion in the car park.

Immediately I recognise her dark green Corsa behind a red Honda Civic and chequered black and white Mini. I spot the boy who's driving the Civic from the stairs and hide my face. Keeping my head down, I scurry towards Mum's car and slip myself in. She has all the windows rolled down and the seats are warm. Mum is chuckling at my shifty behaviour when I put my seatbelt on. Her sunglasses shade her chocolate brown eyes that are shooting me sideward glances.

"Hello darling. How was your day?" she asks, putting the car into gear.

I exhale loudly. Immediately, Mum tuts and pushes her sunglasses up onto her head.

"That bad, huh?"

I shrug my shoulders and stare out into the almost empty car park.

"It's not been the best day ever, I have to say." My voice is heavy with sarcasm which makes Mum stifle a laugh.

"Me neither Rose," she says with a deep sigh. Mum's hand reaches over and squeezes my leg to reassure me. "Well, it's a good excuse for a visit to the beach. Come on!"

Mum hums thoughtfully as she steers the car away. I turn on the radio and we listen to music for the full thirty-minute journey.

Ever since I was little, Mum had never been able to drive and talk at the same time, so we always had music on. She was a good singer too. Somehow, she could sing and drive but not talk. It was funny how her brain worked. Mine was similar.

"Here we are, darling, let's go!" Mum announces as we pull up.

When we get out, we hurry to take off our shoes and socks before starting down the low cliff towards the sandy beach. She's taken me to A Rún (ah-roon) which was a term of endearment meaning secret. My Dad had named it that before I was born. It was his and Mum's secret hideaway.

They met here when Dad was camping out for a weekend away. Mum had been on a long walk and heard him singing to himself. He invited her to join him which led to them talking by the campfire all night. Mum said she knew she was already falling for him, and it scared her. After that night, she wondered if she would ever see him again. But of course, like any fairy tale, they met again by chance and decided to not let this one go. They began dating for a short while and got married the following year. Mum always made it sound so magical.

Now, Mum's thirty-eight but still looks about twenty-eight. With her long, dark, brunette curls and pale, freckled skin, she doesn't seem to have aged at all. In my entire seventeen years of existence, she's never even got a single wrinkle on her face.

"Come on, tell me what's wrong then?" Mum says.

We're about midway across the small beach and the sand is hot beneath our toes. I look at Mum and shake my head; where do I begin?

"It happened again, like at least three times," I sigh.

Mum knows exactly what I mean and stops in her tracks. Her face is covered in concern. "What caused it?"

"I'm not sure," I shrug, "They were the same shocks I had before, but I kept getting anxious afterwards. Jasper," I pause as I mention his name and see the arch rise in Mum's brow, "Well, he kind of found me and managed to keep me calm."

There's a pause as Mum stares thoughtfully into the distance before asking more questions.

"Did you tell anyone about it? Like Ebony or Finn?"

Shaking my head, she lets out a long, deep sigh and wraps an arm around my shoulders. Gently, she pulls me into a warm, reassuring hug and strokes my hair repetitively. It was her way of comforting me when she didn't know what to say. I knew this because I did the same. Hugs seemed to say what we couldn't.

"I'm sorry darling," she mutters, "We'll work it out, I promise."

Nestling my head into her shoulder, I found myself in a state of unexpected peace. Five, ten, maybe more, minutes pass as we stand in our embrace, listening to the waves.

"So," Mum says after a while, "Who's Jasper?"

Nervous laughter escapes my lips as I pull away from her embrace. Mum's concern has been replaced with a child-like giddiness. She loved teasing me about boys, especially now that I had just about gotten over my long-time crush on Finn. It was a secret that only Mum knew about.

"Well?" she says, expectantly.

We both wander along the beach again to find a rock or two to perch on.

"Nobody special," I sigh, "He found me after English and kind of kept me company for the morning."

Nodding, Mum takes a seat on one of the big, black rocks and pats the one beside her. I sit instinctively, confused by the flurry of butterflies in my stomach.

"Rose?" Mum calls my name gently, already knowing I was in another world again. "So, what does he look like? Is he tall? Have you stalked him on social media yet?" she teases.

"No," I squeal in embarrassment, "Oh my days Mum! That's weird…"

"But true," Mum says with a wink.

I'm giggling as I shake my head and start to describe Jasper. I mention his darkened ash-blond hair, juniper eyes and unusual melodic voice which Mum seems to approve of. I also mention that we exchanged numbers before he left. This seems to pique Mum's interest.

"He gave you his number?" Mum says. Her eyebrow is arching so high, it might touch her hairline.

"Yes, we exchanged numbers," I nod, feeling some heat in my cheeks, "I still can't believe he saw me cry though."

"Oh sweetie," Mum tuts, "It's okay, if he's the right boy then he'll understand," she plants a kiss on the side of my head, "Just be careful, okay?"

I nod and smile. Mum rests her head on mine as we sit peacefully. Our attention is drawn to the gentle rolls of the ocean. The soft chatter of the steady waves becomes slightly hypnotic as they reach the beach.

"Come on," Mum says and begins to stand up.

My eyes follow her questioningly.

"We're going to paddle, no arguments."

She offers her hand to help me up and I take it but wince as pain shoots through my palms. Mum gasps quietly.

"It's okay," I wave her concern away, "I'm alright, don't worry."

The tide is almost completely in and so we don't have far to go. The soft, warm sand becomes cool and wet as we approach the open sea. Mum and I look at each other before racing in and squealing as our feet immediately freeze. The salty waves catch the bottom of my jeans. Icey water soaks through the denim but I don't care. Mum is singing and giggling as she tries to adjust to the water. I'm shaking as I navigate my way towards Mum. She smiles at me and pulls the skirt of her maxi dress to her thighs in an attempt to stop it from getting wet.

"Mum?" I call out, stopping in my tracks.

A huge, wild wave is rushing towards her, and I've already started retreating. I'm unable to tell Mum to run and watch helplessly as it soaks her.

"Oh no! Mum, are you okay?"

I apologise through my laughter, but Mum is already storming towards me. A wicked grin leaks from her lips.

"You cheeky monkey!" she says with a laugh. "You tried to distract me…"

"I didn't! I'm sorry, I'm sorry!" I squeal as I try to escape her wrath. "Please!"

My words are interrupted by laughter. I can barely stand up as she tickles me.

"Serves you right!" Mum says, ceasing the attack.

Leaving Mum to enjoy the waves, I find a spot in the sand and try to squeeze some of the salt water from the hem of my jeans. My smile grows as I watch Mum splash with reckless abandon. Nobody understood my Mum the way I did; she was an adult with a child-like approach to life. All I wanted was to be as happy as her.

"You got bored quickly then?" I ask Mum cheekily once she returns.

"No, I just realised I can't leave a child unattended," she replies equally sassy.

"Hey!" I protest.

She always calls me a child. I'm not a child. Technically speaking, yes, I'm not eighteen yet but still; I'm not a child, I'm just not a 'legal adult'.

"You know I don't mean it!" she cuddles me before straightening up again, "Come on, we need to go home!"

She takes my hand, and we wash our feet off in the shallow waves before heading back to the car.

"So Rose, what do you want to do for your big eighteenth?"

My eyes light up; I've been planning my eighteenth since my last birthday. I had always wanted a fun party where it wasn't about being wild and crazy. It's a new chapter in a girl's life and I want to celebrate the ending of my childhood properly... with bouncy castles and ball pools. Mum always preferred something like that because she didn't want me getting into any trouble. After all, it's my last day of being Mum's 'little girl'.

"Do you still want a bouncy castle and ball pool?" Mum purses her lips and waits for me to nod. She already knows my answer. "How did I end up with you?" she chuckles.

I wrap an arm around her waist and shrug, "You love me though…"

"Yes, I do…" she agrees.

"Enough for a ball pool and bouncy castle?" I try cheekily.

Mum scoffs and then thinks for a moment.

"Well… I guess…"

27

Already finishing her sentence before she can, I pull her in for a big squeeze to thank her.

"But on one condition, Rose…" she pauses and gives me a pointed look, "We get to have a go before everyone else arrives!"

Her face crinkles into another wide smile.

"Oh Mum!" I whine.

CHAPTER
Three

Pop music blasts from the radio as we drive back to the house. The sun is lowering in the sky as we get closer to the centre of town. Great Hills tower over the town and cast a jagged shadow that shields us from the sun's light. Greenery smothers the hills whilst delicate wildflowers line the roads. It's beautiful here in Corden. So ordinary yet completely extraordinary.

We pull up to the house and Mum parks perfectly adjacent to the garage. I quickly get out, grabbing the house keys, and run around to open the front door. Mum follows me in with her handbag and damp towels before disappearing into the kitchen. I skip upstairs to put my college bag away. When I notice the mess on the floor, I take the opportunity to tidy my pink palace.

Mum loves the colour of my room. We picked it together when I was about five and it took three days to paint because I accidentally got in and drew on the walls. What can I say? I was a creative child. I loved the bright flamingo and candyfloss pinks when I was still a little princess. Yet now the colours were too bright for my pastel taste. I had grown up and the fairy tale was much less vibrant than the one I had known.

Once everything is back in its place, I grab my books and revise. My phone pings a few times and I check to see who's texted. Ebony's bold name tells me she is waiting for me to update her. I'm reluctant at first and sigh as I press to call.

"Hey," her voice appears after a couple of rings, "Are you okay?"

"Hey, yeah," I reply, leaning back in my chair, "I guess I owe you an explanation."

We talk for an hour as I try to give a vague excuse for my disappearances and strange behaviour. She seems okay about it once I tell her I've seen a doctor. Thankfully, she doesn't ask much more, satisfied I'd given her the answers she wanted. What has really caught her attention is this mysterious Jasper.

"He's just a friend," I assure her.

As we hang up, Mum calls me for dinner. I run down to clear the table and put the cutlery out whilst Mum dishes up. By the smell, I guessed it was Spaghetti Bolognese; one of my favourites.

My mouth was watering by the time we sat down to eat. Manners are left behind as I inhale my food, barely feeling it touch the sides of my stomach. Mum, on the other hand, is far more controlled and takes delicate, small mouthfuls. I guess I was my father's daughter, lacking poise. When Dad was home, he thought I was hilarious. Mum, however, did not.

"Rose?" Mum says abruptly.

"Yes?"

I look up and notice her lips are curling as though she's holding back a smile. Her eyes are gleaming as she reaches over to hold my hand.

"I got a letter today about your father."

My heart begins racing.

"He's coming home in September!" she says, her eyes sparkling with tears.

My heart jumps for joy; I can't believe it. I'd heard the rumours about the government bringing the soldiers back for Christmas, but I didn't like getting my hopes up. Dad's been in the army since I was nine. I was so used to him being away for long periods of time, it was hard to imagine him being back this soon.

"For good?" I ask.

Mum nods, holding a hand to her lips. She had been waiting for news like this for years. She missed him and so did I.

"Mum! That's… that's great!"

My cheeks hurt from the huge smile on my face. Mum is still nodding and laughs as a few tears roll down her face. I get up to hug her and stroke her back soothingly. Then, the excitement comes, and we rock side to side, giggling.

"I'm so happy for you."

"Oh darling, I'm happy for both of us. We're going to be a family again!" Mum wipes her eyes as I sit back in my place.

It's been twenty-one months since we've seen Dad and those months haven't been easy. Mum is a strong woman, but this almost pushed her to the limit. To know that Dad would finally be home for good was like having all the year's celebrations in one.

Motivated by the news, Mum and I start to plan trips and parties and other fun things for us to do as a family. It's so far away, but I already know I want to share my birthday with his coming home party.

"What about your big eighteenth?" Mum asks.

Shrugging, I tell her I don't mind postponing. Dad was coming home and that was worth waiting for.

Together, we stack the dishwasher and I wipe down the table. Everything is tidy and put away for Mum, just as she likes it.

"Darling," her voice is gentle, "Now that we know he's coming back, we need to keep it quiet. I know that might be hard but as they haven't made it official publicly… we'll just have silent parties for now. Is that okay?"

I'm nodding as she squeezes my arm and leads us into the living room. We've exhausted ourselves and decided a film was in order. Mum is still eagerly planning on her laptop what we could do for Dad's return. Tiredness sets in for me as I cuddle into her side. I feel myself drifting and my eyes are lowering by the second until I'm almost asleep.

Gently, Mum nudges me awake and takes me to bed. She's giggling and telling me about her ideas for Dad's party but I'm barely awake enough to listen. We sit on my bed and talk for a little while until I'm practically asleep again. She kisses me gently on the head and tucks me in before whispering, "Good night." As she leaves, she closes the door slightly, so a little bit of light is coming through. I hated complete darkness.

Dad's coming home, I think to myself as sleep takes over.

"GOOD MORNING," MUM'S VOICE CHIMES AS I ENTER THE KITCHEN.

She's dressed in her black trouser suit with a half-unbuttoned white pinstripe shirt. Her face beams whilst she sits at the dining table. Her reading glasses lay beside her on a folded-up newspaper that she's finished perusing. A mug of steaming hot tea, her favourite, is sitting on a coaster on her other side. She picks it up and takes a sip, watching me as I sit down beside her.

"Morning Mum, I like your outfit today," I say as I pick up the bowl Mum's left out for me.

I begin filling it with sugary cereal whilst Mum gets up and flicks the kettle on, anticipating my desire for a hot drink.

"Thanks darling," she says and leans on the kitchen surface, waiting.

Mum's arms are folded across her chest, and I notice a small pendant dangling around her neck. It's the one Dad gave to her before he proposed. She barely wore it because she was afraid that she would lose it, but I assumed it was her way of celebrating Dad's impending return.

"How are you feeling?" Mum asks, and I shrug.

The nerves had finally set in for the exam today and I was hoping that somehow, I would get through it. I'd done a lot of revision and I knew most, if not all, of the potential questions that would come up. I didn't need to worry really and knowing Dad would be coming back soon definitely gave me a confidence boost.

"Thanks," I say as Mum hands me a fresh cup of milky tea.

She stirs the sugar in and taps the spoon on the edge three times before allowing me to take a sip. The steam warms my nose and cheeks as I enjoy the sweet taste of breakfast tea. I swallow more than intended and it burns my tongue and throat. I'm quick to place the tea down as I fan my mouth to cool it down.

"It's really hot!" I pant making Mum laugh.

"Really?" Mum's words drip with sarcasm, "…and there was me thinking that tea was supposed to be cold."

"You know there's iced tea…" I tease back.

"Yes, but why anyone would enjoy that is beyond me."

We burst into giggles as I shake my head at her. She places her hand on mine and squeezes tightly, sending a soothing wave up my arm.

"Right," Mum says, "I'm going to go in early today to catch up with some work I've been putting off."

I frown at her as she starts to stroke my cheek gently. I'd been looking forward to a lift with her. We had more celebrating to do.

"I'm behind in almost everything because Mr Sandwell decided he didn't like my pitch, so I need to go in and get a head start," Mum sighs.

She works at Bonvier, an advertising agency. Most of the time she is completing creative work for them, but her boss likes to make her job far more complicated by being extremely difficult.

"Do you mind?"

"No," I say with a reassuring smile, "I'm sure Finn or Ebony can pick me up."

"If you're sure?" she asks. I nod and she exhales. "Well, I hope it goes well today."

"Thanks, I hope you get lots of work done and Mr Artsy-Fartsy is nice to you," I say with a grin.

"Thanks," she mutters, "And darling? Say hi to Jasper for me," Mum winks as she strides towards the kitchen door. "See you tonight, love you!"

Laughing now, we both blow kisses to one another before she exits. I hear the front door slam behind her a few minutes later and the house is left eerily quiet. My mind drifts to Jasper as I remember our conversations yesterday. I checked my phone when I woke up and saw he had sent a message. I'd not responded yet because my mind was on other things, but now I felt I should finally reply.

Rose: Hello stranger, how are you?

Beaming, I reread his message as I wait for his reply. I notice he's called me 'friend' in capitals. I knew he was being flirty, but I didn't mind. I enjoyed the attention, and it took my mind off all the crazy things that had been happening. Jasper seemed sweet and I knew Ebony would love to hear all about it.

Jasper: I'm good thank you, how are you? Ready for another day at college?

I'm laughing as I reply with a witty comment. He seems to like it and jokes back. Jasper suggests we have lunch together and I agree on the condition that he buys me a milkshake. He appears amused and tells me to meet him after my morning exams. Checking my phone, I see that Ebony and Finn haven't responded to my earlier texts. I'm showered and dressed when my phone finally rings. Finn's name flashes up with an old picture of us and I answer.

"Hey Rosebud," he says cheerfully, "I was going to message you but then I thought it would make more sense to call you. I'll be at yours in ten minutes, okay?"

"Can we make that fifteen?" I ask, hoping I can buy myself some more time to look moderately decent.

"Sure," he agrees, "Oh, will you do me a favour? I need to borrow that book for Performing Arts. It's for the course work…"

"Yeah sure," I reply and there's a long pause. Finn huffs unexpectedly which bothers me, "What is it?"

"Nothing," he says, but I know that's not true. I wait for him to continue, "It's just that I'm worried about you. You seemed really upset yesterday…"

A pang of guilt settles in my stomach, but I will it away. I'm trying to convince myself as well as Finn that it was okay. To put his mind at ease, I decide to tell him about the doctors and my anxiety when he picks me up. It's not the whole truth, but hopefully, it'll suffice for now.

Grabbing my key and bag, I walk out the door. I've assembled myself adequately for the day in a floral, yellow dress and boots. I feel nervous as I think about the exams and seeing Finn. The rush is enough to push me out into the fresh air and take a deep breath.

As I lock the door, I settle my nerves and run down the path. I can hear a car pulling up and see Finn's beaming smile. He lowers his shades to flash me a silly face before opening the passenger door. Slipping in beside him, I barely have a second to click on my seatbelt before Finn has pulled away. Nobody speaks at first and we listen to the low hum of an old indie band. Finn had been obsessed with their original album and I could agree that it was a good one. I hum along and stare out the window, watching the white lines on the road.

"Rose?" Finn says, turning the music off. "What's going on?"

Shrugging, I begin my rehearsed monologue, "I've been not feeling well over the half-term and- "

"What kind of unwell?" Finn interrupts, taking me by surprise.

In the rehearsal of this conversation, I didn't get interrupted once. Every time, Finn would simply listen and accept it. I wasn't prepared for any questions.

"Um," I frown as I quickly think of something, "It's hard to describe," I stumble over the question and try to move on, "But, Mum took me to the doctors, and they said it was some kind of anxiety. It's all very new and I think going back to college triggered it."

"Oh," Finn mutters to himself, "Well," he looks at me with bright eyes, "I guess we just have to work out what's triggering it and avoid it at all costs, hey?"

A joyful smile returns to his face, and I feel my nervous heart steady itself as I nod. We draw closer to the college acknowledging that nothing more needs to be said. Now that Finn has accepted my excuse, I lean back in my chair and close my eyes. Finn turns up the music and we hum along contently. It's a peaceful few minutes before we arrive on college grounds.

"Ready?" Finn asks and I nod.

"Ready."

IT'S A LONG MORNING OF EXAMS. I MEET UP WITH EBONY FOR ONE OF them and she seems slightly off. With the rush of nerves, I try not to overthink it. The rest of the students are all buzzing with anticipation, and I soon catch the feeling too.

Before we go in, I tell Ebony that I'm going to lunch with Jasper which seems to upset her. She turns her back on me as we wait to go to the exam and sighs. I try to ask what's wrong, but she shrugs and starts walking into the exam. I notice that she doesn't sit near me, either. It throws me off and I keep glancing at her throughout the exam.

Hoping she'll wait for me I scurry out of the exam hall and search for her. There's a sea of students which makes it hard to spot anyone. Someone touches my hand, taking me by surprise.

"Rose?" a voice chimes through the bustle.

"Jasper?" I say, confused.

Then I remember; we were meeting for lunch. Could it be that time already?

"I know I'm a little early…"

Jasper extends a hand to help me through the crowd and I stare at it blankly, wondering if I wanted to chance another shock. Much like yesterday, I notice he's wearing a black t-shirt with his skinny jeans and leather jacket. Awkwardly he retracts his hand and smiles politely.

"I'm guessing you're not a physical touch person, hey?" his laugh is slightly forced, and I cringe.

Good job, Rose. I scold myself.

"How was it?" Jasper changes the subject, nodding to the exam hall.

I hear him, but my mind is on Ebony still. I can't help wondering what's upset her so much. Maybe something is going on and I should find her. But then again, I promised Jasper lunch.

"Okay, I guess," I answer instinctively, and spot the searching look in Jasper's eyes, "Sorry, my friend was upset with me earlier and I don't know why," I sigh, "I'm trying to work out what I did wrong."

"Ah," Jasper says, understanding, "Well, if you would like, you can go find her and sort it out now…"

"No, I already tried that," I shake my head.

I know Ebony has another exam soon, so she won't have a lot of time. If anything, she'll come to me afterwards if she's ready. I just hate not knowing what I've done wrong.

"Come on," Jasper says, putting an arm around my shoulder, "Let's go and talk it out," he smiles, "Think of me as your agony aunt."

Resisting the urge to roll my eyes, a smile curls up on my lips as we head towards the canteen. He continues to boast about his ability to help resolve issues, and I simply elbow him in the ribs. This stops him altogether and he stares, mouthing the word 'wow'.

"You asked for it," I tease.

"Okay," he nods, "But you aren't getting a milkshake now."

Gasping, I pretend to be hurt and we both start laughing. We stroll into the canteen and see that it isn't so busy today. That's probably because a lot of the students are in their exams. It makes me thankful for dropping Maths this year. A lot of people I know chose it and would say it was academic suicide.

"So," Jasper says as we sit down at one of the tables near the window, "Tell me what's happened…"

Shrugging, I exhale, "I really don't know."

For some reason, I end up telling him everything about Ebony which is relieving. I explain the feud between her and Finn as well as how I've always been in the middle. He asks me a few questions about her as a person and I begin to feel like I'm doing her an injustice.

"She's a great person," I insist, "I don't want you to think she's bad because she isn't," I pause and notice Jasper is nodding as he listens, "I just think it's weird that she's awkward about... well others."

"Others?" Jasper asks, raising an eyebrow.

"Well, when I mentioned you this morning, she was pretty upset."

"Oh..."

"I mean, the only other time I've seen her like that is around Finn," I explain.

"Ah..." Jasper nods, "I see..."

Leaning back, his eyes flicker to me and then to the table. He plays with his dinner knife in deep thought which makes me wonder if I've said too much. I knew he wasn't going to be offended, but I had no idea what he was thinking. For all I knew, he could be thinking about something completely different.

Perhaps I was overthinking?

"Okay," Jasper says, leaning forward energetically, "I have an idea. How about we all get together after college and spend some time getting to know one another? I can get a sense for myself, and if they start falling out, I'll be there as backup. What do you think?"

Butterflies instantly flutter around in my stomach. I love the thought of them spending time together, especially when Jasper was eager to get to know them. I reckon Finn would appreciate the male company and Ebony might just play nicely if it was presented to her in the right way.

Immediately, we concoct a plan for a day at the beach, and I suggest A Rún. Ebony and I had spent last summer there when Finn went away to see his Mum. This would make it easy to convince her to visit. Then there was Finn. I knew he really wanted to visit as it had been a while, plus he loved the story about my parents. Unbeknownst to all, Finn was a closet romantic.

"Tell me," Jasper says with a pearly grin, "Would you like me to drive us there? Then, if we get some time after then I can take you out for dinner?"

Nodding, I rest my chin in my palm, hoping to hide the giddiness that swirled within. I'm sure he notices my grin, but he's sweet enough to not point it out. Instead, a softened glimmer replaces the hopeful look in his eyes.

"I think you're beautiful," he says.

This time, I can't hide the blushing. I don't dare look up in case he realises how flustered I am. I barely muster up a small thanks before Jasper's attention is diverted elsewhere.

"Right, I need to get going."

Jasper stands, scraping the metal chair legs across the canteen floor. This catches the opposite table's attention and one of the girls shoots a glare and makes a comment about manners. Jasper hears it and waves mockingly, making her scowl even more. He's completely unbothered as he turns and winks at me. I inhale rapidly and accidentally choke.

"Hey," Jasper leans in, his nose almost touching mine, "Don't forget to breathe," he whispers, chuckling as he walks away. "I'll text you, okay?" he calls.

Throwing him a thumbs up, I nod with my face as red as a plum tomato.

Gee, smooth, Rose, smooth.

Why did this fluster me so much? I needed to talk to someone about it, and Ebony seems to be the answer. I feel deflated when I think about her and the way she had been today. She didn't seem bothered about Jasper when we spoke yesterday.

Suddenly, my phone lights up as a text message flashes up on the screen. I'm hoping it'll be Ebony asking if we can meet up. The optimism fades as I see Jasper's name; he's telling me to stop being so glum. I search the room to see where he is and notice his broad shoulders leaning across one of the exits. His gaze captivates me for a brief second before he leaves, waltzing along the corridor against the new flood of students. Smiling now, I grab my stuff and decide to catch up with him. The powerful impulse urges me forward, through the warm, sweaty bodies. I feel so many variations of nerves and excitement from the crowd that I ignore the increasing pins and needles.

"Yes?" Jasper says, amused after I've tapped him on the shoulder.

"Um," the sudden loss of confidence throws me, "I just wanted to ask if I, um…" I feel myself shrink again into the nervous Rose I'm so fond of. "I just, um, wondered whether I could walk with you as, er, I'm going this way anyway and, um…"

"Come on," Jasper smiles, but the mocking glint in his eyes has faded, "I'm going to see our favourite teacher."

"Oh no," I tease in an attempt to recover from the mumbling idiot I had become, "Did he not scare you off?"

Laughing, Jasper shakes his head, "No," he sighs, "Nobody can scare me."

We spend the rest of our day together, laughing and studying. Most of the time, I forget about Ebony and Finn, even though Jasper mentions them. He seems sincere in wanting to spend time with them and this pleases me greatly.

When I finally get home, Mum is waiting in the kitchen with ingredients lined up and ready for cooking. Looking at the flour and water I think I can guess what we're making and get to work. I place my bag down, pull my hair back and wash my hands. Recently, Mum has been trying to teach me how to cook because she thinks I won't cope when I leave home. What she doesn't realise is that I'm *never* leaving home.

Cue the dramatic evil laughter.

"Right darling, we're going to make pizza," she says, pointing to the array of ingredients spread along the countertop.

We start by pouring the flour and water into a bowl and mixing it with yeast. I help her knead the dough and leave it to rise on the windowsill.

"Would you like chicken or bacon?" Mum asks, but we both know the answer.

"Both?"

Nodding, Mum starts to cook the meats. I help by frying off the bacon whilst she puts the chicken in a different pan. We prepare the vegetables by dicing them into small enough amounts to sprinkle on the pizzas. Once they are all done, I check the dough before splitting it in half. Mum rolls out her half and hands me the rolling pin. I make mine into a square and start putting sauce on top. Mum mentions something about the measurements, but I don't take it in. I'm too busy decorating the top with all my favourite flavours.

When it's finished, I look to Mum who has gone for a chicken and veggie pizza and smile expectantly.

"What?" she demands.

"Can I have mushrooms?" I say with big, pleading eyes.

Mum sighs and points to the fridge.

"Tha-anks," I say, skipping.

Mum explains how to cut them, but I already know. Placing them on top, I catch Mum nicking a few mushrooms for herself and I tease her.

"Oh I see! Now you want them!"

Mum nods and laughs, finishing her pizza masterpiece.

"Right then," she says looking at both pizzas, "Let's get you in the oven."

We put them on trays before placing them in the oven. It shouldn't take too long so we wait in the kitchen for them to cook. Mum sits at the table and asks about my day.

"So… how was it?"

How do I answer that? It had been a flurry of exams, laughter, weird best friends and a LOT of blushing. Mum would go giddy if I told her that Jasper had asked me on a date.

"Good," I reply, but Mum waits for more, "Well, actually… I think Ebony is jealous because I'm spending a lot of time with Jasper."

"Jasper?" she says, and I can visibly see her ears prick up.

Beaming smiles spread on both our faces as I begin to tell her about how he found me again today. I mentioned that we'd suggested getting everyone together for a beach trip after Ebony's weird behaviour during exams. Mum gives some positive murmurs and gentle nods, suggesting he's got the approval. I'm halfway through gushing about his eyes when Mum interrupts me to check on the pizzas.

"So, are you going to date him?" she asks, peering into the hot oven.

"I'm not sure," I admit as I watch her waft the steam from her face, "I think I'd like to see how it goes at the beach. He did mention going on a date afterwards."

Mum grabs the floral oven gloves off the counter and slips them on before taking out our pizzas. We grab two plates and decide to eat the pizzas in front of the TV. I've almost finished my second slice when Mum turns to me with concern in her eyes. She places a hand on my knee whilst putting her plate of pizza down on the floor, exhaling slowly.

"Sweetie," she says, "I know you already know this, but I need to tell you something about dating and this new boy, Jasper."

Nodding, I swallow my mouthful to speak, but she shakes her head.

"No, just listen," her voice is gentle but firm, "I know you're excited about this boy and I'm glad to see you happy, but I need you to know that if it doesn't work out, there will be others," she pauses and rubs my cheek with her thumb. "You are so young, and I don't want you getting hurt, so my advice would be to take things slow. Don't rush in because everyone else does, okay?" she pauses long enough for me to mumble an agreement, "Just be you, and I'm sure he'll love you."

As her words land, I feel an uneasiness set in and I can't quite work out why. Mum doesn't say anymore and wraps an arm around me, pulling me into a cuddle. When she kisses my head, the unwelcome feeling disperses, and I'm filled with a reassuring peace. I nuzzle down into Mum's side and let her steady breathing lull me to sleep.

My eyes close as dreams of juniper eyes come like a warm, welcoming embrace.

CHAPTER
Four

It's finally the weekend. Jasper and I have put the last bits and pieces of our plan together. Between study, exams, and a lot of stress, we've managed to organise the perfect day out. We've even got both parties to agree to come.

Yes, I'll admit that neither knows the other is coming, but Jasper insisted it would be better that way. If they didn't know, they'll come with their defences down, or at least that's what Jasper thinks. I'm not entirely convinced, but my excitement is overtaking any anxiety I could have.

"How are you feeling?" Mum asks as I rush into the bathroom.

She's doing her makeup and I can see she's slightly more tired today. I'd noticed she had woken up earlier than normal.

"I'm good, just really nervous," I reply, picking up my phone from the shelf.

In the rush of getting ready, I'd left it there playing music after my shower. It had been a mad dash around the house after my alarm didn't go off when it was supposed to. Thankfully, I was used to getting ready under pressure. Dad wouldn't have approved of my tardiness however, today I felt I had good reason to be.

As I'm about to leave, I catch a glimpse of myself in the mirror and try to spruce my hair up a bit. I've gone for soft waves, but I know they won't last long. My hair was so thick, it needed a bottle of hairspray to make at least one wave stick. Mum notices the growing impatience as my hair doesn't do what it's supposed to and tries to help. She finds a red product from the shelf and sprays it onto her hand. A white, shimmery foam forms and Mum gently rubs it between her fingers, before running it through my hair. Once she's done scrunching and playing, she stands out of the way so I can see. It looks so much better.

"Thank you," I kiss her on the cheek and run out, "You're the best!" I call down the hallway.

"I know," she replies quietly under her breath.

Galloping down the stairs, I check my phone to see if Jasper had sent me a text to let me know he's arrived. I see another text from Ebony pop up and she offers to take me in her car. I politely decline and explain that I have my own way of getting there. It was awkward keeping secrets from her, even if they were for her own good. I knew she would say no if I said Jasper or Finn were coming.

Ebony: Okay girl, I'll see you there.

I exhale as I read the text; she's on her way. Then, another text pops up on my screen and I check it immediately.

Jasper: I'm outside.

The bubbling nerves give way to excitement as I reread the text. I send him one back with a thumbs-up emoji. He sends a heart which sets off a whirlwind of giddiness. I had noticed these hearts growing more frequent in our conversations. It was clear that he liked me, but I wasn't ready to tell him I felt the same.

"Mum, I'm going!" I yell up the stairs.

There's a vague goodbye and good luck before I prance out the door, practically dancing as I lock it. I search for his shiny, black Range Rover that's supposed to be waiting at the side of the road. I notice all windows apart from the front are tinted and spot the driver. His charming smile is the first thing that gets my heart fluttering until he gets out.

He had never looked finer.

Black denim shorts reveal his thick, muscular legs and his half-unbuttoned navy shirt leaves nothing to the imagination. His eyes are shielded by retro sunglasses as he approaches me, car keys jingling in his hand. Jasper embraces me and I feel myself begin to sweat. I'm in a floral playsuit which suddenly doesn't feel light enough. There's a small tingle under my palms as I touch his skin. I'm taken aback by it and let go quickly. He frowns, confused.

"Everything okay?" he asks.

"Yeah," I assure him.

"Okay, good, because you look like an absolute dream."

Rolling my eyes, I pretend not to be flattered and divert my gaze to his car. I give him a cheeky comment about not wearing enough colour and he feigns being insulted. I shake my head and walk to the car giggling.

"Not today," he says, stopping me in my tracks.

Jasper joins me at my side and turns me gently to the left, pointing at a black, green and silver motorbike. My dad had one that he rode everywhere when I was little, but now it sat in the garage getting old and dusty. Only the blue blanket that covered it preserved the memories it held. The prospect of having to ride one now made me incredibly nervous.

"You look terrified," Jasper laughs, reading my expression.

Was I that obvious?

"Yeah, I...I don't think it's such, uh, a good idea," I stutter anxiously.

There's a long, unspoken conversation between us and we look at one another. Jasper won't take no for an answer and wins the silent argument. He thought I didn't 'adventure' enough. In other words, he wanted me to try new things more often, starting with this.

"Trust me?" he says, offering me a helmet.

Nervously, I take it. The smile on his face couldn't get any wider as he winks.

"You'll love it, I promise."

We strap our heads into the oversized bowling balls and mount the bike. Jasper has some fingerless leather gloves which he slips on before telling me to wrap my arms around him. To my dismay and secret delight, I hold onto his waist. I'm still battling the simmering anxiety as he pulls away. My closeness to Jasper holds my attention until I finally relax. I can't believe he's convinced me to ride with him. It's actually not that bad.

When we arrive, we both dismount and Jasper is humming with excitement. He had fastened the picnic and blanket to the back and somehow it had managed to stay secure. I wait for Jasper to untie the knots and look around to see if Finn or Ebony have arrived. The coast is clear, excuse the pun, and I exhale, relieved.

Wrapping my cream cardigan around me, the salty spray of the ocean tickles my face in the breeze. Jasper begins to ascend towards the beach with a picnic in hand and the blankets over his shoulder. He somehow produces towels from somewhere too. I follow and feel the exhilaration of the ride settle into giddy nerves.

"Finn?" a familiar voice finds its way to my ears.

"Ebony?" another familiar voice replies.

As I look up, I can see two faces peering down at me; one smiling and one ready to kill.

"I can explain…"

AFTER A ROCKY START, EBONY AND FINN AGREE TO SPEND THE DAY together. They seem surprised that I've organised this with Jasper. Yet, both play along and smile, even Ebony, who was more than reluctant to stay.

"Please Ebs?"

"Only because I haven't seen you in forever and I miss you," she says, rolling her eyes.

"What's the plan then?" Finn says with a grin.

Both Jasper and Finn had got on with setting up some games which Finn had brought. He'd never go to a beach without some kind of sporty game in the back of his car. Jasper suggests a game of volleyball, but Ebony doesn't want to play. Taking the opportunity, I suggest the boys play whilst I find out what's wrong with Eb.

"Have I done something to upset you?" I ask quietly, watching the ball fly over the net.

"No," Ebony replies sharply.

"Come on," I ask, "I don't understand what's going on. You have been off with me for a couple of days now and I just want to fix things."

Sighing, Ebony turns to me and shakes her head, "Nothing is wrong. I'm worried about you, and I feel like I can't do anything to help because you're not telling me what's going on. You're hiding something from me, Rose. I know you are… and I don't like it."

Sickening guilt prods at my chest and I'm unable to push it away. I'd been figuring out and researching to see if I could find more answers about the shocks. Every path led to insanity or impossibility. Neither was very reassuring.

"I'm sorry," I reply, "I wish I could tell you, but it's too complicated. I don't even understand it myself…"

My shoulders slump and Ebony is quick to put her arm around me. She lets me rest my head on her and begins to stroke my back as though to soothe the growing angst. There's a long, peaceful pause and I believe she's forgiven me. She wouldn't let me near her if she hadn't. This gives me the confidence to tell her everything – it seemed right even if it didn't make sense. I open my mouth as a striped ball comes flying into us.

"Heads!" Finn calls.

We squeal as it hits both of us.

"Sorry," Jasper says, his eyes filling with instant regret, "I think I may have hit that too hard…"

"Y'think?" Ebony sasses.

Tensions are high as I watch Ebony stand, throwing the ball between each hand. She considering how to get him back.

"Would it make you feel better if I let you hit me?" Jasper replies.

Watching the interaction, I can see where this is going. Ebony is already in position to throw.

"Um, guys…" I look between them and meet Finn's gaze. He seems amused by their rivalry. "I don't think this is a good…"

Bang.

The ball hits Jasper right between the eyes. It bounces off with a loud reverberation and deadly silence follows. Nobody can tell how he's going to take it. My eyes search both Ebony and Jasper before there's a huge explosion of laughter.

What the…

They shake hands and begin commending each other on their hits.

"This one is definitely a feisty one," Jasper says, patting Ebony on the back, "A real warrior."

Taken aback by the exchange, I don't notice Finn who has wandered to my side and is watching in a similar fashion. His hands are on his hips as he elbows me and asks the same questions that are running through my mind.

"What just happened?" he whispers, "I mean, she just hit the dude… like she hit him square in the face and he's laughing like it was normal…"

I break out of my daze and resolve my bewilderment with a laugh. I don't know what was so funny, but I knew this had some-how relieved a bit of my stress. Jasper and Ebony's tension had been broken which happened to take away some of my own.

"Rose?" Finn asks, capturing my attention.

"Yes?" I reply and notice he's expecting an explanation, "Look, I don't know what just happened but I'm hoping it means we can all get along."

Quietly, Finn walks away, and I'm momentarily distracted by his saunter. His shoulders are drooping and there's a sense of defeat in his tall frame. I'm starting to follow him to make sure he's okay when Jasper intervenes.

"Oh, I see, you want to play now too?" he calls, and I snap to attention, "Well, how about me and Ebony versus you and Finn?"

Looking at Finn, I wait for his response, and he nods hesitantly. I turn back to Jasper and shout 'sure' with dwindling enthusiasm. Jasper notices and winks flirtatiously to make me smile again.

"Don't worry, I'll go easy on you," he smirks.

Two pairs of curious eyes watch us exchange teasing remarks. Finn is laughing and encourages the burning insults I serve. His joy has come rushing back and we get ready to play.

"Come on you two," Ebony interrupts our gaze, "Enough flirting, time for a competition!" she says with a competitive smile.

"Ready?" Jasper calls and we all nod.

"3, 2, 1… Go!"

THREE GAMES LATER AND WE'RE OFFICIALLY WORN OUT. JASPER AND Ebony make a great team and win the first round. However, Finn and I are determined and win the second and third game. I'm feeling pretty smug as I hug Finn and look over at Jasper. He's pulling Ebony into a hug and talking in her ear. I feel a rush of jealousy and pull away from Finn. He reaches out and grabs my hands, causing a minor shock to radiate down my arm.

Something new about my shocks was that I realised I could read or feel someone's emotions. It was like they took over how I felt in a way. When I had a shock, it replaced my current emotions with the other person's emotions momentarily. Finn's jealousy wasn't far from my own. Clearly, we were both unnerved by the friendship that was forming.

"Come here you!" Jasper's melodious voice breaks the silence, as well as Finn's hold on me. "I'm impressed, you were so good in that last game."

"Thanks," I say, avoiding eye contact, "So were you…"

"Woah, woah, woah, woah, woah," Jasper leans back and pushes the fallen hair away from my eyes, "What is it?"

Finn, who was observing our exchange, wanders off once he notices the tension. We're alone so I know I can talk, but the stubbornness in me wants to stay silent. I didn't even know why it bothered me so much. I wasn't his girlfriend. I was Ebony's best friend. I shouldn't be feeling like this.

Scolding myself under my breath, I inhale and force myself to look at him.

"Nothing, I'm simply overthinking," I exhale with a forced smile.

Okay, so I may have not meant it. I may have been lying to him, but I didn't want to be *that girl*. The one who ruins a good day simply because she's gained feelings for a guy. Especially when she hasn't known him long enough to warrant the jealousy. I won't let him see the green-eyed monster rising in me. I refuse to be *that girl*.

"Are you sure?" Jasper asks, searching for an honest answer.

"Yes," I reply positively.

"Come on then." He says and guides me towards the rest of the group. "Let's get some food in you," Jasper chuckles.

As we approach, an array of food is laid out on the red and white chequered blanket. It looks perfect with the strawberries and triangular sandwiches: a picturesque picnic. Ebony is rooting around the basket and squeals with excitement.

"Champagne!" she pulls out the bottle and grabs some plastic champagne flutes.

"Rose can't have it," Finn says, clearly thinking aloud.

"She can have a drop!" Ebony insists, giggling.

Jasper flushes red. I frown at him when he sighs and whispers, "That was meant for later…"

Pouring us each a whole glass more than a drop, Ebony hands us one each and we sit in a circle around the food. She raises her plastic champagne flute and toasts our new friendship. We clink our flutes together and take a sip. Before the champagne touches my lips, Jasper leans into me and smiles, mouthing 'to us'. I nod in agreement and thank him.

"This wouldn't have happened without you," I whisper.

"We make a great team," he says.

There's a moment as I realise how close Jasper is. His lips are barely an inch away. He wavers and pulls away, his expression conflicted. A warm flutter of butterflies takes flight in my stomach before settling again. I wanted to ask if Jasper is okay but instead, I watch him quickly recover. He starts eating again, telling me he's fine.

Though Jasper moves away, there's a tingle of joy from his hand touching mine. My eyes survey the group, wondering if anyone saw until they're met with Ebony's. I can't read her as she seems lost in a world of her own.

"You okay?" I mouth and she nods, grimacing.

Sweat permeates my palms as I move my hand away from Jasper's. My skin is hot and tingling which is becoming uncomfortable. I take a sip of the champagne quickly, hoping it would help. Instead, the bitter taste ruins the rest of the food.

"Hey," Finn whispers as he shuffles next to me.

"Hey," I smile back.

We talk about Jasper, and he asks lots of questions, mentioning that he approves. He nudges me playfully, and I feel a spark shoot up to my shoulder. It happens a few times whilst we chat together. There's no emotion in any of them, but it unsettles me as the pain increases. This time it's nauseating and I'm starting to get a headache.

Today, out of all days, I had hoped would be one without worry. Yet, I found myself feeling agitated. I wanted to feel normal, but I knew I wasn't. It brought me back to my first problem; the one that was causing all of the anxiety in the first place.

"Guys," I say abruptly.

Everyone stops midway through their picnic and meets my gaze. Ebony's bright, hopeful eyes are the ones I focus on, hoping I won't back out now. I knew I had to tell them. I knew it was going to make it easier.

"I…" I begin, but the words won't come out.

My tongue is tied to the back of my throat where a lump is starting to form. I didn't realise it would be so hard to share, that it would make me feel this upset.

"What is it?" Ebony asks, the concern spreading across her face.

"Yeah, what's wrong?"

Finn takes my hand innocently and I snatch it away. The fear he feels is like an explosion in my head. Tears trickle over the floodgates and onto my cheeks. I try to apologise to Finn, but I don't make any sense. My words turn into sobs and my sobs become uncontrollable. Everyone is concerned and attempting to give me comforting embraces. Shaking my head, I push them off and realise that Jasper is the only one left who is touching me which it doesn't hurt.

"Rose?"

"I can't do this..." I say, rocking back and forth.

Moments pass as my body finds a rhythm. I must look insane to everyone, but I don't care. Holding everything in had become too much, too overwhelming. Concern descends like a thick fog over our lovely day out.

"I'm sorry," I whisper, embarrassed.

"Aw, Rose, no," Ebony replies, "Don't apologise."

She shakes her head making her ponytail swing. Her expression tells me she wants to hug me, but she's hesitant. I want to hug her too.

"It's so complicated, you know," I say as my voice breaks, "I wish I had told you all sooner, but I couldn't, I didn't know how. I've been so scared..."

"Whatever it is, Rosebud," Finn says, "We can work it out, I promise."

His long gaze is earnest and seeking answers; I need to tell them.

"I think I have some kind of power or something..." I exhale; this had been my conclusion after all my research. "I know that sounds totally crazy, but something isn't right. My hands are getting shocks and I can feel other people's emotions. It's like something connects me to their feelings... and I... I can't quite describe it."

Pausing, I scan the circle to check their reactions; Ebony's alarmed eyes stare back at me whilst Finn looks away and Jasper watches curiously.

"I think you're sounding crazy," Ebony says, her voice forceful, and then laughs uneasily, "What I mean is; I'm sure it's just that you're sensitive at the moment. Everyone would be with exams going on and the fact that your dad is away. There's a lot of stress on you."

Ebony reaches out to touch my shoulder, but I shrug her off. This was not the response I had expected.

"Really Ebony?" Finn says, and I think it's the first time he's challenged her in front of me.

"Finn, if I were you, I would butt out right now," she glares at him and returns to me, her expression sympathetic, "I'm not saying you're not feeling what you're feeling. I'm just trying to help you see that there's a lot going on. Don't overthink it."

"Okay," I snap, irritated by her response.

How could she be so blasé? She knew something was going on and I finally tell her, but she won't believe it. It was a stretch of the imagination, but it was me, I wouldn't lie to her. She's brushing it off like it's nothing.

"Rose," Finn says, breaking my glare at Ebony, "I think Ebony is trying to help," he pauses when I look up. "We want to support you," he reassures me.

Studying his expression, I see his eyebrow twitch which is a tell-tale sign that he's worried and trying to hide it. This just upsets me more.

"Really?" I huff, "How, Finn? When neither of you believes me."

"I didn't say that," Finn says softly, "I'm just trying to..."

"Just trying to what?" I snap again. My voice is getting louder, and I feel my hands shaking. "I'm telling you the truth. I know this isn't normal! Why won't you believe me?"

"Hey…" The melodious voice cuts through the fog. "Hey, listen to me," Jasper says, "Your friends don't not believe you, they're trying to eliminate all other contributing factors. Right?" he says and looks around to Finn and Ebony.

Neither respond.

"They don't believe me," I shake my head as the anger reignites.

"They do believe you," Jasper says calmly.

"Do you believe me?"

I swing the question on him, and I can see his confidence falter. He can't look me in the eye.

"Exactly!" I yell, standing up.

Storming off, I traipse along the beach with tears streaming down my face. I wasn't going to sit here and hear this any longer. Once at the cars, I'm finally away from their watching eyes and from the cold waves. There's a chill in the air that makes me shiver. Everything had got so cold, so quickly.

THE SUN HAD MOVED ABOUT THREE INCHES ACROSS THE SKY AS I turned my phone off and on, off and on. I wanted to call Mum and tell her about it all. I wanted her to tell me they were wrong and that everything was going to be okay. Still, I knew she wouldn't believe me. Her eyes betrayed her when she agreed that it could be more than anxiety.

"Mum?" I say as I pick up the phone.

Why had she called me? It was like she knew, and then it clicked. My eyes find the three of them on the picnic blanket talking and looking worried. They glance up and I turn away immediately.

"Darling, is everything okay?" she asks breathily like she's been crying herself.

"Yes, I mean no, but…" I confuse myself, "You're upset, what's wrong?"

"I'm sorry, I'll… I'll tell you when you get home."

"Mum, what is it?" I ask nervously, "Do you want me to come home?"

"No," she insists, tearily.

"Come on Mum," I beg as my heart races, "What is it?"

There's a pause and then says the phrase which scares me most: "It's Dad…"

Immediately, I hang up and yell down to the group for help. I may be angry with them, but right now, I needed them to get me home. I couldn't do it on my own. They gather the picnic and practically run up to find out what's happened. I'm shaking again and trying not to cry as they each ask what's going on. I explain the phone call and they can see how serious it is. Jasper attempts to comfort me, but I don't want it. I don't want any of them to be nice, I just want them to take me home.

"Okay," Finn says, "I'll take her."

Finn pulls out his keys and unlocks his car. I take a deep breath and follow him, unable to look anyone in the eye. Whilst I click myself in, Finn talks to Ebony and Jasper, but I can't hear what they're saying. It's muffled and I can only read their expressions with sideward glances. Ebony looks concerned and regretful, Jasper seemed dejected and confused and Finn is the only one who seems moderately calm.

"Come on then," Finn says as he closes the door behind him.

His smile fades as I refuse to meet his gaze. Instead, I stare out across the ocean and try to not think of the worst. I already know it's bad if Mum has been crying. Secretly I'm praying it's the lesser of the two evils that I'm thinking of.

MUM PRACTICALLY JUMPS OFF THE SOFA WHEN I WALK THROUGH THE hallway. She notices Finn is here and greets him before pulling me into the living room. Tears streak down her face giving life to the fear that was swirling inside.

"Darling, I need you to understand that everything will be okay, and we can't give up yet." She pauses, waiting for me to respond but I don't. "I got a phone call about an hour ago to alert us that your father has gone missing. I'm not sure what happened, but they said that they'll keep informing us as soon as they get more intel. Apparently, he was transferring camps and there was an ambush…" her voice cracks and a few dark curls fall across her face.

"Oh Mum…"

I throw my arms around her. Her pain creeps into me like an unwelcome thief stealing all hope I had for better news. My palms sweat as a heaviness set in the pit of my stomach. It hurts and I can't bear the grief. She's drowning me with her sorrow, and I can barely think straight as I try to process the shock. The dizziness throws me back and away, searching for some kind of peace and clarity.

"I'm sorry…" I mutter.

Unsure of what to do, I run and push past Finn's strong stature. Familiar faces wait beyond the hedges of my garden, and I don't know which way to go. I hear Finn calling my name and Mum is hurrying after him. I glance back and then ahead, and then back before I make my decision.

"Jasper!" I yell his name, running towards him. He had followed us all the way back to collect his car. I barely give him enough time to respond. "I need you to drive. Please, don't ask me anything, just…" my lip quivers, "Just drive, okay?"

I slam the door of the car behind me and avoid all eye contact, already welling up. Jasper is baffled and glances at Ebony who shakes her head. I notice Finn has got through the gate and Mum is not far behind. They all try to reason with me, but the metal casket muffles them out. I lock the doors and take a deep breath in as I try to process everything. My head is whirring with voices as I replay Mum's words.

Before I can fight it, the air is getting thin around me. I don't feel panicky as the light drifts away under my eyelids and I slump into the chair.

Murmurs of voices are all that's left in the calm, quiet darkness.

CHAPTER
Five

"Rose…"
Sunlight streams across my face as I stir awake. My mind is fuzzy about the events before now. Cool sweat clings to my sheets like a stain. I hear the gentle voice call me again, so I force my eyes open.

"Oh Rose."

Someone pulls me into them before I can get a look at who's there. My fingers detect the calm relief that washes over both of us. Her curls tickle against my cheek as her vanilla scent pierces through the damp air. Every event of the beach day before comes flooding back. The picnic, the phone call, Mum crying, hiding in Jasper's car.

"Mum?" I gasp, sitting up quickly, "What happened? Where is everyone?"

"They went home…"

"What day is it?" I ask, confused.

"It's June 1st," Mum responds, appearing slightly surprised by my question. "Honey, are you okay?"

My mind wanders to yesterday and what was said. Nobody believed me that I had some kind of special power. I know I sounded insane, looked insane and, honestly, felt completely, and utterly, insane. But I couldn't deny that I could physically feel my Mum's concern for me. Her worry tingled my skin like aloe vera on fresh sunburn.

"Um… I don't know…"

"Ebony tried to explain what happened, but you started getting angry and you told them to leave."

Unable to recall, I tilt my head and frown, "What?"

"Don't you remember? You woke up whilst we were putting you in bed and you screamed before telling them to get out. Ebony was very upset when she left. I told her I would get you to call her when you were feeling better."

A deep, frustrated sigh blows through my lips. I fight myself internally; do I feel bad for her or not? She was the one who told me I was stressed. She didn't believe me! *Her best friend.* What kind of friend doesn't believe her best friend?

Then again, I had been sort of lying to her this whole time. I had hidden it, so maybe she was feeling hurt. Maybe she was upset because she did believe me, but she just didn't know what to do. *I* don't know what to do. There's a lot of information that needs processing…

"Mum?" I ask her, beckoning her closer with outstretched hands. "Is Dad really gone?"

The redness of oncoming tears swells in the corner of her eyes and it's enough to answer the question. Nausea churns in my stomach as I try to absorb the broken information from Mum's relaying of the story. She reminds me that Dad was moving camps and that someone had ambushed them. I nod, recalling her telling me before. She explains that she's spoken to his Commanding Officer since then. All I hear is the mention of a fifty-fifty chance of

Dad returning and the sudden urge to throw up is almost followed through.

"Darling?" she asks.

Quickly, I stand up and run out of my bedroom knowing what's coming. Mum follows me into the bathroom. My body deeply aches as I throw up twice in the sink. I wash it away and a couple of tears follow. Mum is holding back my hair and stroking my shoulder.

"I know it's a lot to take in, but it's going to be okay. I promise."

"How can you say that when Dad has, what, a fifty percent chance?"

Pushing off my knees, I run the taps again and wash my mouth out. I cup my hands under the cold water and take sips. The water dilutes the taste of bile in my mouth. My nausea subsides once Mum's peaceful energy infiltrates my skin.

"How can you be so calm?" I ask.

"I'm not, but you need me more," Mum replies.

We both walk into my room with a heavy sadness between us. There was so much going on without a moment of release to help me through. Not even the tears seemed to wash away the emptiness I felt. Mum sits beside me and wraps her arms around my curled-up frame. I close my eyes and let the tears crawl down my face, betraying the brave front I was putting on. There was nothing I could do. Dad was gone, my friends didn't believe me, and I couldn't understand what was happening. I felt lost and Mum seemed like the only way home. She knew me, she could tell me what I needed to do.

"I'm so scared," I begin, "I have something wrong with me. I feel emotions that aren't mine and nobody believes me because I sound insane. I'm afraid that Dad won't ever come home and then what if… what if I lose you too, too."

Shaking her head, Mum pulls back and forces me to meet her gaze.

"Darling, no, I don't want you to go down this path in your head. Now, listen to me," she pauses, waiting for my full attention,

"You are *not* going to lose me. I'm never, *ever* leaving you. Do you understand?"

I nod, but my gaze wanders. Mum puts a finger under my chin and tilts it upwards. My focus snaps back to hers and she smiles.

"Sweetheart, I will always, always believe you. No matter how insane and scared you feel. You are *my* daughter, and I will never tell you that you're wrong… unless you are," she laughs under her breath, "But that never happens."

A small, thin crack appears in my lips and a weak smile breaks through. Mum plants a kiss on my temple and pulls me into her chest again. She tenderly strokes my hair and I feel the storm inside begin to subside. The ocean waves return to a stillness that allows me to think straight.

"So," Mum holds me at arms-length and sighs, "Tell me from the beginning."

MINUTES TURNED INTO HOURS AS I EXPLAINED TO MUM WHAT WAS going on. I could see in her eyes that she couldn't quite understand, yet she nodded, encouraging me to go on. Her face lit up as I told her about Jasper and how I'd grown to care for him more than I had let on. Jasper's name rolled off my tongue a few times and my emotions were torn.

When I spoke about my theory of having some kind of power, Mum's expression didn't falter. I explained that I thought the doctors had only got half of it right. Yet, I argued that something more was happening beneath the surface. She listened quietly and only asked a question here and there, mainly to see if I was okay.

"Does it still hurt?" she frowns, now looking at my hands.

"Not anymore," I reassure her.

This was partially true. I didn't like the shocks it gave but I was used to it. The pain was merely an unpleasant side effect. Continuing, I explain what happened at the beach and why I was so angry. Mum said she could understand and gave more encouraging murmurs. The weight of my secret began to lift as I told her everything. It felt good to finally be honest. All my fears burned in the light that had been cast on them.

"So," Mum says after the conversation falls silent, "What are you going to do now?"

She slowly takes my hand and rubs it with her thumb. I'm not sure if she does this on purpose as I can feel her emotions. Her pulse is steady and calm, and her eyes tell me what I should do next.

"Call Ebony?" I grimace.

Nodding, Mum squeezes my hand and plays with my hair. She encourages me to have a go and gives me a quick kiss before standing up.

"Right," she exhales, smoothing out her shirt.

As she begins to leave, I call her to turn around. She pauses and turns, her smile thin and fading. I know she needs to hear this, too.

"It's going to be okay," I nod, "Dad's going to come back, I believe it."

The truth is, I have no idea. Dad could never come back. I could see through her mask of strength and poise that she was struggling too. It made me feel selfish knowing she was putting on a front to console me.

"I know," she says softly. "Thank you, darling."

Once she's left, I listen as her footsteps disappear down the stairs and into the hallway. I dwell in the conversation, wondering how I could possibly fix things with everyone. Did I want to fix it? I wasn't sure, but I did need my friends whether that meant putting aside what happened before.

Grabbing my phone, I open it to find six messages: two from Ebony, one from Finn and three from Jasper. Each holds some kind of apology, and some have a question of forgiveness to which I know I'll need to reply to. Ebony asks if I'm feeling any better whereas Finn tells me to call when I feel better. Jasper's texts are endearing as he tells me he's worried and wants to meet.

Holding the phone up to my ear, I try to think of how to start the conversation. 'Hello' seemed strange when I didn't feel like saying anything at all. I exhale loudly and soon her familiar voice appears.

"Rose?" she says sounding croaky, like she's been crying.

"Yeah, hi," I reply, and all anger dissipates. "Are you okay?"

"Yeah, yeah," she sighs, "Are you? I was worried when I didn't hear from you yesterday. Your mum said you weren't feeling yourself still."

"No, I've been sleeping it off mostly."

There's a long, uncomfortable pause as the conversation runs dry. Neither of us knows what to say without apologising first. The reality is, we were both too stubborn to give in leaving us in a stalemate. I knew I should apologise. No matter how angry she had made me, I didn't need to be mean. She didn't understand and Mum was right when she said I shouldn't expect her to. Nothing about my situation was normal.

"I'm sorry."

"What?"

I'm taken aback by hearing the words I was planning to say.

"You heard," she sasses me but there's a subtlety to her voice, "I know I shouldn't have dismissed you the way I did. I should have listened and believed you and maybe you would've been okay. I was just trying to protect you."

Taking a deep breath in, I also take in her sentiment and allow it to wash away any residual anger. I didn't need to be so upset when we both knew we had been unkind to one another.

"I'm sorry too. I shouldn't have got so angry with you. I'm just really scared and overwhelmed."

"I know you are, and the stuff with your dad..." she hesitates; I know she's worried to say anything to upset me again.

"It's okay," I reassure her.

Taking my time, I describe everything that I know about Dad and his situation. My voice quivers slightly when I mention the attack, but Ebony doesn't interrupt, clearly taking it in. I tell her what Mum said about the fifty-fifty chance and she gasps.

"Are you sure you're okay?" she asks for the fifth time once she's heard it all.

Sighing, I shrug and try to give her an honest answer. The truth was that I was afraid and uncertain and angry. It was a poisonous mixture for any hope that I had left. Yet, there was something in me that couldn't give it up, maybe for Mum or just selfishly so that I had something to hold onto.

"I have no idea what to think, but I'm going to believe that Dad is coming home. I have to."

Her lack of response confirms she is still concerned, but she won't dismiss me. Instead, she tells me she will support me and that if I need her, I can call her. As we finish our conversation, I hear the strain in her voice.

"Ebony?" I say, "It's okay. We're going to be okay," I remind her.

She replies breathily with a 'thanks' and we both hang up.

Gently, I put my phone on the table beside the bed and close my eyes. My thoughts are racing and I'm struggling to keep up with them. Images of Dad flash to the front of my mind and a sharp pain cuts through my chest. A weak groan escapes my lips as I push the pain away. There's no space for fear.

"There's no space for fear…" I mumble repetitively.

RETURNING TO COLLEGE WAS EASIER THAN I'D HOPED. I HAD BARELY any classes left, and my exams were almost over. Everyone knew, unsurprisingly, our situation with Dad so I was treated with extra special care. It felt overbearing at times, but it did mean I could leave class or exams early if I needed to.

"Yeah, sure," Nya, the exams lady, smiles and dismisses me.

Before the exam, Nya had told me that if I wanted to have extra time, I could. However, I was more likely to get it done and get out of there. Nobody wanted to spend more time in an exam than they had to.

Nobody.

"Thanks," I whisper, grabbing my things.

I exit without looking back and find myself heading towards the stairwell. A dark, ash-blond-haired boy sits waiting for me to arrive. We had been texting all week and this was the first time I had been able to see him. Things were back to normal between us, and I was excited to meet him. His head was down whilst he stared at the steps below his feet, completely lost in his own thoughts. There's a concern in his features which overshadow the brightness of his smile when greets me.

"Hey!" he says, standing up.

"Are you okay?" I ask, talking over him.

Nodding, he walks down the steps and pulls me into a hug. His warmth envelops me, and I sigh, relieved to be in his arms. I touch his skin to read his emotions, but there's nothing there. He was the only one whose emotions barely showed. It was refreshing in most circumstances unlike now.

"What's wrong?"

Jasper's pearly smile fades as he leads me back up the steps. We sit down together on the stairs, and he takes my hand in his palm. For some reason, it's colder in here than usual. The hairs on my arm start to prick up as the uncomfortable atmosphere continues to grow.

"What is it?" I ask.

"I... I need to tell you something," he begins, breaking eye contact, "I haven't been completely honest with you, and I have to tell you this now before anything happens because I... I like you and I don't like keeping secrets from you."

My heart starts to flutter. I like him too. Then the warmth fades as I consider the secret that is about to be unveiled.

"I..." he stops and meets my gaze.

I must look concerned because he chews his lip tensely. Some of his dark, ash-blond hair falls across his eyes, but he pushes it back rigidly.

"I... I know about your power, Rose, I've known about it all along."

Silence. His confession sinks in like a dark stain on a shirt, spreading slowly and concealing the colours that were there before. It permeates the conversations we've had and the lies I have told to cover up all that I had shared. It made no sense.

Why was he telling me now?

"What?" I ask in shock, "What do you mean you knew? That was two weeks ago and now you're saying that you always knew?" I shake my head, "Are you mocking me?"

"No," he mutters, his head hung in guilt.

"I don't understand…"

Trying to even out my breathing, I pull myself back around and sit beside Jasper calmly. He's looking ashamed and hurt, and all I can do is place a hand on his. For the first time, I feel his emotions swirling around under my fingertips. His sadness breaks through with tears dripping silently down his chin. There's a quiet tap as one tear hits the concrete steps.

"I'm sorry," he says, unable to look at me.

"No," I reply, the guilt setting in heavy, "I'm sorry, I have a lot on my mind, but that doesn't mean I should yell. I just don't understand, what do you mean you knew?"

Nervously, he meets my gaze and rubs his palms along his thighs. I can tell he's worried that he'll upset me further.

"The people I live with, they're kind of… knowledgeable in this whole power thing," he pauses. Jasper seems really uncomfortable. "I can't tell you much more, but I promise, I won't lie to you again. It was killing me not to tell you, but I was afraid of what they'd think… and I was already in enough trouble as it was. I…"

Jasper hesitates and glances at me. His expression looks as though he had forgotten I was there.

"Sorry, I just didn't know how to tell you."

"You're afraid…" I state, clearly reading his expression.

"No, I, uh," he stammers, "I…"

Placing a hand on his shoulder, I force him to stop and look at me. The tears have stopped but his gaze is glossed over with anxiety.

"Come on, what is it?" I ask again.

"I… it's… I can't say."

Smacking my hands down on my knees, I let out an irritated sigh. "Seriously? I tell you something crazy, you tell me that you believe me and that you won't lie and now you're telling me you *can't say?*"

There's a long exhale that flows from Jasper's tight lips as the fear disappears. He seems angrier now that I've snapped, and it provokes my frustration.

"It's not that simple, Rose," Jasper says and I can hear the strain in his voice to keep calm.

"Isn't it? Because I have no idea…" I say and bury my face in my hands. "If you know something, help me."

Minutes pass in the eerily empty stairwell. My irritation is fed by the absence of Jasper's reply. There's a shuffle and I look up to see he's put some distance between us.

"So, you're just going to say nothing?" I tut.

Jasper avoids eye contact and shrugs. It's enough to make me want to scream, but I withhold…. Barely.

"Fine," I hiss.

Each footstep echoes through the empty stairwell. I sigh heavily, reminding Jasper that I was furious with him. Part of me wondered if he was just saying things to make me feel better. Or maybe he was telling the truth? It didn't matter because he wouldn't tell me.

"You're a pure power, Rose…"

Pure.

That word pulls me back in. I stop and glance at Jasper to see his reddened, puffy eyes staring back. His face was a picture of regret. I couldn't conjure up the sympathy that he desired. Instead, I wanted more answers and to go home.

"What do you mean?"

Shaking his head, he remains silent. Tears and frustration continue as he stays seated, battling his own better judgement.

"I don't have time for this," I growl and force myself to keep walking.

Looking around, I feel the adrenaline of our encounter trigger more anxiety. This was a real anxiety attack now. I break into a jog, finding a way to get outside so I can breathe again. I trip and someone catches me as I collapse into their arms. They appear shocked at first and then concern clouds their focus.

"Hey," the voice breaks through, "Rosebud? Rosebud!"

Realising who it is, I straighten up and look him in the eye. I hadn't seen him since the beach as he said he had needed to visit some family. We had made up over the phone, but I hadn't seen him until now.

"I'm okay," I reassure him, "I'm fine, I just got a little overwhelmed."

"What happened?" he frowns, pulling me from the flurry of students.

His eyes are watching me earnestly and I can see he's searching for a clue or something to give away why I was running.

"I need some air," I gasp.

Immediately, Finn nods and takes my hand so he can guide me to the nearest exit. My head is fuzzy as the air inside my lungs fail to steady my breathing. Once I'm outside, we both stand in the warm glow of the sun. His gaze washes over me as if to see how he can help more, but I reassure him that I'm fine.

"Are you sure?" he presses once I've finally got my breath back.

Nodding, I tell him not to worry.

"Okay," he nods with apprehension still in his eyes, "I would stay if I didn't have an exam in like five minutes…"

"It's fine, Finn, go if you need to."

"Er… okay," he says and pulls me into a warm embrace, "I'm worried about you. Please wait for me, I want to see you after college so we can catch up. Alright?"

"Okay," I agree.

Pulling me into the tightest hug, Finn kisses my forehead and I'm almost certain I feel a tingle of something. Before I can read it, the feeling disappears, and I'm left still searching for air.

FINALLY, THE DAY WAS OVER, SO I MAKE MY ESCAPE TOWARDS THE double doors. A warm, spring breeze washed all the anxiety away and I'm met with hot sunlight. It was a perfect blue sky with not a cloud in sight, enough to melt all my frustrations. The time between seeing Jasper and now seemed like aeons and for once, I was actually *thankful* to be busy with college work.

As I inhaled the fresh air, I walked towards Ebony and Finn who were clearly talking about me. Their body language said it all.

"Rose," Finn greets me, breaking off from the intense conversation they were having.

"Hey," Ebony beams, turning to hug me.

They both give me a squeeze and ask me about my day. I shrug and tell them a basic overview, hoping they won't ask questions. Ebony had decided to take it upon herself to check on me daily. It was obvious that Finn had been roped into it, possibly by a guilt trip from his 'enemy'.

"Okay, so what's the plan?" Ebony smiles at Finn and then to me, "What do you fancy doing this afternoon?"

"Maybe we could go get some smoothies, or go to Annie's Diner?" Finn replies, "Your favourite!"

Their eagerness and sparkling eyes make it difficult not to laugh. I don't mean to. I know they are trying to help, yet in doing so, were becoming comical. I still couldn't quite believe that they were working together. This new partnership was somewhat, disconcerting.

"I'm sorry," I giggle, "but you guys need to chill out. I'm fine, I really just wanted to go home tonight. I've got the exam tomorrow and it's a big one…"

"You need a distraction," Ebony insists, "Come on, it'll be good for us to hang out. Won't it, Finn?" she hesitates before hitting him gently on the arm.

Looking at his arm, and then to her, and then back again, Finn frowns. He nods slowly and meets my gaze.

"Yeah, totally."

"So, what do you say?" Ebony says, but I know she won't take no for an answer.

"Fine," I shrug, "Let's go into town."

It doesn't take us long to get there, especially as Ebony is driving. They fought about who was going to drive, typical, and as it was 'her idea', Finn and I were stuck being the passengers of the death-mobile. I loved Ebony, but I did not like her driving.

Once we arrive, we all get out, slamming the doors behind us before strolling towards the shopping park. It's bursting with life as people mill in and out of the shops, like bees on their way to their hive. I hear Finn say something to Ebony and she elbows him and moves towards me. Linking her arm through mine, she pulls me towards the dress shops.

"Come on, we should look for your birthday," she beams, giggling with excitement.

Sighing, I smile and nod reluctantly. She pulls me forward and I look over my shoulder at Finn who is falling behind. He looks mildly uncomfortable but changes once our eyes meet. I turn back to face where Ebony is taking us and stop. My smile falters when I see half our year is also here, shopping and getting ready for the end-of-year dance. Ebony sees my disappointment and reassures me that I should go inside.

"It's not that bad," she whispers, "I promise…"

An array of colours bursts through the racks of dresses hanging along each wall. There's an upstairs, which sells suits, and I notice a few boys from our English class running up to have a look. Pristine, white, oval tables decorate the centre of the room with handbags, jewellery and shoes adorning them. Strangely, there are no mannequins except for the ones in the windows. The air is filled with a floral fragrance which intensifies as we walk further into the shop.

"Can I help you?" an older, pale-faced lady asks.

Ebony explains what we're doing and before I know it, we're both being whisked away to the dressing rooms. Another two ladies, one wearing red lipstick and the other with glasses, have come to help us choose a dress. They separate Ebony and me into our own dressing room and consult us individually. I get asked a few questions about my preferences and I hear Ebony get asked the same.

"Okay, ladies let's go find these girlies some birthday dresses to die for," the pale-faced lady, called Jaqueline, winks.

"We'll be right back," the lady with glasses, Rosemary, says to me.

As the calm returns, I peer over to Ebony who is plaiting her hair in the mirror. She notices me and turns around, giggling with bright eyes like a toddler.

"Isn't this exciting?"

"Yes," I agree, but she knows I'm humouring her.

Pouting, she stares at me until I fake a smile. She knows it's forced, but it is enough for her to return to her excitable ways. Her fingers play with the end of her newly finished plait as she looks into the mirror.

"I was thinking of doing this for your birthday," she says, watching me in the reflection for a response.

"It looks pretty," I reply, and she sighs heavily. "I'm sorry, I'm not trying to be unenthusiastic. It's just that…"

My mind thinks about the plans we had with Dad and my heart drops to the bottom of my stomach. The thought is too painful that I must force it away immediately before it ruined everything.

"What is it?" Ebony asks, concern blooming on her face, "Is it your dad? Mum?"

Shaking my head, I stop her by giving a reassuring smile. Her bright eyes are dimming, and it makes me regret opening my mouth. This wasn't the time or place to be sad. Ebony had planned this to cheer me up so mentioning Dad was only going to ruin the experience.

"You know what?" I say, "It doesn't matter."

There's a break before either of us speaks. Ebony stares in the mirror and chews the inside of her lip.

"If, you're sure?" she mutters.

"Hey, I thought you had brought me here to have fun," I tease, hoping it'll make her laugh.

Her lips curl at the edges and a glimmer of light returns to her face.

"There's that smile," I whisper, wrapping an arm around her shoulders.

Ebony opens her mouth to reply, but we get interrupted by cackles of laughter. The ladies have returned with armfuls of colourful, flowing gowns. Excitement hits easing the pain momentarily so that I could enjoy the present, for now.

CHAPTER
Six

"See you tomorrow," I yell as I close the car door behind me.

Wheels spin as Ebony and Finn drive off to collect Finn's car from college. The smile on my face doesn't fade as I saunter up the garden path towards the house. Low, evening light warms my back like the glow of a dwindling fire. I pause and take a deep breath in, looking at my home. The house seems quiet and still when I open the red-painted door.

"Mum!" I call, my spirits high from my time with my best friends.

Placing my bag down, I realise there's a strange smell in the air. The more I get into the house, the more I realise something is burning. I run into the kitchen and turn everything off. The hob is smoking, but thankfully nothing caught on fire.

"Mum?" I call again.

"In here," a croaky voice replies from the living room.

Anxiously, I rush to find Mum on the couch sobbing. Her hair is pulled back in a messy bun as she wipes away the floods of tears. Makeup is smeared across her face and rivers of mascara trickle down her cheeks and chin.

"Mum!" I gasp.

In the sadness, I sit beside her with an arm wrapped around her. She turns and nestles her head in my embrace, weeping heavily. She shudders in my arms. I don't know what to say or do, but I don't want to let her go.

"I'm sorry…" she cries, "I'm so sorry…"

"No, it's okay," I reassure her, holding back my own tears.

A dark, heavy emotion fills my palms and cuts straight through the centre of my being. It feels like someone is tearing me apart, vein by vein, inch by inch. I'm struggling to breathe under the intensity of the emotion so much so that I want to let go. A lump builds up in my throat as the conflict battles on within.

"He's not coming back," Mum sobs.

"You can't say that, you don't know that."

"But why haven't they found him yet?" she trembles with each word.

Silent; I don't have the answer or the words to make her feel better. It's as though I'm being pulled apart, between the hope and truth of what we were facing. We had been so strong until now, despite not hearing any update on Dad's whereabouts. The lack of control we had over this situation was dragging us down, crushing the hope we had left.

"I never meant for you to see me like this," Mum says, pulling herself away.

"Oh Mum, it's okay," I reply.

"No, it's not," she snaps, wiping the tears away.

Standing now, Mum pulls herself together and asks if I've had anything for dinner. I tell her that Ebony, Finn and I ate during our time in the town centre. She seems relieved and tells me she is going to make a cup of tea. Once she's left, my mind races with concern. The problem was this wasn't the first time Mum had been like this. It was the third time this week. I hadn't told anyone because it was something I'd hoped would go away. Mum's mental health was deteriorating, and I could barely save my own from drowning.

"Sweetheart?" her voice is calm and collected when she appears again, "I'm sorry for earlier. I shouldn't have snapped at you."

Sitting down beside me, she places a hot, steaming tea on her knee and reaches for my hand. I look up at her and see her saddened gaze. She quickly forces a brave face and nods, telling me that she loves me. I tell her that I know and I'm thankful that she is there.

"I'm thankful I have you," Mum says, "Without you, I don't know how I could carry on."

The weight of Mum's words rests heavily on my shoulders. We don't talk much about Dad and when I stack the dishwasher, Mum decides to go to bed early. I'm not far behind once I've finished tidying up.

Turning the lights off, I slip into bed and close my eyes. Warm, salty tears stream into the pillow as I rest my head. The tiredness overwhelms me and pulls me under. A dreamless sleep quickly follows.

RIBBONS OF YELLOW, MORNING LIGHT BREAK THROUGH THE GAPS IN my curtains. Birds sing their morning song proudly outside my window, reminding me that it's another day. The radiator hums quietly from the night before for a few moments before coming to a sudden stop. The sweet, smoky aroma of bacon beckons me downstairs. I throw off my covers and slip on my pyjama hoodie to greet Mum in the kitchen.

"Morning," I say, breezing through the doorway.

My resolve is that it's a new day. Mum wasn't going to always struggle like this, and so I needed to cling onto hope, for both our sakes'.

"Good morning sweetie," Mum replies.

Dressed in black, I notice the silver necklace and bracelets adorning her wrists and neck. Her wild mane is pulled back into a sleek, slender ponytail with a thick, silver cuff surrounding the hair tie. She must've been up for hours, but she's hidden it with a mask of beautiful makeup. She hides her freckles and lines with blusher and concealer. Her lips are layered with a shiny red lip gloss and her eyes are shimmering in brown and gold.

"Would you like me to drive you to school today?" she asks between sips of tea.

"Um," I hesitate; I had asked Finn to pick me up yesterday, "Yeah, sure."

Finding my phone, I text Finn and let him know the plan has changed. His reply is instant as he says he'll see me at college.

"Sweetheart?" Mum says softly, making me look up at her. "I know yesterday was a lot and it's clear that I'm not handling things very well," she sighs, "It will get better, and I will try harder. I promise."

"It's okay," I smile at her, "I'm finding it hard too."

Relieved by our shared understanding, we quietly eat the bacon sandwiches that Mum had made for us. Mum is the first to finish and rushes out to organise her bag and folders. In the quiet of the sunlit kitchen, I ponder on the events of the past few weeks. My mind drifts to Finn, Ebony and the fun evening we had yesterday. They had stepped up hugely to support me during such a difficult time. Thoughts of a boy with darkened ash-blond hair dampen my increasing positivity. Jasper had texted me twice last night, but I had ignored them. I didn't need to talk to him. I needed time to think about what he had said. Finishing my second bacon sandwich, I put my dishes and cutlery in the sink and pour out the now-cold tea. I spring upstairs and grab my towel before jumping into the shower.

Makeup and effort didn't appeal to me this morning. I was tired from worry and my face needed a break from unwanted chemicals. Instead, I grab my phone to text Ebony; I wanted her to meet me when I got to college. There was a lot I wanted to talk to her about and process.

"Ready?" Mum's round face appears around my door, smiling. She has her sunglass on her head, but immediately pulls them over her eyes. "Come on, darling."

Following her out to the car, I reach out for my bag and throw it into the footwell once the doors open. I close myself in when I'm in the passenger seat and click my seatbelt on. I'm suddenly reminded of the impending exam and my stomach churns.

"Are you okay?" Mum frowns, noticing my sudden discomfort.

"I've just realised, it's the final exam this morning," I reply.

Understanding, Mum places a hand on mine and her confidence radiates out of her palms. There's a calmness that washes over me and I relax.

"You are going to be amazing," she says, "I have every faith that you will do your absolute best, and that's all I'm expecting from you. Okay?"

Nodding, I take a deep breath and let her words rotate in my mind. She rubs my hand gently before turning the car on and reversing off the driveway. We turn the radio on and Mum sings along, burying her worries in each lyric. I join in once we're closer to college and the music infects me with a temporary joy. Busy students congregate at the double-door entrance, filtering like ants on an anthill.

"Darling?" Mum calls, lowering the passenger window, "You *are* amazing, you are going to *do* amazing, and I *love* you."

I'm smiling as I reply, "I love you too, Mum."

"Good," she winks over her sunglasses, "Have a great day! I'll see you later," she says as she slips her sunglasses back on, "Let me know how it goes!"

As she drives away, I look to the college and search for Ebony. It wasn't until the bell that I found her, and she grabbed my arm, pulling me into one of the stairwells. Wrapping her arms around me, she gives me the biggest hug and asks me how I am. It's as though she senses something was up and waits for me to talk. I begin to explain that I was worried about Mum when a voice interrupts us.

"Rose?" he says, and conflicting emotions arise.

Ebony's face watches my own and I can feel her uncertainty tingling my skin. A pang of anger appears but disappears as soon as I start talking.

"Hello Jasper," I say with false warmth.

"Can I talk to you?" he says, looking over at Ebony, "Alone?"

Hesitating, Ebony comes to my rescue and answers for me.

"Sorry, we've got an exam in a minute so we can't be late," she says, smoothly, "I'm sure when it's over, she can text you?" her eyes flicker to mine and I know she's read them correctly, "...or not," she adds.

Looking rather dejected, Jasper shrugs and nods disappointedly. He locks eyes with me, and I notice the thin, tight-lipped smile faltering. I want to apologise and talk to him and pretend everything was okay, but it wasn't. He was the least of my problems, and I couldn't handle any more stress right now.

"Rose?" Ebony says and pulls me out of my thoughts, "We need to go."

Her strong intonation rests on the word 'go' and I immediately start walking.

"What was that about?" Ebony asks as we get closer to the exam hall.

Locking arms with me, she guides me through the last few students who are rushing to their classes. I shrug at her question and stare, wondering if I should have heard Jasper out.

"I don't know, Eb, it's complicated," I say.

"Why?"

"I..."

An awkwardness falls between us when I don't respond. I didn't want to tell her about Jasper because it meant bringing up the power I think I have. It was a conversation that would only lead to more uncomfortable conversations. I didn't need that today.

Ebony guides me outside to where the benches are. The sun is still warming up the air, but it's a beautiful day. We find a place that's half-shaded by the willow tree and sit. Ebony hasn't let go of me since we left Jasper.

"So, tell me everything," she says, her face full of intrigue.

Beginning with Mum, I explain everything that has happened since we found out about Dad. Some of which, I know Ebony knows, but I don't leave out the rest. Coming clean about the struggle at home has somewhat lightened my burdens. When I mention Jasper, she asks a lot of questions. Instead of getting into it, I simply explain that my feelings had changed after the beach trip. Ebony doesn't appear suspicious when I explain all of this and gives me some advice.

"Maybe you need to talk to your mum tonight," she smiles, "Sometimes, it's better when you get it all out there. She's your mum and she loves you, right?"

"Yeah, I know," I nod.

"Plus, I'm glad you're kicking that Jasper boy. I was *not* a fan."

This makes me giggle, albeit a little sadly, because I knew how much she had disliked him from the start. It was good comic relief, though.

When I finish saying everything I need to say, Ebony is quiet and reflective. She squeezes my hand a few times and then asks if there's anything she can do. Shrugging, I tell her I will start with Mum and leave the inevitable conversation with Jasper for another day. I wanted things to go back to normal, but nothing about my life was normal right now.

"I just feel helpless," I sigh, "I can't make any of this go away, and I don't know how to help Mum..."

Ebony smiles and tugs at my hand, forcing me to look at her.

"Let us help you," she says, "Stop trying to be strong on your own. We love you, and we want to help."

I'm not sure what about her voice makes me cry, but the tears instantly fall, and Ebony gets up to hold me. She wraps both arms around my crumpling frame and pulls me into her. Sobbing now, I can barely breathe and gasp for air, but the pain only gets worse.

"It's going to be okay," Ebony says repeatedly, rubbing my back, "You are going to be okay."

Moments pass as the tears dry up and I'm left feeling empty yet again. The salty taste on my tongue makes me thirsty and I'm exhausted. Ebony is still holding on tight, so I thank her and gently ask her to let me go.

"I'm sorry," I say, pointing to her sodden shirt.

Ebony brushes it with her hand and tells me not to worry.

"It'll dry," she replies.

Birds chatter in the willow tree as a natural lull in the conversation arises. This time, it's not awkward or sad, it's content. I inhale the fresh air and let the sun warm my back and neck, re-energizing me for the day ahead.

Looking over towards the Great Hills in the distance, I see clouds covering the peaks. Black and brown dots fly up and through the white mist before diving down in between the valleys. I'm focused on my breathing when Ebony shakes my arm.

"We *have* to go," she says with alarm.

"What?" I ask, startled.

Handing me her phone, she flicks it on and reveals the time. It's 11:00. Our exam is in fifteen minutes!

Rushing now, we jump up from our table and run inside towards the exam hall. Thankfully, students are lining up for the exam and nobody has gone in yet. We pant and laugh as the relief floods over us. I lean against the cold, white wall to cool off. Ebony mutters something, but I miss it and giggle anyway.

The exam goes smoothly, despite my pens running out of ink and having to ask for a new one, twice. I close the paper and realise I have completed all of my work for the year. This was it. I was free! Now all I wanted to do with my freedom was spend it with my friends and Mum. Ebony was still busy and had another exam, so I decided Finn would be my best bet. He'd already texted to say he wanted to meet up once I was finished.

Wandering through the quiet bustle of students, I look to see if anyone is still in the classrooms. He had double P.E. usually, but they had made it optional since the exams had started. It was good because Finn was always worried about not having enough time to complete his coursework as well as fit in his revision.

When I get to the Sports field, I notice there are only a few people running around and the rest are sat either eating lunch or watching. A couple of the boys are shirtless, and I can see a row of girls fawning over them. Rolling my eyes, I search again for Finn and finally spot him in the goal. I take a seat on a patch of grass that isn't infected with giggling, hysterical girls and wait. I take out my water bottle and sip it slowly as the game unfolds.

By the end, nobody has won and the boys have given up. The coach blows the whistle and instructs them to go inside and change. Finn only notices me when he walks off the field and I wave at him. He points to the door and mouths to meet him there after he's got changed. I nod and smile, excited to spend some quality time with him.

My skin is almost burnt by the time Finn finally comes out of the changing rooms. He's beaming and has designer shades covering his eyes. Dressed in basketball shorts and a tank top, he looks like he's just walked out of a 90's American sitcom.

"What are you smiling about?" he asks, and I shrug.

"Oh nothing," I smile.

Putting an arm around my shoulder, Finn begins to walk with me through the college halls. A contented smile forms on my face; it had been a while since things had felt normal between us.

"So, how have you been?" he exhales.

"Not good," I reply, "How about you?"

"Meh," he shrugs, "I've missed my best friend."

A warm sense of comfort flows through me and I lean my head on his shoulder. He pulls me into his side and squeezes as if to reassure me.

"I missed you too," I beam up at him.

His big, watchful eyes meet my happy gaze. There's a stirring inside me as forgotten feelings come out of hiding. They return to where they once lay in the pit of my stomach. I forget to breathe as a blush rises on my cheeks, surprised by the sudden influx of emotions. Finn notices I haven't breathed and breaks the contact.

Inhaling, I look away and tuck the fallen strands of hair behind my ear.

"What is it?" he asks, trying to understand what he had witnessed.

With everything that had been going on, I had become vulnerable to these feelings again. They had been shut away for so long until now. My attempt to force them back is only to ensure they don't become something I can't return.

"Nothing," I smile, plastering it on.

There was a big chance Finn was going to see straight through me considering he knew me so well. Yet, he was still a teenage boy. When it came to feelings, I knew he wouldn't realise until it was either placed in front of him or too late.

"Come on," he says.

Dammit, I sigh in my head. He paid far too much attention sometimes.

"No, honestly, I just really missed you."

Frowning, Finn scoffs and tilts his head to the side.

"We were always friends, Rosebud," he says, returning the arm around my shoulder, "Although I wish you would tell me what was going on with you."

With one big inhale, I start the story again. Explaining everything was easier the second time around after speaking with Ebony. I told him that Mum wasn't coping because Dad was still missing and that it was worrying me. I even briefly mentioned Jasper which seemed to make me uncomfortable and shy. However, we breezed over it and continued to talk about how I felt about the situation. Once we had finished talking, Finn had to go for his final exam. Reassuringly, he planted a kiss on my forehead and told me he was proud of me.

"See you!" Finn calls, "And well done, you're free!" he adds, disappearing into the crowd of students.

The rest of my day was quiet. I didn't see Jasper all day after Ebony and I blew him off. It was nice to have the tension taken off the situation, and the sunshine was certainly helping lighten the mood. The butterflies for Finn had stopped and I tried to bury the feelings that had resurfaced. I forced them down with one big swallow and busied myself with other thoughts. Jasper crept back into my mind, instantly filling me with a flurry of mixed emotions. I decided that would need burying too as I wasn't ready to deal with it.

Ebony met me at the end of the day to take me home as Mum had said she wasn't able to. Something had come up, so I was to make my own way home. I'd guessed she wasn't in the best place which filled me with anxiety. Ebony kept reassuring me that there was nothing I could do and that was okay. Her words eased my mind and settled my stirring worry. A few cars fly past as Ebony does her best to drive carefully to my house. She had been pulled over the night before and told to watch her speed. It didn't surprise me as I knew it would happen eventually. At least now I could rest easy knowing she was more considerate on the roads.

Loud sirens startle us from behind. I stare as an ambulance and two other vehicles rush by in haste. The light traffic parts like the red sea and gives way to the emergency vehicles. Only when we turn down the same road does Ebony give me a look of concern. Billows of smoke rise above the houses, and I realise it's coming from my street. There's a gathering of people at the end of the row, next to my house. My heart starts to race as the vehicles also stop next to my house. I'm reluctant to look and see the roof now glowing red.

Fire.

Ebony speeds down the street and emergency breaks to let me out. In a panic, I throw my bag down and begin to run, my feet pounding against the watered-down pavement. I can hardly breathe as I push my way through the gathered neighbours. They all look at me with pity and fear in their eyes, but I push by and ignore them. Horror fills me when I hear someone whispering about getting 'her' out.

Mum!

Flames engulf my house like a blanket of orange and red. There's a shared gasp as we hear a window shatter somewhere in the back.

"Mum?" I call, "Mum!"

I'm panicking.

Searching to see if I can see her, I glance at every face that will look at me. Their unfamiliar stares cause a nervous itch in the back of my neck. No one looks like Mum. I realise my worst fear is coming true. She must still be in there.

"Rose…" Ebony's voice cuts through and I look at her.

Tears are welling up in both our eyes as I tell her that I think Mum is inside. She shakes her head, knowing what I'm going to do and tries to hold me back.

"Let me go, Ebony." I cry, dragging my arm from her grip.

"This is madness, Rose."

"I can't lose her too…"

With Ebony's sad gaze in my mind, I force myself towards the house. Running up the footpath, I feel the intensity of the fire's heat prickle my skin. A fireman tries to stop me, but I duck and get away from his reach. The adrenaline makes me faster as I run through the open door and search for Mum.

Toxic smoke smothers my lungs. I cover my mouth for some protection and call for Mum. I'm choking as I listen. I can't hear anything above the crackling of burning wooden beams. Even the sound of protesting firemen is muffled inside the house. The heat is making me sweat, but I push on and find a way to climb the scorched staircase. Suddenly, something falls and there's a familiar cry. I hurry to her rescue.

Mum.

Bursting into her bedroom I see her under the beam that has fallen. It's burnt and smouldering as the flames die down. I try my best to move it off her, wrapping my jacket around to protect my hand. The beam lifts momentarily, and then it slips out my fingers as tears sting my face. Mum flinches under the impact, her eyes remaining shut.

I feel sick.

Screaming for help, I check to see if Mum is still breathing, but I can't tell. My shaking hands are unable to find a pulse and I can't think straight. There are no emotions in her touch. I notice blood is pouring from the back of her head. I press on it, still choking on smoke, and hope to stop the bleeding until someone finds us. I call out again and cough into my arm. My hands become bloodied, wet and trembling as I wait.

My face is drenched with tears when emergency service personnel finally come. I try to fight against them as they tear me away from Mum, but their grip is too strong. I look up at the fireman, who is in fact a woman, and demand to stay. She ignores me and forcefully leads me out. I struggle feebly as I'm too weak from the lack of oxygen. The smoke in my lungs tickles every time I try to breathe.

Two medics pass by with a stretcher which I assume is for Mum as we walk down the stairs. Hope floods over me; now that they've found her, she might be okay. There's a muffled radio call which makes the firewoman quicken her pace. I ask what's happened, but she doesn't respond. All I know is that whatever they said, it wasn't good.

Once I'm outside, I begin to choke on the fresh air. My body had become accustomed to the carbon monoxide that was trying to smother me. Three medics run towards me with a blanket and guide me to the ambulance. Ebony rushes through the crowd in floods of tears. She squeezes me tightly and I begin to cough more violently. She immediately lets go and apologises, rubbing my back. She tells me I was silly for going in there, but I know she's just afraid. My head is blurry with smoke and my chest feels like it's too big for my ribcage. They give me a bottle of water for my dry mouth, and I take it anxiously.

Pushing Ebony to one side, a paramedic asks specific medical questions, but I'm not listening. The image of my Mum is haunting me, and I can feel the sickness rise. Bile threatens at the back of my tongue and before I know it, I throw up. A female medic rushes into the ambulance and grabs a bowl for me. She smiles at me, but her reassurance is wasted.

"They're going to get her out of there," Ebony says, finding her way back to my side, "It's going to be okay."

"I want it to be okay," I sob, "I want her to be okay."

Another blood-curdling scream makes us look up and turn to the house. My eyes don't believe what they're seeing. Smoke, flames, glass, and brick blur as the house falls to its knees. Every memory was lost, now hidden in the rubble, and engulfed in hungry flames. People are panicking whilst I search for any sign of Mum's stretcher. I spot the firewoman who walked me out and she is calling for anyone who is inside. Each time, she waits longer for a sign of life. Her shoulders droop and she turns to face her fellow firemen. Our eyes lock at the last second.

Lowering her gaze, I finally understand.

"No!" I scream, "No! It can't… it can't… no…"

Pulling me into a hug, Ebony firmly holds me as I sob. Fighting her, I tell her it's not true and that she was wrong. There was no way that Mum had gone. It was impossible.

"Rose, she's gone," Ebony utters between tears.

"No," I reject angrily, "No, she isn't. She can't."

Ebony squeezes me tightly as she tries to soothe me, but she gets caught up in her own tears. Her body is shaking as she clings on, not wanting to let me go. Neither of us wanted to accept the reality which was; Mum was gone. She was buried with every other piece of home I had left.

"Miss O'Donnell?" a voice appears beside us, "We need to take you to the hospital."

Shaking my head, I refuse and latch onto Ebony even tighter. Her emotions overwhelm my fingertips and coarse through my arms. I'm taken aback by the impact and feel a dizziness setting in. Ebony asks if I'm okay, but I'm unable to speak. My tongue is heavy, and my eyes won't open.

"Miss O'Donnell?"

CHAPTER
Seven

"I'm so sorry," Another officer says for the hundredth time. I sit unresponsive on the hospital bed stuck in a trance. The tears are unrelenting, and my heart still races. They tell me they think it was an oven fire, but they can't be too sure until they do further investigations. The shock of what had happened hadn't sunk in yet. It felt like a dream, a horrific, sickening dream that I couldn't wake up from.

When I finally came around, the paramedics wiped the blood off my hands in the ambulance and treated the burns I had obtained. There were a lot of questions and awkward gaps when I refused to speak to anyone. They told me Ebony was following in her car as though to comfort me.

Now, surrounded by officers and medical staff, I was thankful Ebony was allowed to stay whilst I was assessed. I'm holding her hand tightly as I close my eyes and wish for them to leave. The officers keep asking the same questions about my family, especially my dad.

"And your father's name…?"

"Thomas O'Donnell," Ebony replies for me.

We both stare blankly at them as they continued their examination. I think Ebony was in shock, her hand shaking faintly in my grasp.

"And you say he's in the army…?" the officer asks.

I nod and it was clear they didn't know what had happened.

"He's missing," my voice croaks.

They start whispering to themselves. I'm not sure what to expect next. I've lost all my family in such a short amount of time. Everything I owned was in that house. All I had left was my college bag and the clothes I was wearing. Anxiously, I begin rubbing my arm where they've stuck a needle in me to give me fluids. It's meant to replace everything I've lost through being sick. Yet, the more they spoke, the worse the nausea got.

Suddenly, an officer rests his hand on my shoulder making me flinch. I don't think he sees my surprise as he continues to talk down to me.

"We are sorry Miss O'Donnell for your loss. We will find your dad and make sure he is sent straight home to collect you. Until then, do you have any family members you can stay with?"

I shake my head; we didn't keep in contact with our extended family. Mum and Dad's parents weren't around anymore, and any aunts and uncles lived in different countries. They might as well have not existed.

"Okay sweetheart, what about your friend here?"

They look to Ebony who's whiter than a sheet of paper. I've never been to Ebony's house as she had said her family didn't like having people over. It was strange at first, but I accepted it quickly. I'd preferred staying at mine anyway, it was safe and familiar, and we had way more fun.

Everyone stares at Ebony, waiting for an answer.

"Yeah, she can, um," her lip quivers, "She can stay at mine."

"Brilliant," the officer beams, "We will talk to the doctors and Social Services. They can release you when they think you're ready," he grabs his hat and looks at Ebony, "Can we speak to you and find out some details, please?"

Glancing at me, Ebony checks to see if I'm okay. I nod and squeeze her hand before letting go.

"I'll be okay," I reassure her, and she agrees to leave with the policeman.

My gaze follows them as they talk about addresses and other details. It's hard to hear once they leave the ward. I'm left with an empty feeling and unwelcome watching eyes. The nurses busy themselves, checking me over for the second time.

A lot had been said this evening. The police explained how they weren't expecting to find a body in the wreckage for a short while. However, they assured me they would let me know if there were any changes. Not that it mattered. If I were honest, I didn't know if I really wanted them to find the body. I didn't want to have to see my own Mum like that. Nobody should have to see their parent like that. I wouldn't cope knowing my last memory of my mum was seeing her laying on a metal table. Seeing her once loving, chocolate brown eyes sealed shut by death itself, her skin cold to the bone.

"We think that it would be best for you to stay here for the night, is there anything we can get you?" a nurse asks.

Their probing eyes scratch at my skin with their continuous stares. I shake my head and tell them that I was tired. There's a long pause before they decide to talk 'privately'. Once they've left, I crumble. Thankfully, nobody returns to watch me cry. I let myself sob into my pillow and curl up under the itchy blanket. The ache in my stomach is unbearable. I hold myself, knowing there weren't many more tears left in me.

In the end, Ebony didn't return to say goodbye. She texted me to say 'goodnight' and explains that she was asked to leave. Her promise to visit in the morning is reassuring as I want to see her as soon as possible. I didn't like it here. I also receive texts from Finn and two missed calls. He knew and wanted to make sure I was safe, but I didn't have it in me to reply.

What do you say? I'm okay, I'll survive? It was pointless, everything was gone and there was nothing I could do. The nightmares had already started, and I wasn't even asleep yet. The thought of not having Mum was tattooed on my mind and there was nothing I could do to erase it. All I could see was Mum under the rubble and ash, helpless.

Eventually, I close my eyes and the exhaustion forces me into a haunting sleep filled with fire and blood. Nurses rush to my aide as I call out and try to relax me. I can feel the smoke again and I'm choking uncontrollably. There's the smell of burnt wood and iron blood tickling my nose. I'm unable to get away as sickness returns.

"Miss O'Donnell," a nurse's voice gasps.

Her panicky emotions are prickly on my skin. I shake her off, but she returns immediately with a tighter grip. We wrestle momentarily and she tells me to calm down. The anxiety is too much as I'm gasping for air again and wishing the sickness would settle. Firmly, the nurse tells me to take a deep breath and I inhale automatically. At the same time, I feel a needle in my arm scratch my skin. I hear the nurse tell me to calm down, reassuring me that 'this will help' and darkness follows.

7:00 AM WAS AROUND THE TIME THEY DECIDED TO WAKE ME ON MY second day in the hospital. A soft, calming voice was chosen to call me out of my slumber. I recognised her from the night before, but I couldn't picture her face at all. Reluctantly, I open my eyes. The sunlight stings my sensitive eyes forcing me to shut them again.

"Is everything alright, Miss O'Donnell?" she says, and I nod.

As I sit up, I stare in surprise at the presence of two women standing at the foot of my bed. The one I recognise is dressed in a crisp navy-blue uniform and her hair is pulled into a blonde ponytail. I look at her name badge and read her name, April Marston. She smiles and starts a routine check before writing on her clipboard.

"All good!" she says brightly.

I stare at her blankly. How could I be *good?* I was a wreck.

The second lady was shorter than April and her hair was in a pretty pixie crop. She also looked quite young and so I assumed she must be a trainee nurse. It made sense but her outfit said differently. I looked at April for an introduction and she smiled, understanding.

"This is Lucy, she's our resident support worker," her voice, ridiculously chirpy. "She will be looking after you when we're not around."

April gestures for us to shake hands and I offer mine half-heartedly. I'm not looking forward to this. Lucy and I look at each other and her face turns to pity. I sigh; I've seen so much of that face. It didn't bring Mum back so why did they do it? I lie back down and stare at the ceiling. It was too much energy to get angry, and instead, I wanted to be left alone.

"I guess we'll do this later," April says as she guides Lucy away. "Your breakfast should be here soon," she says softly and starts towards the door.

Relieved, I close my eyes. All of a sudden, April stops and turns to me.

"Please eat it," she says thoughtfully before she and Lucy both exit the ward.

Sitting up again, I wait for food as my stomach groans. Against my better judgement, I would say I was hungry, though there was a sickening taste in my mouth. A male nurse appears at the door and hands me a tray. I take it and thank him, gratefully. Just as I'm about to take a bite, the same nurse appears at the door.

"Sorry Miss O'Donnell, but we have some visitors for you."

Now?

As I look to see who it is; relief overwhelms me. It's Ebony and Finn. Tears are evident on Ebony's pale cheeks and Finn's eyes are red and bloodshot as though he's not slept. They both look how I feel; haunted by the sudden loss of Mum. Finn is holding a plastic bag with something in it, but I'm distracted as Ebony approaches me. I welcome her embrace.

"Hey," she says.

"Hey," I reply, taking in her familiar smell.

A few tears trickle down my face as I hold her tighter. Finn stands watching us, but his mind seems to be elsewhere. When Ebony lets go, I call Finn over. I say his full name which snaps him back into reality. There's a glistening in his eyes and I can see he's holding back tears.

"I'm sorry Rose. I… I'm so sorry."

Finn falls apart, unable to look me in the eyes. I get up and wrap my arms around him, and he pulls me in. His warm tears trickle onto my cheeks as we hold one another. Ebony sandwiches me in between them and their sadness forms a bubble around me. I'm able to feel their pain, but this time they can also feel mine.

Ebony had always felt like a second child to Mum. Without her parents here, Mum was the mother Ebony went to for advice and wisdom. Mum could see through the hard shell that Ebony put on and welcomed her into our home. My heart ached for Finn, too. He had known my family his entire life. Mum was his 'cool' Auntie Emma who helped him through his parent's divorce. Mum and Dad spent hours with him when his parents began fighting. Our home was his safe place to escape. Mum loved both Ebony and Finn as if they were her own. They were family, blood or not.

Finally, Finn manages to hold it together and we all pull away at the same time, wiping our faces of the tears. Ebony grabs my hand and squeezes it gently, her eyes reassuring me. Finn kisses my forehead to comfort me, and I inhale his familiar scent. Gratitude overwhelms me as I realise that some of my family still lives.

"Thanks for coming."

My lip quivers as I try not to cry again. Ebony shakes her head and smiles sadly. She picks up the plastic bag and joins me on the hospital bed.

"We couldn't let you deal with this on your own," she replies.

"Thank you…" I sniff.

Ebony's long, dark hair falls and covers her face as she looks into the plastic bag. She opens it up so that I can see inside and starts explaining the items.

"I also brought you some clothes, they're as colourful as I could find," she says, handing the bag over to me.

"Thanks," I reply with a smirk; she barely wore anything bright.

Taking the bag, I hug her again and she squeezes me tightly. Finn is not as receptive and seems lost in his own trail of thought. His expression suggests he's holding back from saying something which is bothering him.

"When is Eli coming?" he asks abruptly.

I frown. I'd never heard that name before. I turn to ask Ebony about him but notice a silent conversation between them. There's a warning in her eyes as Ebony glares at Finn and shakes her head, mouthing 'stop'.

"What?" he asks, defensively.

Glancing between them, I feel as though I've missed something important.

"Who is Eli?" I ask, forcing Ebony to look at me.

Her emerald eyes look me over, but she still won't meet my gaze. She licks her lips nervously and glances at Finn.

"Tell me," I demand, pulling her focus back to me.

"He owns the place I live at," she sighs, "I don't live with my aunt and uncle, I live with Eli. It's… it's like a…" she pauses as she tries to think of a way to describe it, "It's a place for young people to stay. Like a hostel but better."

Confused by her explanation, I don't quite know what to think. I thought she had family here, but obviously, that wasn't the case. She was living in a hostel, and she was clearly embarrassed by it. I needed her to know it was okay. Grabbing her hand, I open my mouth to speak but immediately get interrupted.

"Here she is!" A bright voice bursts through the doors and I see Lucy beaming at me.

Finn, Ebony and I all stare as she accompanies a brunette lady who has a Social Services lanyard around her neck. An elderly man follows them in a dark, grey suit. Though he had white and grey peppered hair and beard, the man walked with energy and poise. There was a grace about him that gave me a sense of ease.

"Hello," I whisper, already standing to greet him.

He beams, taking the hand I had unknowingly offered to shake it. No emotions flood my fingertips except peace. Lucy gestures to the man and squeezes his arm as though she knew him. She glances at us both and turns to the Social Worker. The brunette lady seems to be staring vacantly at Finn and Ebony.

"Sorry, I didn't realise you had visitors..." Lucy says, embarrassed.

"Would you two mind waiting outside for a moment?" the Social Services lady says pointedly.

Finn looks at me and then at the elderly man. They exchange a look I can't quite work out. Ebony does practically the same thing.

"It's okay, they can stay," the man says softly, "Ebony, Finn," he nods a greeting to them.

I'm piecing everything together when we get introduced.

"Okay," the lady says nervously, glancing at Lucy, "Rose, this is- "

"Eli," I mutter, cutting her off.

"Yes dear," the lady nods, "He's going to look after you whilst we get in contact with your father. We understand that it is of the utmost importance that we get you settled into somewhere soon. You can't stay here, obviously."

The lady snorts rudely and I notice Lucy wrinkle her nose at her.

"We don't think that you will find much better than Eli as he is…"

By this point, I'm not listening. I'm staring at Eli as he leans on the arms of his chair. He rests his chin on his hand whilst politely listening to the Social Worker. There are creases around his eyes which tells me he's kind. Dad always said that the placement of wrinkles was a tell-tale sign of a person's character.

"We've completed the paperwork, but it will take a day, or two, to process. Mr. Blakewood has been excited to meet you and we hope you will feel it is a good fit. His record is excellent on the system. I know he's very good with orphans like you…"

The word *orphan* captures my attention.

"What Ida is trying to say is that you're in safe hands," Lucy chips in and smiles, reassuringly.

The brunette lady, Ida, looks at Lucy over her glasses and screws up her lips. Understanding, Lucy looks at me and smiles again.

"I'll let you get acquainted, but I'll only be outside if you need me," she gives me a meaningful look.

I nod and Lucy quickly leaves. Ida smiles as she sits down on the chair in the corner. She gestures for Eli to introduce himself properly.

"Hello Rose," his voice is gentle, and it draws my attention. "I'm so sorry for your loss," he says to me.

It sounds so genuine that I'm slightly taken aback, but I'm not sure why. Everyone had said this to me over the past 24 hours. Yet, there's something in his cadence that is different. An aching pain returns as I think about Mum, but I'm not upset. I'm just sad, and hungry.

"Ebony's has told me that you need a place to stay…"

"I do…" I reply, glancing over at my breakfast tray.

"It's okay," Eli says softly, "You can eat if you want."

Thanking him, I grab my tray and have a mouthful of toast. Its welcomed buttery taste is immediately curing my aching stomach. As I sit down, I realise Ebony hasn't looked up from the floor since Eli started talking. Neither has Finn.

"What's wrong with you two?" I ask suspiciously, making Ida look up from her notes.

Everyone is staring at me.

"I'm sorry," I mumble.

"Oh, my dear, are you alright? Do you need some water with that?" Eli says meaningfully to me.

Immediately, Ida stands up, offering to get some, and leaves without another word. Eli looks back at me and then to the window behind him. He stands up and opens it, muttering something under his breath.

"So, how are you doing, Rose?" he asks, returning to his chair.

Eli looks at me with patience in his eyes and waits quietly. I'm soothed by the space that follows his question.

"I'm okay," I reply after a short while and he nods again. "Thank you," I add, politely.

"Has Ebony explained anything to you?" he glances at her, and she shakes her head, "Ah," he says, locking his hands together, "No wonder you're confused. I'm sorry, this is a very difficult time for you. I hope you understand that I'm here to help. I can offer you a room, clean clothes, some hot food…"

"She knows I live with you," Ebony mumbles.

"I know," Eli replies, "She has a lot to learn, but for now, she needs to know that she is welcome at the Manor."

Manor?

This was much fancier sounding than the hostel Ebony suggested it would be.

"Here we are, one glass of water!" Ida returns, disrupting the unspoken tension in the room.

Eli stands up and walks over to Ebony and Finn, placing a hand on their shoulders. They look up at him and nod, as though there has been a silent agreement between them.

"These are two people who love you very much, Rose. Please don't forget that." Eli says, before approaching me, "I'll be back for you tomorrow morning."

"Is everything okay, Mr Blakewood?" Ida asks, confused.

"Yes, thank you, Ida," he looks over at me, "I think we will be perfectly fine," he smiles, "I look forward to seeing you tomorrow."

Eli strolls towards the doors with Ida leading the way.

"Goodbye Rose," he says with a wave.

"Bye!" I call after him.

The room quietens as he leaves and I'm not sure what to make of him. His whole presence is unlike anyone I'd ever met before. I think it was the deep greyish blue of his eyes like a stormy ocean.

They make me think about A Rún and it catches me off guard. His words leave me more confused as I replay them in my head.

"Rosebud?" Finn says, his voice is gentle but urgent, "We really need to talk to you."

Both of their faces are red and filled with shame. Neither of them can look me straight in the eye and I know it's not good news. I'm not sure if I'm ready for any more revelations and shake my head at them.

"Please don't, I'm not ready for anything more."

Grabbing a hand each, they come around me and I feel their urgency and love surge through my skin. It's warm and prickly, kind of like having hot bristles brushed along your arm.

"It's important," Ebony sighs, "We know about your Gift."

Speechless, I stare at them both in disbelief. Did I just hear them correctly or was I imagining it?

"What?"

Shaking my head, the shock dissipates into anger. I had said that I didn't want any more revelations today. Why was she doing this now?

"Rosebud?"

"Don't!" I hiss, "Don't touch me…"

Heat fills my body as I rip my hands away from them. I stand up and put distance between us, knowing I didn't want to feel any more of their emotions. Ebony tries to reassure me that it was okay and that she was trying to help me. Finn also trying to do the same, but it's not working.

"How could you both lie to me? You made me think I was crazy! First, it was Jasper, now you two…"

Frustratedly, I exhale and throw my hands up in the air.

"What about Jasper?" Ebony says, fear clouding her eyes.

"What?" I snap.

"You said 'first it was Jasper'." Ebony turns to Finn and then back to me. Her expression is concerned but her voice is stern. "What has he told you?"

Guilt trickles like thick oil into my chest; I hadn't been fully honest either.

"Jasper told me believed me and that he had friends who knew about powers," I sigh.

Reluctantly, I retell the story of what happened with Jasper and watch as the blood drain from their faces. Fear grabs me by the neck after they exchange a nervous look.

"Does he know where you are now?" Finn asks.

"No, we haven't spoken since…" I reply, "Why?"

"Okay," Ebony says. She sits beside me again and grabs my hand, forcing me to sit down. "You need to listen to us carefully. There are some things we need to tell you and it's important you don't get angry, just listen. Please. I am *begging* you."

My heart rate is increasing as I glance between them. They're scaring me.

Ebony inhales anxiously before starting her explanation. She describes something called a Gift, something that she and I and Finn all have. She says that Eli doesn't like calling it a power as this implies that we use it to control others.

"It's supposed to help others," Finn assures me.

Finn then goes on to explain that Eli looks after Gifted people and protects them. However, most of the people who live with Eli weren't Gifted. Finn talks about another family who already lived there. The father of the family was good friends with Eli and had known him for a long time. They knew about the Gifted children, but they didn't mind. There was a clear mutual respect for Eli and the Gifted children that he protected.

When Ebony's family had kicked her out, she moved in and to my surprise, so had Finn. They had been working together to look after me under Eli's instructions. They mentioned that I was different to any other Gifted. I had no idea what that meant, but the outcome didn't sound like it led to anything good.

"You're basically going to be hunted," Ebony says bitterly, "They know you're vulnerable, so we need to get you out of here."

"What?" Finn and I both say in unison.

Ebony is already handing me my coat and producing something that looks like a blade from her boot. Alarmed, I raise my eyebrow and look at Finn. He seems just as confused and grabs her by the arm.

"What are you thinking?" he says.

Instinctively, she bats his hand away and tells him to never touch her again. It's as though I see a glimmer of their old selves, but it quickly disappears.

"We need to keep her safe, *here*," Finn insists.

Ebony calculates her next move before returning the knife to her boot. I watch her fold her arms across her chest and sigh.

"Fine," she glares at Finn, "Do you have a better idea? They're going to come for her sooner rather than later."

"I know," he snaps back, "But we can't just break her out. We have rules and Rose still needs to be treated, remember."

"Remember?" Ebony growls and squares up to him, "Did you forget that your job is to protect her? I'm trying to do that. You could at least try…"

An argument breaks out. They're antagonising each other by talking over one another. Finn is desperately trying to be heard whilst Ebony gets louder and more aggressive. I haven't seen them fight like this in a long time. I'm not sure if I have the energy to break them up.

A white noise invites me into an unexpected darkness as the thumping in my head gets louder.

"Rose!" their voices call, but everything goes silent.

CHAPTER
Eight

Midnight.

I've been waking up almost every hour. Finn and Ebony promised they would stay close by whilst I was in the hospital. Unsurprisingly, it didn't calm my nerves to know this. In fact, I was terrified. Suddenly I was in the middle of something, and it was all because of some Gift. A Gift that I *did not* want.

What I wanted was my parents back and my normal life again. I wanted my house and my bedroom and my space. This room was too empty and cold. The hospital's quiet bustle and the consistent beep of machines reminded me that I had lost everything.

"Rose?"

The whispering voice makes my heart race. It's unrecognisable which forces my breathing to increase rapidly. Looking up from my phone, I search the room and see a figure at the doorway.

I'm hoping it's one of the nurses, but the thought of an intruder creeps into the back of my mind. Ever since Ebony and Finn told me about being hunted, I've been unable to get it out of my head. *You're going to be hunted...*

"Please don't panic!" the voice assures me, but it isn't helping. The figure moves closer with their hands up in an attempt to show me they mean no harm.

"It's me," he says.

Exhaling, I realise who it is. In the low light, his hazel-forest eyes twinkle, giving him away.

"What the actual heck, Finn!" I scold him.

Pushing his curly, chestnut hair back, Finn smiles sheepishly and apologises. My heart is still racing as I welcome the hug he gives. He squeezes me and tells me to move up so he can sit with me. There's not a lot of space on the bed and we end up balancing ourselves precariously side-by-side.

"I'm sorry about everything," Finn whispers, "I never wanted to hurt you or give you a reason not to trust me."

As we lay there, I rest my head on his shoulder. We both stare at the ceiling, our minds in completely different lands. Somehow, we were trying to make sense of the situation. Finn said he knew more than he felt was necessary for me to know and that was okay right now. His priority was being there for me, and that was enough.

"It's okay," I whisper back, "I know you did what you had to because it was your job."

"But I'm not just here to be a protector," Finn replies, taking my hand in his, "I love you and you're my best friend."

"I know," I nod.

Closing my eyes again, my heart flutters momentarily and then a quiet peace returns. Finn was quite comfortable telling me he loved me since we were little. It was what made me fall for him in the first place. I realised after a few years that his love for me was different, though. I was like his little sister, or really, *really* close friend. Finn made it clear that he never wanted to be more and that's why I had to get over him. It was hard at first, but Finn kept me safe and protected, and I didn't want to lose that, ever.

Quietly, Finn plants a kiss on my head and puts his arm around me. I bury into his chest and feel his heart beating steadily. The gentle, steady beat almost rocks me to sleep. He strokes my hair as I rest and take in his comforting, familiar scent. The tiredness comes back, and I find myself drifting off into a welcomed bliss.

Get up.

A voice wakes me from my slumber. It's getting louder, pulling me urgently from my bed. I'm barely awake when I open my eyes to dim light and footsteps.

"Rose! Get up!"

Finn looks back at me, holding me behind his back so that I can't see what's happening. He's poised, ready with his tightly-fisted hands beside him. There's an exchange happening as Finn talks slowly, fiercely. I'm almost certain there's a hint of threat in his response which is unlike the Finn I know.

"She comes with us, or I'm going to have to take her from you."

The voice is coming from an unfamiliar female, and I try to take a glance at her. Her black and ruby red-haired is shining in the low light as the girl leans by the door, glaring. She sees me and pauses, and then her smile grows more calculating. Another body appears from the shadows which takes me by surprise. He grunts and glares almost animalistically, ignoring Finn completely. His orange marble eyes are locked on mine.

"Don't you dare," Finn warns, continuing to shield me.

The impending fight breaks out into one blur of shadowy bodies, grunting and hitting one another. I try to focus and stay alert, unsure of what to do if I have to defend myself. Finn is closest to me and is landing quite a few heavy punches on the beastly man. There's a growl but Finn ducks, avoiding the clawed hands of the intruder. This irritates the creature-like man even more. My eyes keep checking for the girl at the door as she approaches me. Finn notices and swings to kick her in the chest which throws her back. She curses at him and gets up, running towards me.

"I don't think so," a familiar voice bursts through the doors.

Gasping, I look up and see Ebony, kitted out in all black, already throwing punches. Her unmistakable black hair brings a flood of relief. Ebony eyes lock onto the unfamiliar girl as she attempts to disarm her. There's a struggle, but Ebony seems to have the upper hand. She wrestles the girl into a headlock and pulls her hair to get her to listen. There's an exchange of insults, but the unfamiliar girl seems to be losing consciousness. Her eyes are rolling back when I try to tell Ebony to stop, unable to cope with the thought of watching someone die tonight.

"Rose!" Finn yells as something sharp hits my head.

Collapsing on the ground, I know whatever hit me was not good. Dizzy and losing my own consciousness, the reality of the situation hits me. Someone drags me by my shoulders and throws me back down to the ground. My spine is throbbing as I lay, unable to get up. There's a darkness that comes which I have become accustomed to so I welcome it. I didn't want to see how this fight ended anyway. I just wanted Ebony and Finn to win.

"Hey!" A voice draws me out of my slumber, holding my hand tightly. I feel their worry in my palms like a cold, morning dew. "Hold onto me, okay? Rose?"

The voice pants wearily as it tries to bring me to. I recognise the stern tone as Ebony's. It's the voice she has when she's trying not to panic.

In the stillness, I feel my headache fade away and the dizziness subsides. An unusual energy flows through my hands and awakens the rest of my weak, bruising body. Forcing my eyes open, I stare at the two concerned faces watching me. A chestnut blur waits beside me as Ebony quietly checks for injuries.

"I'm okay," I reassure them, "I just got hit really hard, I'll be fine."

Touching my head to find the cause of the dull ache, I feel a warm, sticky liquid on my scalp. Shaking, I look at my hands and see dark, crimson blood decorating my fingertips. I wipe it away and try again, but Ebony blocks me and pulls my hands away.

"Don't," she says, "Let me do it."

For half a second, I'm sure Finn gives Ebony a look, but it's gone before I can ask. He sits beside me and holds my hand, wiping off the blood with wipes he had found in the cabinets. His knuckles are bloodied and bruised, but he doesn't seem to be in pain. His expression is calm, collected, as he meets my gaze again.

"I'm sorry you had to see that," he whispers.

Shaking my head, I squeeze his hand. "Thank you for protecting me," I say and turn to Ebony, "Both of you."

A moment of relief is shared between us. Finn puts his arm around me and lays my head on his shoulder. I reach for Ebony and pull her into my side so we're all being embraced. Their tiredness was tingling my senses, making me feel drowsy. Then I remember what had just happened and it chases the sleep away. Part of me still couldn't believe what I had witnessed.

"Will they be back again?" I ask, sitting up and looking between them.

Finn is hesitant as he replies, "Probably, but they won't get to you. You're safe with us."

"Well," Ebony chimes in, "You're safe with me, but Finn needs to try a little harder…" Her eyes flicker up at Finn.

"Thanks, Ebony, I feel so much better now," Finn says, scowling at Ebony, "As if I didn't already feel bad enough…"

"Hey," I say, calming them before another fight breaks out, "I don't think it's quite fair that we start blaming each other. Yes, something happened to me but I'm fine. I trust you both, and you proved that tonight," I stop and sigh, "I just want to know why… why did they come? What did they want?"

"You," Ebony says softly, "But we won't let that happen, ever."

Ebony and Finn look at each other before nodding and wrapping their arms around me. Squished between them, I feel safe and somewhat dizzy again, suggesting I was still concussed from the head injury.

"Okay, get off," I laugh, elbowing them off.

Smiling, Ebony gets up and picks something up from the floor. I watch her, realising there are pools of blood where I must have passed out. Nauseated by the sudden faint metallic smell in the air, I try to focus on the walls. To my horror, there's also blood splattered on them too.

"Look at me," Finn says, holding my face and turning it towards him, "Don't stare at it. Just look at me. Focus on something else, like what do you want to know?"

It's a good question, but my mind goes blank. All I can think about is the blood. I wrack my brain to think of a question, something that would take my mind off it, but I can't. There's so much blood, tears are starting to well up...

"Tell her about your Gift," Ebony says.

We both glance at her and she shrugs, continuing to clean the floor. She's taken the wipes from the cabinet by the door and used them to remove the stains. The now-crimson wipes make me feel nauseous again...

"So," Finn grabs my attention, "My Gift is the Protector's Gift. I have superhuman strength and intelligence, and I can adapt to other people's abilities. So, like, if someone can do something superhuman, there's a good chance I can do it too."

Processing the information, I stare blankly and repeat his words in my head to keep my mind focused.

"Only temporarily, of course," he adds.

As I think about it, I realise it makes sense. He is ridiculously smart, that had always been Finn's thing. I'd never really thought anything more of it. It would also make sense that he was super strong. Finn was always at the top of his P.E. classes and could do all the flips, jumps and weights like an Olympic athlete. He said it was because he enjoyed it, but now I see it was because he had the upper hand.

"I know it's a lot..." Finn says, trying to read my expression, "But I'm telling you, it's not as crazy as when I first got it. I was..."

"He freaked out," Ebony cuts in, raising her eyebrow at him.

"I did not..." he defends himself, "Okay, I did a little bit."

A small smile grows on my lips and I can't help the light chuckle that comes out. Finn seems relieved and laughs too. Ebony simply sits next to me again, holding the crimson wipes in her hands. She sees my eyes linger on them and gets up to throw them away.

"Tell her about your Gifts," Finn says, and Ebony stops in her tracks.

Turning around, I see Ebony's face go pale. She stares down at her hands before continuing towards the bin by the window. There's a clink as she lifts her foot off the peddle and the lid closes. She is quiet, deep in thought, as she considers telling me about her Gift.

"What is it?" I ask.

"I'm sorry," she says, sitting beside me, "I don't want you to be upset with me, but you know the whole 'I can feel your emotions' thing? Well, that's part of my Gift, too."

Again, I'm silenced by the revelation. Ebony's tight-lipped smile suggests this isn't the only surprise she has in store for me.

"I'm a Healer which means I can heal things, like... your head. It's not bleeding anymore, is it?"

Ebony indicates for me to touch my head again. As she has stated, there's no blood on my fingers and there doesn't seem to be any open wound. I press harder, expecting some kind of pain or wound to appear, but there's nothing. Gasping, I don't have the words to express how freaked out I am. Instead, I just stare at her, wide-eyed and in complete disbelief.

"Please don't panic..." Ebony says, squeezing my hand.

Calming sensations fill my body. I'm almost certain Ebony's using her power and it's unnerving.

"You're doing something," I say, "Aren't you?"

Ebony lets go, her shoulders drooping, and her gaze fixed on the hands in her lap. She rubs them repeatedly as if to remove the power they possessed.

"I'm sorry," she mutters, "I could see you freaking out and I didn't want you to be afraid of me."

Sighing heavily, I consider what she says and shake my head, "I'm not afraid," I reassure her, "It's just a lot to take it, you know?"

"I know," she agrees.

"I still love you both."

Exhaling, I look at each of them. Their weary, deflated expressions won't meet my gaze. Guilt hangs in the air and I'm not willing to let it win. They had said they were sorry, now I need answers.

"I do have one question though."

"What's that?" they ask in unison.

"If Ebony and I have similar powers, does that mean I'm a Healer too?"

They exchange a look and shake their heads.

"Not exactly…"

DESPITE KNOWING THAT THE MORNING WAS COMING, I STILL FELT RE-luctant to wake up. Everything between the fight and the conversations with Finn and Ebony in the early hours seemed to blur together. I had only slept for forty-five minutes before one of the nurses had arrived.

Jumping awake, I hear April's voice sing. I look around, knowing for sure that I had fallen asleep with Ebony and Finn both in the room. My heart races as I realise, they've gone. No idea how, but I take a few deep breaths to calm my shaking nerves.

Probably the same way they got in.

"Oh, did I scare you?" April asks, approaching me cautiously.

No, but my friends did.

Bright, chirpy faces flurry in and out of my room for the rest of the morning. Lucy and April both come to say goodbye, even though Eli still hasn't arrived. I've changed into a new outfit that Ebony had brought me. It's a dark blue, denim dress and cream cardigan with brown, suede dolly shoes. I can tell she's never worn the cardigan as it still has its label on it. The wait is finally over when I see Ebony and Finn arrive. Eli is not far behind them, confidently striding through the door with a beaming expression on his wrinkled face. His deep ocean eyes look over the room and there's an atmosphere of calm which is soothing.

"Come on then, Rose," Eli beckons.

Sunlight glimmers off the three of them as they begin to help me move my things. I don't have a lot, but they still make sure I don't forget anything. Looking between Ebony and Finn, I know I have everything I need.

"Come on then," Eli says, walking us out of the room.

There was an excitement that fizzed in the air as Eli lead me to his car. It was an old silver Bentley with white leather interiors and ornate wheels. I didn't know a lot about cars, but this definitely wasn't cheap.

"How are you feeling today?" Eli asks once we're buckled in.

"I'm okay," I nod.

Understanding my slightly glossed-over expression, he assures me that I can relax for the journey.

"It won't be too long, take a nap if you need it."

"Thanks," I yawn as we drive away.

A GENTLE HAND WAKES ME TO LET ME KNOW WE'VE ARRIVED. Opening my eyes, I see the beautiful Manor and sit up to take it all in.

As we pass through the gates, I read a large, slate plaque with beautifully engraved, white letters, which says: Blakewood Manor. Behind the gates is a long, gravelly road which leads to a large, grey, stone house. It was bigger than I had expected. With several chimneys at the top and floral grounds decorating the front, I found myself staring in awe. The windows were framed with more slate and limestone, and a huge wooden door invited us in.

The crunch of the gravelled driveway continues underfoot as we get out of the car. We climb the large, stone steps towards the front door and wait for Eli. Trees line the grounds like a fence and when I looked over my shoulder, I could see the Great Hills in the distance. We weren't in Corden anymore. My eyes glance across the exquisite front gardens. A large, Roman fountain sits in the centre of the road to the house, catching the sunlight and creating a delicate rainbow. The grass is freshly cut, tickling my nose with a sweet, dewy aroma. Taking it all in, I couldn't quite believe this was someone's home.

"Would you like to go in?" Eli asks, joining us.

Nodding, I stare at the large, wooden doors. They are giants in comparison to me, the taller-than-average girl that I am. Eli unlocks the door and pushes it open. I expected them to creak, but they swing with ease on their iron hinges. Calmly, Eli waits for me to go in before following with Ebony and Finn. He shuts the door behind us and takes my jacket. I stop in awe as I see the large, maroon, carpeted staircase. The large foyer is a pasty white with numerous old paintings on the walls. There's a large mirror above a desk which has a single, corded phone on it and a notepad. Two hibiscus trees guard the staircase with their flamboyant flowers in full bloom. This house was far too elegant to be someone's home. It was more like a castle that time had forgotten.

"This is incredible…" I mutter.

There's a low chuckle as Eli removes his grey coat and hangs it on the wooden coat rack. I notice a few coats are also hung on there and remember Finn telling me about the other family who lived there. Suddenly the nerves come rushing back. Eli places a hand on my shoulder and tells me to take a deep breath in.

"Don't be afraid, Rose," he reassures me, "Why don't I let Ebony and Finn show you to your room?"

Beaming, an excited Ebony is already taking my arm and walking towards the staircase. I run my hands over the thick, glossy, wooden banister as we climb to the top. Ebony is talking a mile a minute, but I'm too distracted by the house. My eyes can't process it fast enough. I find myself looking back and checking that it wasn't a dream.

"Cool, isn't it?" Finn says as he follows behind us.

"I thought you said this was a hostel…" I ask Ebony and she laughs.

"I'm sorry, it's not easy to describe," she replies.

"Yeah, I get that…" I say, staring at the wooden beams above us.

Once we get to the top of the stairs, I see that the walls are filled with bookshelves and wooden panelling. Huge, arched bay windows pour light into the landing. The flooring is also wooden with a patterned rug that lays square towards some doors. Ebony and Finn guide me to one of the doors where they tell me they've prepared a room for me. Ebony pushes the door open and tells me to look inside.

The room is light and filled with the scent of fresh lavender. A large, four-poster bed, draped in soft lilacs and a white, sheer curtain, is placed in the middle of the room. The headboard is leaning against the wall opposite the entrance door. A pastel purple wall is decorated with little silver wicker love hearts that have dried lavender hanging in the centre. The rest of the walls are a bright, fresh white which gives off a new paint smell.

As I walk in, I see there are some double doors behind more sheer white curtains which swing out onto a small, square balcony. I look around and notice there's another door which seems to lead to an en suite. Next to the door are some white chests of drawers with smooth, silver knobs on. A large vase with dried lavender is placed on top and I take a deep breath in to capture the scent.

I *love* lavender.

Ebony starts to draw the sheer curtains back and opens the balcony door. A warm breeze flows through the room and onto my skin. It reminds me that this isn't a dream. It can't be.

"I'll be right back," Ebony says, rushing out of the room.

Finn and I nod, and I approach the balcony to see the rest of the grounds. I couldn't believe how far the gardens extended. Finn laughs to himself and leans on the doorframe, watching me take the view in.

"You can't believe it, can you?" he says, joining me.

"No, I really can't."

Finn laughs again and nods in agreement. We stare into the garden without feeling the need to say another word. He wraps an arm around me and squeezes gently. I know he wants to say more to me, but he decides against it.

"Right!" Ebony returns abruptly, beaming and holding something in her hands.

Immediately, Finn lets go of me and we both turn to face Ebony. We are puzzled by the bag which makes her roll her eyes, waving at Finn to move out of the way. He steps aside, still confused, and watches as Ebony explains.

"So," she starts, "I've made you a survival pack. It has all your toiletries, first aid and emergency snacks," her voice lowers to a whisper, "For when you need a midnight pick-me-up."

Filled with an overwhelming sense of gratitude, I throw my arms around her and pull her into a hug. I thank her and take the bag before placing it on the bed. I unpack the sweet treats and disappear into the en suite to put the toiletries away. Unlike the bedroom, the bathroom is all white and has sparkly grey flooring. There's a mirror above the wash basin and a cabinet hidden within. I put the remaining toiletries in the cabinet and explore the rest of the room. There is a toilet and shower which are both pristine white. I run the taps and shower head and let the water wash over my hand for a moment and sigh contentedly.

I love this.

Peering into the bedroom, I look at Ebony and Finn who are in quiet discussion. I clear my throat to let them know I'm there. They look up immediately with a fixed smile as if to hide their guilty conscience.

"Come on," I sigh, "What are you two talking about?"

Shaking his head, Finn approaches me.

"Nothing," he says.

Unconvinced, I look to Ebony who says the same. Folding my arms across my chest, I lean on the bathroom doorway and wait for one of them to crack.

"I'm not having you guys keep any more secrets from me."

Glancing at each other, I notice their now fallen smiles are now barely hanging on. Finn swallows hard and finally gives in.

"There's someone else we want you to meet," he says, "We aren't the only two Gifted here…"

This doesn't surprise me as much as they seem to expect. I open my mouth to respond when we're interrupted.

"Talking about me, are we?"

A calm, strong presence appears at the door. We all look to see a young man with steel-blue eyes staring at us. Rich brown strands of hair fall across his face as the rest is pulled back in a messy ponytail. I notice his tank top and khaki green jeans are well-worn. The stubble on his face suggests he's older than us.

"Will," Ebony greets him.

"Hey Eb," he pulls her into a side hug.

As he lets Ebony go, he extends a hand to Finn and pulls him in and pats him on the back. They exchange a 'hey man' and pull away, all staring at me.

"So, this is her?" Will asks, approaching me with curiosity.

Stepping back, I hold his gaze and ask what he means. He laughs and shakes his head, calling me sweet. His expression doesn't falter as he leans his arm on the chest of drawers near the door.

"You're a Pure Gifted, a kind of rarity if you'd like," he says as he rubs his chin, "Although, you're not what I expected. You're very endearing."

In an attempt to hide the blush on my cheeks, I stare at the carpet in front of us. Will's tone doesn't seem flirtatious as he speaks, yet I find myself incredibly flattered anyway.

"Right," Will says, "Why don't you get settled and we can talk about the rest later?"

He pushes himself off the drawers and wanders out, nodding at Ebony and Finn as he leaves.

"Great," Ebony beams, approaching me.

She places both hands on my shoulders and rubs them reassuringly. I know she doesn't need to use her Gift to know how I was feeling.

"I promise you," she says softly, "Everything will become clear, but right now, as your best friend," she pauses as Finn coughs purposely, "I am ordering you to go and have a shower. You stink."

My mouth flies open as they both start sniggering. I glare at them individually and march around the room trying to find a towel. The drawers are full, and I realise everything is exactly like what I would have chosen for myself.

Damn, they know me well.

"The towels are in the bathroom," Finn says, pointing.

"Thanks," I reply, still pretending I'm insulted, "I expect both of you out of my room by the time I'm finished."

As I close the door, I watch them leave and break into a smile. They were good friends. Without them, who knows what would have happened to me?

A stab of pain hits me in my gut as I think of Mum. The sadness is overwhelming. I envision her again; still sitting in the car on the way to college singing her favourite songs. The last thing she said to me runs repeatedly in my head. I can almost see her precious smile and chocolate gaze, telling me how proud she was of me. She brushes the hair from my eyes, tells me she loves and drives away. Tears weren't enough to express how much I missed her.

CHAPTER
Nine

After my shower, exhaustion comes rolling in like a tidal wave. I crawl under my soft, cosy duvet and let my aching bones rest. The faint scent of lavender filled the air around me as I lay in the darkened room. Each drape was drawn so the only light came from the crack in the doorframe.

My mind kept rerunning the past week, over, and over, and over again. The torment of discovering an entirely new world with nothing of my old life seemingly surviving the whiplash. The hurt, pain and anxiety of it all was a toxic concoction for my fragile heart. I wanted to wake up and for it to all be a terrible, cruel dream.

Unfortunately, when I woke up, the world hadn't changed. Yet, the heaviness in my head had been relieved and the anxiety had retreated. Before any sadness could return, I decide to find the others and explore the Manor. The sun was lowering and cold, evening air was blowing through the drapes. I close my balcony doors before putting on some warmer clothes.

Running down the stairs, I almost miss a step and stumble into the foyer. I take an immediate right and pass the single desk I had noticed when I arrived. Through a wooden archway, I find myself in a wide, open kitchen. An island sits centre of the room surrounded by eight stools and has a bowl of fruit in the middle next to some flowers. Pots and pans hang on hooks under the cupboards trailing along the walls. A white light shines above the sink, illuminating the silver taps and basin. In the corner, I notice a short woman with her back turned to me. She appears to be quietly humming to herself whilst she cuts something on a chopping board. I begin retreating back into the foyer in hopes that she doesn't sense my presence.

"Hello dear," she says, turning around to face me.

A warm, kind face greets me. The older woman has short, thick, silver hair and beautifully golden honey skin. She has rosy cheeks and light grey eyes that sparkle as she introduces herself.

"My name is Ava, mother of the household," she says with a light chuckle, "You must be Rose."

Waiting for me to nod, she slowly approaches and extends her arms.

"Can I give you a hug?" she asks.

Nodding, I lean into her loving embrace. She smells of hyacinths and vanilla, and I immediately think of Mum. The hug lingers as Ava asks how I am, but I'm too busy thinking about Mum. Tears prick my eyes and I swallow them down before she lets go of me. I didn't want to cry again.

"Hello sweetheart. It's lovely to meet you," she beams at me and then her expression turns sombre, "I'm so sorry for your loss," she says, "I hope we can make you feel at home."

The same sad smile drifts onto my lips. I don't know what to say. I'm grateful for the warm welcome, yet there's nothing I can say about the rest. All I knew was that I felt empty inside.

"Can I get you something?" Ava offers, "Maybe a drink?"

"Um," I hesitate and look around, "I don't know. What do you have?"

"Well," she beams.

Walking over to one of the cupboards, she opens it and bends down. She reads off all the different squashes and soft drinks they have stocked. Then, she moves to the fridge and lists the fresh juices and a couple of milkshakes.

"Wow, you… you have a lot of choices."

"That's just the cold drinks, dear," Ava giggles, before listing off the coffees, hot chocolates, and teas. "So… what can I get you?"

"A fruit juice would be nice," I decide, "Can I have the orange, pineapple and passion fruit, please?"

Nodding, she opens the fridge again and grabs a glass from one of the top cabinets. She places it down and turns to me.

"Would you like ice?"

"I would love some ice," I say as I sit on one of the stools, "Thank you."

Once the drink is made, Ava slides it to me and asks how I'm doing. I explain that I had just woken up from a nap and that I was hoping to explore the house a bit more. There's a short-lived attempt to talk about Mum, but I insist that I don't want to talk about it now.

"Look," Ava says as she grabs my hand, "I understand that I'm just an unfamiliar, old lady who you've only just met, but if you ever need to talk," she pauses and looks into my eyes, "I'm here."

My lip quivers. I'm touched by her kindness and compassion as it radiates through her fingers. A tear escapes down my face and I can taste its saltiness on my lips. My strong exterior is being quickly demolished by this kind, gentle woman. Thankfully, Ava sees my stronghold crumble and catches me in her arms with a reassuring embrace.

"It's okay," she hushes me, rocking me slowly, "It's okay."

"I'm sorry," I say and scoff in embarrassment, "I didn't mean to burst into tears."

"You're okay," Ava reassures me.

Sitting back upright, I wipe the tears with my sleeve and force the pain back into its box. I focus on controlling my breathing and count each second slowly. If I don't pull it together, I know I'll lose it completely. Ava watches me closely, still rubbing my back to soothe me. I thank her and apologise again. She waves it away and tells me to 'never apologise for being sad'. Her words are comforting, and I thank her a few more times.

"Stop that," she scolds me playfully, "Now, go and find your friends. You need a distraction. I will not hear any more apologies, do you understand?"

"Yes," I reply, and add, "Sorry…"

We both start laughing and Ava shakes her head at me as the stillness returns. There's a sadness that hangs in the air, but it doesn't bring any more tears.

"You're going to be okay," Ava says, looking deep into my eyes.

"Thank you," I reply.

"Come on then, your friends are waiting."

Pointing to the door, Ava explains there's a games room where everyone should be. I follow her directions – straight ahead, the first left after the stairs and then a quick right. The room erupts with chatter and laughter when I open the door. Everyone is watching a game in the middle of the room between people I don't recognise. I think it's ping pong. Whatever it is, the room goes quiet once they realise, I'm there. A sea of eyes watches nervously, and some curiously, as I stand alone by the door.

"Rose!" Ebony calls my name and I exhale with relief, "Come over here!" she smiles and pats the seat next to her.

Self-consciously, I keep my eyes on Ebony as I pass through the curious looks. Ebony throws an arm around me when I sit down and asks how I am. She says she had come to check on me earlier but had found I was asleep. Concern clouds her eyes momentarily before her confidence reappears. I know she wants to ask more so I tell her that I'll be okay.

"Are you sure?" she asks.

"Yeah," I reply.

"Good, because you're about to meet everyone," she whispers before raising her voice, "Everyone!" she waves to get the room's attention, "This is Rose!"

The instant embarrassment ties my stomach in knots as I listen to Ebony introduce me. This was not the way I had hoped to meet everyone.

"She is shy and a little goofy- "

"Thanks, Eb," I mutter.

"Single-"

"Ebony…" My tone lowers, mortified, "Why would you say that?"

"So, play nicely, she doesn't bite…"

"Thank you, Ebony," I sing and grab her arm, clearly indicating that I would like her to stop.

An indistinguishable laughter whispers throughout the room. Ebony is looking pleased with herself, and I continue to glare at her, unable to meet the amused sea of watching eyes.

"What?" she asks, innocently.

"You are so dead," I say, but laughter escapes my lips.

Giggling, I feel the focus move from me and onto the game that had paused for my unfortunate introduction. I scan around to see if I can find Finn and notice he is sitting with Will. They both nod and smile, Finn's eyes sparkling with amusement.

In the middle of the room, there are ping pong tables where a girl with golden brown hair and a tall, lanky boy are playing. They tease one another with competitive smiles, clearly related by their similar button noses.

"That's Amber and Solomon, but we call him Sol," Ebony whispers, "They are Ava and Jesse's two eldest. Amber is a couple of years older than Solomon."

I notice their eyes are both a greyish blue, yet Amber has her mother's pink lips.

"Cool," I reply.

My gaze lands on two other probing eyes who are watching me intently. Her brunette bob and fringe frame her little oval face. She couldn't be older than six or seven. I give her a smile and her quizzical expression falters. Instantly she looks away, searching the room for someone else to focus on.

"That's Lily-Grace," Ebony whispers again, "She is one of Ava and Jesse's youngest. She and her twin are the sweetest duo you will ever meet."

Lily-Grace stares at a boy with a similar oval face and short brown hair. He has a frown printed on his freckled face and refuses to make eye contact with me. His lips tighten as he turns away and folds his arms across his chest.

"That's the other twin, Cole," Ebony laughs, "He is a little bit grumpy, but he has a good heart."

Solomon notices his brother's behaviour and calls him over whilst still playing Amber. A reluctant Cole lowers his head as he approaches the table, knowing he's in trouble. Sol leans down and whispers in his brother's ear and Cole immediately looks up.

"I'm sorry for being rude," he says to me.

"It's fine," I say, warmed by his guilty pout.

"I'm sorry," Sol says, approaching me once the game is over, "It's really nice to meet you, Rose."

Offering me a hand, I stare at it blankly. His outstretched hand reminds me of when Jasper introduced himself. Ebony nudges me with her shoulder to snap me out of it and I shake away the weird memory. His hand tingles with a flurry of emotions but I don't hold on long enough to read them. I exhale and smile, telling him not to worry about Cole.

"I can take a glare or two," I assure him.

"Oh good, because he has plenty of them," he laughs, looking back at his brother.

Cole looks puzzled before realising we're talking about him. Ebony stares at me whilst Sol and I interact, so I meet her gaze in wonder. She raises one eyebrow and I already know what she's thinking. I shake my head at her and gently kick her on the leg. She rolls her eyes and mutters a 'whatever', clearly entertained as a smile curls in the corners of her lips.

"Hey, little brother?" Amber calls, interrupting our conversation. "I think you and I have a score to settle, don't we?"

Lifting the ping pong bat, she spins it in one hand and gestures to the table. Sol looks at me and then back to his sister before shrugging, getting up and picking up his bat. They taunt one another, playfully, and begin. Both of them dance around the ends of the table to stop the ball from flying past.

"Would you just give up already? You're never going to win," she says halfway through the game.

"Oh please, like you've ever won against me before…" Sol scoffs.

There's an 'ooh' as the room goes silent, waiting for Amber's retort. She utters an insult and he scoffs, pretending not to be offended. Dramatically, Sol covers his chest but at the wrong moment and the ball flies past him.

"What was that, young Solomon?" Amber says, arrogantly.

"Whatever," Sol laughs, "You got lucky."

"Maybe," she replies, "But now you owe me."

Everyone is laughing and talking as the siblings begin bargaining with each other. It's nice to be involved in their game and feel like I can relax around them. Ebony has got up to talk to Amber when Finn quickly takes her place. He looks at me with his big eyes and tilts his head to the side.

"Are you okay?" he says, "We missed you earlier."

Summoning a smile, I nod and rest my head on his shoulder. He wraps an arm around me and rests his head on mine. His comfort calls the secret butterflies to come out of their hibernation. I can't afford to let them get out of hand, but for a moment, they comfort me with what was once there.

"I am now."

By THE TIME THE TWINS HAVE GONE TO BED, WE HAVE ALL PLAYED A game of ping pong against one another. Someone suggested doing a tournament to find the 'ultimate winner'. I'm terrible, unsurprisingly, so thankfully I only play once against Will. He takes it easy on me, but I'm still embarrassingly uncoordinated.

In the final match, Ebony and Finn get into a heated debate so much so that I have to intervene. Eventually, they agree to disagree, but only when I stand up, frustratedly, and approach the table. Ebony apologises as Finn serves the ball, finishing the debate once and for all.

"I guess they really respect you," Will says when I sit down beside him.

"No," I assure with a laugh, "They just know I don't like it when they fight."

Carefully, Will listens as I explain their long-standing feud over their friendship with me. However, Will did say that it made sense, and I agreed. There had been a complexity to our friendship that I had been completely unaware of until now. Finn had said many times that he wished he could have told me. It was Ebony who seemed unrepentant. She was stubborn in believing it was for the best.

"Do you think you would've believed them if they had told you?" Will asks with a confident stare.

Slightly taken back, I think about his question. I'm not sure what the answer is. If they had told me any of this, I would've probably laughed in their faces. It was beyond anything I could have ever imagined. The world I lived in wasn't anything like I had believed it was. I preferred what it was before, so I wouldn't have wanted anything to have changed that. Even if it meant Ebony and Finn had to hide who they truly were…

"Probably not," I admit.

It's fair to say that once Ebony and Finn decide on a draw, we have had enough of the game. Amber is exhausted and decides to head upstairs to bed. Sol follows shortly after. The four of us talk for a little while in the games room. I learn more about Will as he explains how he encountered Eli. He and his brothers, Luke and Jason, were in care, like me. Eli adopted the eldest two, but unfortunately, Jason had already been fostered by another family, probably because he was the youngest. Will seems saddened when he talks about Jason. He hadn't seen his youngest brother since he was five. Eli said that when he tried to find Jason, he had been officially adopted and was happy. Will had accepted that it was the best place for him to be, even if it meant the torment of never really knowing who or where he was now.

"He must be so different today," Will says, "I always remember him being scruffy and silly. We played lots in our parents' garden and caused all sorts of mischief. Luke and I were never that close, despite being a year apart."

"Why isn't Luke here now?" I ask.

"It's… it's complicated."

Casting my eyes across the room, I notice there's an uncomfortable silence that has descended. I want to ask a question, but their expressions are telling me not to. I decide to with my better judgement and quickly move the conversation along.

We discuss Will's Gifts and I find out he's called a 'Dreamer'. It means that he has dreams and visions of the future and can see light and darkness in people. I ask if he means literally and he nods, pointing to the contacts in his eyes. They're to give him a rest as it can overwhelm him sometimes. Eli had taught him to only use his Gifts when necessary and to always note every dream down in a notebook.

"I would show you," he laughs, "But none of it would make sense. Although, I did see you coming."

"Oh really?" I reply, intrigued.

"Yeah," he nods, "It's kind of an abstract dream but there were these colours and symbols…"

Confused, I try to make sense of his ramblings, but it's no use. It was obviously something I would understand if I had the Gift myself.

"I'm sorry," Will cuts himself off, "I'm doing a terrible job of explaining it, aren't I?"

"No," I lie, "It's just more complicated than I'm used to. I'm still getting my head around Gifts. I think what you're telling me is amazing."

"Thanks," he replies bashfully.

There's a comfortable lull in the room and I lean back, exhaling. Being around people who also had Gifts was giving me a sense of understanding and comfort. It was reassuring to know that they didn't find their Gifts easy to use, nor did they fully understand them when they first got them. I had no idea what I was capable of, and yet the fear lessened with the knowledge that nobody knew when they first started out.

"Come on," Ebony says, grabbing my hands and pulling me up, "We're going to watch a film. You two coming?"

Finn and Will's gormless faces stare up at us as they process the question. Finn stands to his feet and suggests we watch something scary. I immediately shut it down and he pleads, grabbing me from behind and hugging my waist tightly. Telling him no, he lets go and starts rubbing my shoulders muttering an 'okay fine'. It feels good as he loosens the tension in my body and I lose all concentration for a minute.

Dragging me along, Ebony leads me into a living room that's just past the kitchen. I immediately notice the conservatory-type ceiling which is in the shape of a dome. The sky is filled with stars in a dark, purple-reddish sky. Large candle sticks stand in the far corner of the room and green, velvet sofas are spread out along the walls. A few cushions are scattered on the floor and there's a DVD near the TV which has been left out.

"Right," Ebony says, still holding my hand.

She beams as she kneels down on the floor to flick through the DVDs. She pulls me down with her and appears to be an indecipherable mix of emotions.

"You can let go now," I tease in hopes to make her laugh.

Shaking her head, the bun of jet-black hair moves loosely. She adjusts it quickly, letting me go, and then grabs my hand again. I'm unable to read her properly and I think it's why she won't let me go. The light flickers in the corner and I turn to see Will has begun turning on the lamps. It gives off a warm, yellow glow which makes the room cosy and intimate. Finn grabs a fleecy cream blanket from a wicker basket and hands it to me.

"You'll need that," he says.

Pressing play, we settle in our chosen spots. Ebony and I have sat together as Will and Finn have taken a sofa each. The boys lay spread out, their arms folded across their chests. I'm not sure they're thrilled to be watching a rom-com, but they don't argue. Instead, their heads lean back and slowly they fall asleep. I keep glancing at them throughout the film, but Ebony and I are the only two left awake.

It was around 11:45 pm when Ebony suggested we watched another. Will had got up at some point to go to bed and Finn was out cold. I didn't have the energy to argue and let Ebony put on an action-adventure film. I didn't care too much as my eyes were already closing. The shrill sound of growing, excitable music and powerful gunshots were all I heard before sleep took over.

IN THE EARLY HOURS OF THE MORNING, I WAKE AND NOTICE THE GREY clouds above us. There is a promise of sunshine coming from behind the cottonwool sky, but I don't hold out hope. Everyone is asleep in the living room still. I notice Ebony has moved to a separate sofa to give herself some more space. She and Finn both mirror each other on the opposite sides of the room; covered in chunky, knitted blankets and heads propped up with cushions.

Making sure I don't wake anyone; I tiptoe across the room towards the kitchen. I'm thirsty and aching from the position I'd slept in. The sofas were not as comfortable as they looked. I grab some juice from the fridge and press the button for ice. The fridge erupts as it wakes up and I panic, immediately letting go.

"Do you have to be so loud?" a voice teases.

Turning around rapidly, I'm met with two juniper eyes. I gasp, recognising the dark, leaning figure as Jasper. His familiar hands are laced together, and I sense something different about him.

"How did you get in here?" I ask, glancing at Ebony and Finn over his shoulder; they're still asleep.

"It's complicated," he sighs, "I'm here because I need to tell you something…"

Jasper runs a hand through his hair and leans back on the countertop. He's in the same clothes as when I first met him. His eyes sparkle when they meet mine and then, the light goes out. I don't know what he's trying to say because I keep missing it. A white noise is filling my ears making me feel disorientated. I'm nauseated by the vibrations and cover my ears to stop it. Eventually, I cry out, but there's no sound. I try again and the same thing happens inducing more fear.

Did Jasper do this?

"Breathe Rose," Jasper's voice cuts through the dizziness.

He lays a hand on my arm, tentatively. My breathing slows as my heart stops beating loudly in my head and pulsating under my fingers. I'm able to open my eyes, but something doesn't feel right.

"Better?" he asks, and I nod slowly, "Good. I didn't want to scare you by using my powers, but hey, it worked!"

"Powers?"

Immediately, my body shivers at the word. I knew he said he was aware of them, but this was different. He had never admitted to having his own.

"Please," he says, reading my expression, "Please don't be scared. I'm not here to hurt you. I have to tell you something and it's really important that you listen to me."

"Why should I?"

"Please?" he begs.

Pushing past him, I head to the living room to warn Ebony and Finn of his presence, but I get stuck. My feet feel heavier as I get further away from Jasper. I turn around, glaring.

"Are you doing this?" I ask.

"No, I promise. This is how these things work."

"These things?"

"Rose, please listen to me," Jasper says, ignoring the question, "I know you don't trust me. You're scared, but this is minor in comparison to what I'm about to tell you."

Concentrating on breathing evenly, my eyes keep flicking to Ebony and Finn, wishing they would wake up. There wasn't anything I could do except listen now.

"Someone is coming for you, and you need to be ready," Jasper says calmly.

"Too late," I sigh, "If this is about the girl and the beastly guy…"

Slowly, he shakes his head and chuckles under his breath bitterly. There's a long, tired sigh as he contemplates his reply, unable to face me.

"They won't stop, Rose," he mutters, "That's why I'm telling you. They will never stop until they have you."

"Who are they?"

"I… I can't say."

Frustrated by this, I throw my hands up and turn away. I have no idea why he can't tell me. It makes no sense.

"Rose?" Jasper's voice pleads, forcing me to turn around. "I'm sorry for not being honest with you," he pauses, "I never intended for us to fall out or to scare you. I'm on your side. I don't want to hurt you."

I can see his tortured mind ticking behind tired eyes and for a second, I want to believe him. He touches my hand slowly and strong emotions surge up my fingertips, his warmth, love, earnest desire. This was the first time his emotions had been this clear and it threw me. I knew deep down that Ebony and Finn would tell me not to be so easily fooled by this. Yet, it seemed so real.

"I don't believe you," I insist.

Letting go of my hand, Jasper's head lowers and shoulders droop. A long, frustrated exhale blows through his lips as he considers his next move.

"How can I?" I continue, "You've lied to me, hidden things from me and now… I don't think I know who you are."

"Okay," he nods and meets my gaze, "Well I have to go. I'm sorry."

The white noise increases, making my ears and head ache. I'm unable to see straight and cry out as the dizziness pulls me to the ground. All I can hear is an echoing apology and see his pleading face begging for forgiveness. I force the image away and force open my eyes again.

"Rose?" a voice asks, peering down at me.

Three blurry shadows hang over my crumpled frame making me scream again. Covering my eyes, I hide my face and plead for them to go away. I couldn't trust if this was real anymore.

"Rose…" Ebony's voice soothingly calms me down, "Hey… You're okay."

Now staring, I look between them and frown, puzzled by what had happened. Somehow, I was still on the sofa and my throat was exceptionally dry. Yet, dizziness still clung on whilst my hands were throbbing.

"What's happening to her?"

"She's had a nightmare."

There's a pause, a silent exchange. Finn gives her a look and then shrugs before getting a glass of water. Something feels off about Ebony's touch as she lets go of my arm. She says she'll be back, but it's barely a second before I feel another presence beside me.

"Rose?" Will's voice fills my ears, "I need you to tell me exactly what happened."

I try, yet all words have dissipated in my mind. I can barely remember what was said. I'm left with an unwelcome stare burned on the back of my eyelids and swirling nausea in my stomach.

"Rosebud," Finn rubs my back and hands me a glass of water, "Come on, we need you to say something."

Taking a sip, I lick my lips, swallow the lump in my dry throat and try to say something. I'm met with their concerned gazes and feel Ebony's tingling energy trying to reassure me.

"I…" my voice is still croaky, "I saw Jasper. He was in… in the kitchen."

"Where?"

"Who?"

Will and Ebony talk over each other and exchange glances. Filling in the gaps, Finn explains who Jasper is and why he was an alarming detail, but Will doesn't seem to understand. His steel blue eyes latch onto mine as he asks me more questions. I explain the warning, but that's all that I can remember. It seemed blurry now that I was awake as if it was just a weird dream.

"He told me he has a power and he used it on me," I mutter.

"What?" Ebony gasps, "What did he do to you?"

"I… I don't know. He used his hand and I started to feel re-laxed… a bit like when you used your Gift on me…"

The anxiety in the room was evident. Ebony and Finn share a tense look and I ask if they knew about Jasper's ability. By their apologetic grimaces, I have my answer and it doesn't make me feel very good.

"What is it? Tell me." I demand.

"He can…" Finn's gaze shifts between Ebony and mine, "He can drain you, uh, like take away your energy until you're d- "

"We're still learning though," Ebony chips in, "So, we didn't tell you in case we were wrong. But it sounds like he was using it to calm you down."

"How long did you know?"

"We didn't- "

"How long did you know?" I repeat.

The long, uncomfortable silence feeds the growing tension between Ebony, Finn and me. How could they have known and not said anything? I had held hands with this boy unaware of his damning ability, yet they said nothing.

"What is happening?" I mutter.

"Rose?" Will's voice captures my attention. "The dream you had… I think it was a vision. That's why you could see Jasper."

I'm barely able to look up, my hands trembling as the anger bubbles inside. This served as another reminder that I had no idea about anything. The things I knew were more like a dream and I was being rudely awakened into some kind of nightmare. Why couldn't it all just go away?

"Rose," Ebony says, rubbing my hand, "It's okay."

"No," I snap, "It's not okay, Ebony. None of this is okay."

My lip wobbles and I bite it, hoping I can keep the tidal wave inside. I stand up and push the blankets off forcefully, unable to pretend any longer. I needed some time to think, figure it out, and find someone who will give me answers.

"I can't do this," I sniff, "I don't understand what's going on or why, and no one seems to be able to be honest with me. I can't... I need answers..."

Walking hastily, I can sense their eyes on me as I storm into the kitchen and collide with someone. Her floral fragrance washes over me and I hear her ask if I'm okay. I shake my head and throw my hands over my face, feeling the tears fall. My feet guide me up the stairs, one by one. I crash into my room, climb on the bed, and bury my head into the pillows. It was too much. Seeing Jasper confused me. I remembered what he said, and it made no sense. It filled me with fear and anxiety. His distinct eyes and repentant plea wouldn't leave me alone.

How could he have felt so real?

I didn't want to believe it was a vision. The thought of being alone and potentially having another vision was terrifying. How could I know what was real and what wasn't?

My heart starts racing as someone comes to the door. Before I can think about it, I tell them to go away and ask for them to give me some space. The person lingers and I look to see who it is. Opening the door slowly, his peaceful presence brings immediate calm to my brewing storm. Eli stands there in a crisp, white shirt, navy waistcoat and some smart, navy, pin-stripe trousers. His hair is combed back and he's wearing glasses. Respecting my wishes, Eli doesn't enter my room but waits for me to tell him what's happened.

"I'm fine," I tell him.

"You're afraid," he says softly.

Exhaling, I force a smile and insist that I'm fine. He doesn't argue and nods, saying 'if you're sure'. I shrug and he turns to leave, putting his hands in his pockets. He glides towards the staircase and stops at one of the bookshelves. His hand searches and lands on a dark red and gold book. He presses it into the wall and a concealed door pops open. The inquisitive nature in me watches, intrigued by what I've witnessed. Surely, he knew I had seen what he had done. Eli disappears into the secret room and closes the door behind him. I find myself wondering where it leads, but the curiosity ceases when I think of Jasper again.

A frustrated growl escapes as I throw my fists down as sit back on the bed. There's nothing that made sense; not in my life nor the lives around me. It was suffocating. I wanted to breathe again. I wanted straight answers, *honest* answers. The only person who would know would be Eli. He had been around enough of us, surely, he would know. But was he willing to tell me?

Sneaking across the landing, I head straight for the secret door. I notice it's been left open slightly, so I run my fingers down the gap and pull the door towards me. I slip inside and turn around, quietly gasping in awe. Yellow light bounces off glossy, wooden walls, framed with a few bookshelves. There's a large oak desk situated in the middle of the room on an old, frayed rug. A large golden globe sits on the desk with a few books scattered around it. I conclude it must be a study. It's surprisingly tidy considering how much paperwork is piled up on the desk. In fact, the desk is the only messy part of the entire room.

"Who's there?" a voice asks.

This was a bad idea…

Realising my mistake, I back out of the room and try to find the door. Before I can grab the handle, Eli appears from behind a bookshelf. He raises an eyebrow disapprovingly.

Definitely a bad idea…

"Yes, but you're here now," Eli says, reading my regret.

Eli walks gracefully across the room and pulls a huge, golden chair out from behind his desk. He sits down quietly and faces me. Interlocking his hands, he rests his elbows down on the arms of his chair and smiles.

"How about you come and take a seat," he says, indicating to the red-velvet chair across from him.

Cautiously, I approach him at the desk and sit, fiddling with my hands. I'm hot with embarrassment; I really shouldn't have followed him.

"Okay, so you want answers?" he sighs and then beams, "Let's start at the beginning."

CHAPTER
Ten

"Many hundreds of years ago, Gifts were bestowed upon particular human beings. Their hearts aligned with a Higher Being; strong, adventurous, kind and fearless. They were named the 'Gifted' and integrated themselves into society. The purpose of giving these Gifts was to enable mankind to thrive. However, the one condition of these Gifts was to not abuse them or other humans with them. Otherwise, they would be taken away. On agreeing to this, the world began to thrive as a Gifted community."

"For a long time, the earth lived in harmony with the Gifted. They continued to use their Gifts to protect, help and enable humans to create a good and fruitful life. Mankind and the Gifted worked alongside each other for centuries. Thus, every being became accustomed to the peaceful life that the Gifts had given."

"Then one summer, an unruly, dark-minded being came to appeal for a change." Eli's tone changes, his eyes lowering. "Severian, the leader of the new rise, began to question and oppose the Gifted. He believed that Gifted people deserved to control human beings instead of living among them. In his eyes, his Gift was power. This power was all he needed to control and manipulate humanity."

"War broke out across the Earth as Severian began slaughtering anyone who refused to join his new campaign. He washed the land with the blood of the Gifted. Most humans were too afraid to rebel against such a powerful being. For one hundred and seventy-two years, Severian reigned supreme. Nobody knew how he kept himself young, but a few believed it was through the blood of a Gifted. Humans feared him whilst his followers revered their new leader. His people swore an oath of loyalty to Severian, honouring his power and greatness. Any who dared question their leader was immediately put to death. This was one of the great Severian Laws."

"Finally, the Higher Being decided to intervene and removed all of the Gifts from every Gifted being as well as their leader, Severian. As a weak, old, lost man, he was quickly disposed of, and his followers were exiled for their crimes. The Higher Being promised from that day on, all Gifts were to be withheld until humanity could prove themselves worthy."

Eli speaks quietly, his eyes glistening with faraway tears as he retells the tragic history of the Gifted. There's so much I didn't know, yet I felt this was the start of understanding. Not only about myself and who I was but about all Gifted people who had lived before me. A sorrowful chuckle passes Eli's thin, pale lips.

"Time passed, and the humans began to forget the Gifted. It wasn't written in many history books and thus, each generation lost a little more knowledge of the Gifted. In ignorance, they lived their lives separate from all understanding of the Gifted and the Higher Being."

An extended moment of reflection follows a deep sigh as I process Eli's story. I couldn't believe that there had been so many murdered because of one man's desire for power. Eli had made it clear that Gifts and powers were different. One could turn a person mad. There was disdain in Eli's tone when he mentioned Severian. Like a bitter taste on his tongue, he seemed sickened when he mentioned the death of all the Gifted. It was nauseating to think someone could kill for power, yet it made me think of Dad. He was in the war to protect others, yet Severian killed for gain. The more I spoke to Eli, the more I realised the magnitude of the oncoming chaos.

"So why now?" I ask, "Because if the Gifted had been wiped out and the Higher Being wasn't going to bestow any more Gifts, then why now? Why do we have Gifts?"

Chuckling, Eli smiles and places a hand on mine.

"Dear Rose, you raise a good question. Why now?" he inhales sharply, "Humanity had to prove themselves worthy. Do you think you are worthy of your Gift?"

Lowering my gaze, I stare at my hands in my lap. This was a question I could answer all too quickly.

"No," I sigh.

"Yet you still have one," Eli chuckles again, tapping the desk, "So maybe you've got this Gift because you're more important than you realise."

I shake my head and shrug. That wasn't it. My Gift was a burden if anything. Or maybe I was the burden.

"Rose?"

My eyes flicker up to meet Eli's deep gaze, calm and composed as he smiles. Creases around his eyes and lips crinkle and he offers a hand across the desk towards me. He takes hold of my hand as I lay it in his palm, bracing myself for whatever he had to say.

"Look," Eli says, "You are capable of far more than you could ever imagine. That's how you were made and that is how you will be. Don't doubt that." He nods reassuringly, lets go of my hand and adds, "This is with or without your Gift."

Mustering a smile, I thank him graciously and lean back in my chair. I exhale as I run his words through my mind. They seem to bring a quiet reassurance, even if I didn't fully believe them. It was undeniable that I was part of something much bigger than I could understand.

"Um, this morning, I think I had a vision," I begin.

"Oh?"

"Yeah, so there's this guy… Jasper. He was a friend of mine and we kind of dated… ish, but yeah, things kind of got messy," I stumble over my vague explanation of him, "Anyway, he talked with me in the kitchen and uses his Gift on me. He said that 'they were going to keep coming after me'. He said he wanted to warn me of who was coming."

Eli sits back in his golden armchair and rubs his chin thoughtfully. He exhales heavily as he considers Jasper and his concerning message. After a few moments, he asks if I'm okay, clearly seeing I was shaken up by the whole experience.

"I don't know" I reply, "Knowing that Jasper can communicate with me and use his power, I mean, Gift is kind of scary."

Understanding, Eli nods and beams, "Whilst you are here, you are safe with us. Though you may feel afraid, you needn't be."

Chewing my lip, I listen as he tries to calm my nerves. Something was eating away at me. It wasn't clear what the feeling was or what it meant, but it just wouldn't go.

"Rose," Eli whispers, "Only *you* can decide what you fear and don't fear. We won't let you do this on your own," he smiles again, "You have my word."

Inhaling and exhaling slowly, a sense of peace washes over me as I think about his promise. His warm, beaming smile was reassuring, and it gave me a sense of security. I felt it when he first spoke to me. I could see now that he cared, a lot.

"Okay then," he says, sitting upright, "Shall we get breakfast?"

Drumming his fingers on the edge of the desk, Eli slides back his chair and stands. He gestures to the door, and I get up, walking beside him as we head to the kitchen. Morning light pours through the hallways. I notice the cotton clouds have disappeared and a clear, blue sky remains. Black birds fly and perch on the tops of the trees, watching the grounds. Warm sun rays cast themselves across the stairs as we descend, talking about the plans for the day. Eli seems eager to show me a place called Ashmoore.

When we enter the kitchen, a cheerful face is the first thing I notice. Ava is cooking a traditional English breakfast with sausages, eggs, bacon and more. She greets us both with a hug and ushers me to the next room. A sea of green grass and rainbow flowerbeds can be seen for miles as I stare through the large, living room windows. The grounds seem to go on and I get lost trying to see where it ends.

"Hey!" Ebony bounds up to me, "Where did you go?"

"Yeah," Finn says, following Ebony. "Are you okay?"

Looking between them, I explain my outburst and apologise for leaving. They understand, apologise about not telling of Jasper's Gift, and ask that I trust them once more. I shrug, what else was going to do?

Ava calls for breakfast and we crowd around the kitchen. We're told to help ourselves to the food. The delicious smell of hot, greasy bacon and baked beans fills the room. There's even a pot of tea and coffee at the end of the table with some mugs and some glasses for fresh orange juice. My mouth waters as I look over the platters of fresh, hot food.

"Thank you, mum," Sol says, reaching an arm around to his mum.

Tenderly, he pulls her into his side and kisses her on the head. Ava's face lights up.

"You're the best," he whispers.

Giggling, she bats him away and mutters 'I love you too'. They both beam as Sol continues to fill his plate. Ava watches over us with pride and wipes the sweat from her brow. Finn is piling his plate to the full and I playfully tell him off, laughing. He starts to put the food back, but Ava forces him to stop. She insists that he eat as much as he likes. I jokily tell her that it would be all of it if he could.

"It's true," Finn agrees.

As we settle down in the conservatory living room, we eat our breakfast in-between conversations. Eli, Ava and a man I don't recognise sit in the kitchen at the breakfast bar cracking jokes. I'm curiously watching them when I get caught by two steel blue eyes. "That's Jesse, Ava's husband," Will says, leaning over. I recognise the name from Ebony's introductions yesterday. "So, are you okay? You seemed pretty upset earlier." "Yeah," I reply, "I'm just a little overwhelmed. It's all good now."

He nods thoughtfully and tells me he's glad before sitting back and eating the rest of his breakfast. I've cleared my plate and stand up to wash it. I brush past Ava on my way to the sink and she stops me. She stands and holds her hands up, still finishing her mouthful.

"Absolutely not!" she says, "What do you think you're doing?" Awkwardly, I take a step back and tell her that I wanted to wash up. She shakes her head and waves me out of the kitchen. She's tutting as I walk away. I meet the gaze of Jesse who laughs and winks at me.

"She's a bossy one," he teases, "Don't worry, she won't even let her own husband help."

"Tell me the last time you tried to help," Ava sasses him with one raised eyebrow.

"But sweetheart," he says, putting his hands dramatically across his chest, "I would do anything for you…"

"Yeah…" she rolls her eyes, "… right…"

Eli and Jesse burst into roars of laughter, and Ava is giggling to herself. Their joy is infectious, raising a smile on my own lips. When they settle again, Eli turns and asks me where I was heading. I tell him I need to get ready, so he says to dress comfortably and to bring a change of clothes. I nod and ask when we'll be leaving.

"How about we leave at 10:00?" Jesse suggests.

They all nod.

"Great," I smile, "Thanks, I'll be back in a bit."

Running up the stairs, I return to my room and hop straight into the shower. The warm water trickles over my face and I rub it in, washing away the tiredness. I roll my shoulder back and feel the heat relax my aching muscles.

Had I really been that tense?

Quickly, I wash my hair with a fruity shampoo and conditioner. Watching the bubbles drain away, I breathe in deeply. The steam catches in my throat, and I decide it's time to get out before I start choking.

There's a knock at my door and I waddle in my towel to answer. I yell through a thin gap, asking who it is. I recognise the giggle and sarcastic tone. She pushes her way into the room and looks me up and down.

"Sexy!" she teases.

"I know right…" I reply jokily.

"Yeah, you might be a bit cold when we get to Ashmoore," she replies, already grabbing clothes for me to wear.

Diving into each drawer, Ebony searches for an outfit and throws a few t-shirts on the bed. She goes to the hidden wardrobe behind the mirrors by the door. Her fingers run across all the different fabrics until she finds something she likes. It's a black pair of joggers with a white and red stripe down the side.

"It has colour," she says, pointing as she sits.

This makes me laugh aloud as I join her on the bed, rooting through her choices. I agree to the joggers and insist that I find my own top. I'd spotted a white crop top earlier which matched the joggers. I find it and run into the bathroom to get changed. There's a noticeable lack of conversation from Ebony which is unlike her, so I ask her what's wrong.

"Hey, you…" I whisper playfully as I sit beside her.

She seems lost in her own thoughts, so I nudge her with my shoulder.

"Yes?" she replies, blinking.

"What is it?"

Turning to face her, I tilt my head hoping I won't have to drag it out of her. Ebony leans back and looks at me with her pretty, emerald eyes, but they're misty.

"I'm sorry that we didn't tell you anything," she begins, gesturing to the house, "About this I mean…" she sighs heavily, "Finn and I… we disagreed. I thought you didn't need to know anything, but Finn thought you needed to know everything. That's why we didn't get along. That's why we didn't like each other. We just wanted to protect you, you know?"

She looks at me with a tear-stricken face and I nod in agreement, knowing her intentions were pure.

"See, I thought I was protecting you *because* you were my friend, but I guess it became all about protecting you and never really being your friend… a-and I'm sorry. I never wanted to hurt you. I'm so scared that I've ruined our friendship…"

Sobbing, Ebony pushes away the hair that's fallen across her eyes with shaky hands. She wipes the mascara trails off her face, and my heart can't take it.

"Stop," I insist, "Just stop it, okay? I'm not angry with you. There's a lot I have to take in at the moment, but I know who my friends are. You, being one of them."

"Really?" she sniffs.

"Yes, you're my best friend," I reassure her, "Who else is going to be my sidekick?"

"Finn?" she says, sadly.

"Come on Ebs," I tut, "I love you both. You *and* Finn. Nothing could change that."

My reassurance is working as the worry in Ebony's eyes fades. The tears fall silently, and I wipe them away with my thumb.

"Please stop crying, Eb."

Ebony murmurs an agreement to try and pulls away to wipe her face with her sleeve. She stands up, clears her throat and walks to the dressing table chair. She looks at herself in the mirror as a small smile rises on her lips. Looking at the reflection, she teases, telling me I ruined her make-up.

"Well, you shouldn't cry then, should you?" I retort.

"I learned from the best," she sasses.

Giggling now, I sit down beside her and rest my head on her shoulder. We both listen to the birds chirping outside my window contently. It's a beautiful day. Cool air washes over our backs, beckoning us to go outside. I peer over at Ebony and smile, ready to give her more sass.

"You really need to sort out that face, you look a total mess," I tease.

"Thanks, Rose…" she says sarcastically, "Clearly won't be going to you for a confidence boost today."

Elbowing her to move along, I shimmy so I can see myself in the mirror too. Ebony finds some make-up she left for me in a painted woven box. She lifts off the lid and passes it to me, and we start to decorate our faces. I'm still finishing my eyeliner when Ebony gets up and sits on the bed.

"You look pretty," she says, admiring me.

Waving her comment away, I shake my head and stare at the mascara. I hated hearing compliments from Ebony. She was the most stunning girl I knew, and there was no way I could be considered pretty in comparison to her.

"Take the compliment," she insists.

"Fine," I tut, "Thank you,"

Just to wind Ebony up, I critique my handiwork and list how I could look better. Before I can make any adjustments, Ebony grabs my shoulders and pulls me away from the mirror. She hands me some spare clothes and my phone, muttering about being late. As we head towards the stairs, we assume everyone is waiting. Someone clears their throat from behind us and we practically jump through the ceiling. There's a very handsome Finn watching us as we turn around with a smirk on his lips. He's in grey joggers and a sleeveless black top. I've seen him like this before, but this time it lands differently. Maybe because I still haven't been able to bury the remnants of butterflies in my stomach.

"Hey," Ebony says.

"Hey girls," he replies and points to the stairs, "Are you going down to meet everyone?"

We nod and I wait for Ebony to sass him, but she doesn't. I think we all feel mildly uncomfortable, so I drag them both downstairs and try to make conversation. Finn walks off to talk to someone else once we get to the foyer. Yet, Ebony's gaze lingers on Finn, and I frown at her as a sense of jealousy sets in.

"Oi," I whisper, "Stop that."

"What?" she asks with a dazed look on her face.

In hopes to change her focus, I force a laugh and pull her down the rest of the steps. Eli is waiting for us with Ava and Jesse near the front door. Everyone is holding a rucksack either in their hands or on their backs. I notice there is one bag left at the front which Ava is filling with snacks.

"Right then," Jesse says, clapping his hands together, "We are going to Ashmoore. My lovely, beautiful, radiant wife has put together a wonderful lunch which we are going to enjoy later. You should have also been given snacks in your rucksacks..." he pauses and smiles at his youngest who are stood near the front, "Don't eat them all at once."

The twins, Lily-Grace and Cole, listen to his gentle warning and nod, trying to hold in their giggles. I notice their blue and pink rucksacks tightly fastened on their shoulders, ready to go.

"Rose, we have a special rucksack for you," Jesse continues.

My heart stops momentarily as all eyes turn on me. The sea is unmoving and curious, watching as I weave through the bodies. I quickly grab the pale purple rucksack and thank them. I shove my spare clothes in the bag and return, head down, to Ebony's side.

"Right! Finn?" Jesse says.

We all turn to Finn who looks up and nods.

"Can you take Ebony and Rose? Can you, Sol, take Will and Amber? I will take Ava, the twins and my brother here," he pauses to place a hand on Eli, "Will make his own way."

"Okay," Ava cuts in, "Anybody who needs to use the facilities, speak now or forever hold your peace!"

I glance at Ebony and she nods. It would be us; the last ones to get ready and the first ones to need to pee. Cackling, we both run back up the stairs and Amber follows us. When we return, there are three cars parked outside on the gravel by the fountain. I jump into Finn's car with Ebony, and Amber gets into her car with Sol. We're all set and ready to go when Sol pulls up beside us. Finn and Sol wind down their windows and look at each other with devious smiles. Jesse has already left which is probably why they have the idea.

"I'll race you!" Sol says.

Loving the challenge, Finn nods. They wind up their windows and Amber counts down on her fingers before shouting 'go!'. Tyres crunch against the gravel as Sol overtakes and makes a left turn. He leads us out of the grounds, and we start our journey to Ashmoore. It's about a forty-minute journey through the Great Hills until we get to a clearing. I can see Corden in the distance and immediately feel homesick. Blakewood Manor is slightly closer to where we are and is hard to miss with its beautiful, kaleidoscopic gardens. From this high, I can even see the sea and it reminds me of my family.

Dad always said that when I see the sea, I need to remember that it connects us. No matter where we are in the world, we can always find our way to one another. I thought he was joking but right now, all I wanted was for Dad to come home, to appear on the shore. I want him to hug me and tell me everything is going to be alright.

"Hey, are you okay?" A voice asks as I stand looking out over Corden.

We've parked up on a rocky edge and there's a lake behind us. Sol won the race in the end, but I didn't care. It was beautiful where we were. I had come to the edge to think, but time has sped up and people were worried.

"Hey, Rose?"

I glance around and I'm met with a charming, warm smile. Something tickles my face and I brush it off, instinctively. I'm surprised to find my fingers are wet with salty tears.

"I said, are you okay?" Will asks again and sees the glistening on my cheeks. "Wait, what's wrong?" his voice softens, "Hey…"

Will bends down so that he can look me in the eyes. He searches my face for a clue as to where my mind had been. Not really knowing me didn't help, but it was clear that he cared all the same.

"Don't cry," he says, rubbing my shoulders.

I hadn't thought about how much I missed my Dad until now. My heart ached for him to come home.

"Rose?" Ebony calls, "Will? What's happened?"

Ebony comes bounding toward us and wraps her arms around me. She holds me tightly as her warmth begins to ease the pain. I guess she's using her Gift but it's welcome here. I didn't want to hurt like this anymore.

"I'm fine," I assure them.

Will watches me closely but doesn't ask any more questions. He moves out of the way so that Ebony can speak to me more privately. There's a crease in his brow and his gaze moves from me to something over my shoulder. An overexcited Lily-Grace appears next to us and looks around curiously. It seems as though she's about to ask a question when Will cuts her off.

"Come on," Will says to her, "Let's give the girls some space, hey?"

He reaches out for her hand. Lily-Grace smiles as she takes his, skipping away and rambling about how excited she was to be at Ashmoore. Ebony mouths a thank you to Will and turns back to me. We talk for a short while and Ebony simply listens, knowing I didn't need anything except for maybe a hug. We return to the group shortly after. We walk past Finn and Sol who are standing, arms folded across their chests, and listening as Jesse talks us through what will be happening today.

"Okay, we are here for the day which means we have no set plans," Jesse's voice echoes in the basin of the hills, "You can walk around the forests or stay here near the lake, but I want you all to look after each other. Don't be reckless or leave anyone alone. No one is going anywhere without at least another person with them, apart from you two. You're not going anywhere," he looks at Cole and Lily who seem disappointed by this. "It's only because I love you so much," he says, ruffling their hair affectionately.

"Sounds good to me!" Will chimes in, "I will be going for a walk then, who would like to join me?"

Lily-Grace and Cole nod enthusiastically at him, but Jesse shakes his head and repeats himself about them staying here. I can see Jesse is adamant for them to stay so Ava tries to convince him otherwise.

"Come on darling, they'll be with Will for goodness' sake. It's not like they're alone," she says.

"Yeah, we can go too," Finn says, volunteering me and Ebony as well.

Not really my plan, but okay…

"You will look after them, won't you?" Jesse asks us with fatherly concern in his eyes, and we nod. "Okay fine…" he gives in, "but, if anything happens to them…"

"I promise you, they are in safe hands," Will assures him.

"Have fun," Jesse exhales, "My little loves."

Waving us off, Jesse is called by Ava to help with getting the blankets from the car. Sol and Amber also stay behind, unloading and setting up the picnic tables.

"Remember to stick together!" Jesse calls once we're near the tree line, "We have lunch in an hour!"

We nod and smile, waving for one final time.

AFTER A WHILE, WE'RE DEEP IN THE FOREST TRAIL. SUNLIGHT STREAMS through the leafy canopies and dances across our heads. Ebony is with Lily-Grace and they're talking about school. She seems to know the family well and I can see the twins love her.

"Yeah, it's going okay. I can't wait until I'm in big school," Lily-Grace says.

She smiles up at Ebony who strokes her hair and puts an arm around her.

"Which subject is your favourite?" she asks.

"Music," Lily-Grace says without a second thought.

"That's amazing, what music do you like?"

I watch them in awe. This was the first time I had seen Ebony interacting with someone younger than her. She was a natural big sister, and it was endearing. Ebony had a softer side which I knew of, yet she rarely showed it so publicly.

"Hey Rosebud," Finn whispers, interrupting my earwigging. "So, what was up earlier?" he asks smiling with a hint of concern in his voice, "I saw you with Will and Ebony, are you okay?"

"Yeah, I'm… I'm fine."

Unconvinced, Finn wraps a hand around my wrist and gently pulls me back so that the rest of the group can go ahead. He brushes the hair from my eyes and tucks it behind my ears so he can see my face. I know he already can tell but he wants me to talk, to let him into what was going on in my head.

"Talk to me, please?" he urges.

Shaking my head, I tell him I'm too tired to talk. Secretly, I know if I speak about it, I'll cry and there had been *so much crying*.

"It's nothing," I sigh, "I don't want to talk about it."

"Come on," Finn presses, "I want to help."

His eyes bore into mine as a lump formed in the back of my throat. It dawns on Finn that this conversation is upsetting me and apologises. I tell him it's okay; he was only trying to help.

"I miss them…"

"I know," he nods, understanding the little that I share.

Finn exhales as he pulls me into his chest and kisses the top of my head. His arms are secure around me as he rocks us from side to side. I hear him mouth something to the others who are waiting, and I assume he's told them to go on without us.

"I don't want to feel like this anymore," I admit with a wobbly voice.

"It's okay," he says softly.

Silent tears stream down my face, but I don't tremble as I had done before. My body had become accustomed to the same motions; crying, stomach ache, a lump the size of a fist in my throat. Somehow it had become mechanical, like breathing. Finn's heavy sigh makes me look up.

"I'm sorry," I sniff.

Firmly, Finn shakes his head, his eyes glimmering, and tells me not to worry. I can see the redness on his nose, a tell-tale sign of his own pain.

"I don't know what I'm going to do without them, Finn. I've never been on my own before… what do I do…who do I trust… I just… I just don't know…"

"I know," Finn whispers, "I know…"

"Why did this happen?"

Finn wraps his arms around me again and his voice cracks.

"I don't know," he says, resting his chin on my head, "But I promise you, we will find out. I promise."

There weren't many times that I had heard Finn cry or get angry because he was one of the happiest people I knew. It took a lot to make him upset, but this was different. He was angry and I could feel it radiating through his skin. I knew that if anyone were to find out what was going on, it was Finn. His promise was as real as the feelings I had held for him for so long.

As long as I had Finn, I knew I was protected.

CHAPTER
Eleven

W e venture through a thick, green forest in deep, remi-
niscent conversation. The canopy of large leaves protects us from the sun's light, giving off a yellowy-green
glow. Our shoes melt into the moist, dark soil paths as we walk
along the trail. A few rabbits cross the track, flashing their little
white tails before diving into more succulent undergrowth.

"Thank you," I say after a while.

"Why?" Finn asks, looking over at me.

"You listened, and that's all I wanted. This is why you're one
of my best friends."

Shrugging, Finn smiles and continues walking with his head
down. I nudge him on the shoulder which makes him laugh. He
immediately takes the opportunity to shove me back and runs off.

I chase him through the trail and manage to keep up. This surprises both of us enough to stop altogether.

"Interesting..." Finn says.

"What?" I frown.

"I wouldn't be surprised if you had superhuman speed..."

A laugh bursts from my lips. That's impossible. I've already learned that I have an emotion-sensing Gift, that was enough for me. No more Gifts, please.

"Come on, let's put you to the test."

"No," I say, reaching out to stop him, "Can we please just walk like regular people?"

"Fine," Finn replies, but his hand doesn't let go of mine.

After a short while, we spot Will and the group. Immediately, Finn lets go of my hand and waves to them. Lily-Grace and Cole are pointing upward, so we instinctively look up to see what they've spotted. A small, jet-black blur runs along the winding branches that hover above us.

"What was that?" I whisper.

"That's a black squirrel," Lily-Grace giggles.

Frowning, I check again and see two beady eyes peering down at me. His little blackish-grey nose wiggles as he watches our every move. I'm drawn to the dark, careful creature. His fluffy, black tail lifts up gradually once he's certain we weren't going to hurt him. He produces an acorn from his cheek and starts nibbling it.

"Snack time," Cole and Lily-Grace say in unison.

It's only then that I realise that I've left my bag in the car. My stomach rumbles as I watch everyone begin to eat their snacks. Ebony has sat down with the twins, grabbing her own food and Will is beside her. Finn joins them and I follow, sitting down cross-legged to complete the crooked circle.

"You can have some of mine," Will says, offering me a chocolate and peanut protein bar.

Taking it, I thank him with a grateful smile. As we eat, I learn more about the magical creatures that are hurrying along the trees above us. Will explains that they are usually quite rare in most parts of the world, but Ashmoore has a large population of them.

Whilst I listen, I glance up to see where our furry, little black friend is. He doesn't seem to move from his perch. I watch him toss the shell away as he produces a second acorn. It taps the roots of the tree as it falls before landing and rolling next to me.

"Do you like it here then?" Lily-Grace asks, looking directly at me.

"It's great," I smile, slipping the acorn shell into my pocket as a keepsake. "I'm really glad I came."

We leave shortly after the squirrel has scurried away. I'm still hungry, but Ebony and Finn reassure me that it's not far until we get back to the lake.

Thankfully, they're right. It's not long until we're back at the clearing with everyone. The twins decide they wanted to play tag which Will runs to supervise, leaving Finn, Ebony and I at the edge of the forest. We discuss what Finn and I had been doing before we saw the black squirrels. Ebony says she's glad Finn and I could figure it out and offered to talk when I was ready. She already knew and it was time I stopped repeating myself.

"Race you," Finn says suddenly, sprinting off before we can respond.

Ebony and I burst into laughter as I race after him, my legs carrying me faster and further with every foot. I surpass him and squeal with delight knowing I had finally beaten him. Everyone stares at me when I turn around in victory.

"Interesting…" a calm voice whispers beside me.

I look over to see Eli has been watching our race. He mutters something about being faster than expected. I want to ask, but my throat is too dry. The strain on my lungs hits me and I gasp for air. It's as though my body is delayed in its response to the sudden burst of energy I had expelled.

"I am so unfit!" I pant.

"That'll change…" Amber chips in.

From what I knew of Amber, she appeared really sweet but had a bad resting face. It got her into all sorts of trouble, apparently. I decide to ask her what she means, and she tells me about the training they all take part in. Sol chimes in, saying how important it is that they can protect themselves. They had never had a problem, but they knew my presence at the house would attract attention.

"Great…"

"Don't worry," Will says, overhearing our conversation, "We won't let anything happen to you."

"Yeah," Ebony and Finn say as they join us.

We all take a seat on the blankets that have been laid out for us. Ebony and Finn sit opposite me whilst Will intentionally finds a space next to me.

"Hey," he says.

"Hey," I reply.

"Thought we could get to know each other," he smiles, "I don't really know anything about you."

"Why don't you use your powers and see if they tell you something," I joke which makes him laugh.

"As amazing as my *Gift* is," he replies with heavy sarcasm, "I would prefer to talk to people."

"Okay," I smile, "What do you want to know?"

"Well, have you always been in Corden?"

This begins a long conversation about where I grew up and how my parents met. When he notices the strain in my voice, he changes the subject to college. I find out that he left college and went straight into working for Jesse by fixing cars. He seems happy when he talks about his job and asks what I want to do when I leave school. The honest answer is I have no idea.

"I'm sure you'll figure it out," Will grins.

We continue to talk about Will's family and what he remembers about his parents. He sympathises with me as his dad was also in the military. Though he was young, Will says he still remembers what he looks like. It was his mum who seems to be blurry to him.

"Would you want to find them again?" I ask.

"No," he replies, "They… they died a long time ago."

"I'm so sorry."

Telling me it's okay, Will's gaze drifts towards the lake. He watches the twins with a furrowed brow and exhales before excusing himself. I ask if I've upset him and he shakes his head, saying he appreciated getting to know me better.

"What did you do to him?" Ebony asks, scooting next to me.

"I'm not sure," I shrug.

Ava finally calls us for lunch, and we all gather around the picnic table. The food is delicious and was worth the wait. I finish my plate and go for seconds, then thirds. Everybody looks like they're going to slip into a food coma once we've finished. I was surprised at how much I was able to squeeze in despite my lack of appetite. Something told me I would regret my decisions later.

"Who wants to play Frisbee?" Finn pipes up.

"We will!" Ebony says, nominating both of us.

I immediately turn to her and give her a look that she should not need words to decipher.

"What?" she asks; clearly, she's unaware or simply choosing not to understand.

"I've just eaten…." I groan, rubbing my bloated stomach, and she laughs, "Please don't make me…."

I peer up at her with big, pleading eyes.

"Fine…" she tuts, "I'll go on my own!"

Ebony sighs and flicks her hair over her shoulder dramatically, pretending to be upset.

"Have fun!" I call as she runs to join the boys.

GRADUALLY, THE SUN MAKES ITS WAY ACROSS THE SAPPHIRE SKY. Clouds stroll by and cast temporary shadows over Ashmoore. They're a welcomed intermission under the intense sunlight. Eventually, the heat gets too much on my face and I roll over onto my stomach. I keep my eyes closed and bury my face into my elbow. I can't help replaying my walk with Finn and how he held my hand. The feelings he gave me were unlike any other. I never really believed they could be reciprocated until now. So much had changed, and I wanted to know if he felt the same, or whether I was simply looking for something that wasn't there. If Mum were here, she would know what to do.

"Right, you have had enough time, come on!"

Ebony runs over and orders us all up. I open my eyes and stare at her, unimpressed. She notices my expression and laughs, telling me to stop being so lazy.

"Excuse me, missy," I reply, "I am enjoying myself."

"Well enjoy yourself a little more actively!"

Rolling my eyes, I push myself up and stretch out my arms. I reluctantly follow Ebony with Amber and the twins towards the lake. Finn and Sol are currently racing whilst Will stands as the referee.

"Why are they doing this?" I ask quietly.

"My dear, it's called 'peacocking'," Amber mutters, "It's when a man wants to show he's the best but ends up looking like a complete and utter idiot."

"Oh," I nod and giggle.

I'm still learning about Amber, but her humour is my kind of humour. She makes it easy to be around her and I like people like that.

"Amber! Help me!" Sol calls out as he pretends to struggle in the water.

Shaking her head, Amber stands next to me with her arms folded. We giggle as she tells him to hurry up and win although Finn has almost finished.

"Aw, come on!" Sol whines when Finn wins.

"Maybe you should stop messing around!" Amber teases.

We watch as the boys start to splash and mock one another. Finn is parading around with his arms up, claiming victory. Yet, Will is determined to prove himself.

"Ready?" Sol says, "Go!"

The race begins. There's a lot of splashing, to begin with, but Will and Finn find their rhythm. I watch Finn intently, hoping he wins, and chew my lip. Ebony appears beside me and makes a comment about how good Finn is looking.

"I thought you hated him," I frown.

"I do," Ebony replies, confused, and there's a hint of defensiveness. "I just think he looks good, is that a problem?"

Her eyes bore into mine and I feel my lungs tighten. My stomach twists as I realise, I've come across too jealous. It gives me away and I need to change the tone.

"No, of course not," I shake my head, "He does look good, doesn't he?"

Ebony nods before waving to the boys. It seems it was a tie but they're fighting over who should have won. Sol is refusing to pick a side which appears to put him in a prime position for a playful tackle. We attempt to intervene which causes retaliation.

"Oh really?" Will says.

As they approach us, we back away and warn them of their next move.

"No… Don't you dare…"

Cackling, we all run in different directions to get away from the boys. I feel there's someone close behind me and glance back. It's a rookie's mistake and Finn instantly grabs me. Ebony, Amber and I are thrown into the water and we're laughing through our protests. We challenge them to a race, but I know I won't win. Ebony offers to take my turn and Amber also forfeits. It ends up being Ebony against the boys and we take the opportunity to climb out. We both shiver as the cool breeze hits and hurry to grab our towels. Mine's in Finn's car still so I take his key and let myself in.

Wrapping up, I join Amber and the twins on the embankment. We watch entertained as Ebony attempts to goad the boys into a three-against-one race. They're shaking their heads, but Ebony won't give up that easily. She's stubborn, even I know that.

"Just race!" Cole calls out next to me.

Surprised, I glance down at him. He shrugs and tells me he's bored. Lily-Grace takes that as an opportunity to suggest a game. I share a look with Amber which lets her know I want to politely decline the sweet suggestion.

"How about you and Cole go and play?" Amber suggests, "I think Rose and I need to dry off and get changed."

I mouth and thank you and Amber nods before returning her attention to the lake. There's a commotion in the water and the boys' laughter echoes across the clearing. Ebony frowns and punches the water with her fists. I think she's lost. She glares down at the water as though it had betrayed her. She was always so theatrical.

"Right!" Ava calls, interrupting the laughter with her own, "Come on, you rowdy lot, it's time to get changed and go home!" she points to the forest.

We each take our rucksacks and get changed in a make-do towel changing rooms. Ebony and Amber are talking about Sol whilst my mind wanders to Finn. I don't realise how long I've been lost in my thoughts until Ebony snaps me out of it.

"Ready?" she chirps.

"Yeah!" I smile back.

Leisurely, we make our way back into the clearing and wait for the boys. Ava, Jesse, and Eli have left with the twins leaving only two cars remaining on the asphalt. Time passes and we begin to wonder what happened to the boys. There's no sign of movement in the forest so we take it upon ourselves to investigate. We warn them of our approach so there are no awkward surprises, but no one replies.

"Boys?" Ebony calls.

We see some of the wet clothing strew across some fallen logs. Their bags have been abandoned on the ground and left open. I can't see the boys anywhere.

"They're probably just trying to scare us…" Amber mutters and continues further into the forest. "Sol! If you're hiding, this isn't funny!"

We stop, listening out for any sign of life but it's eerily silent. Even the birds have disappeared. The trees stand still, and the cool shade sparks a chill down my spine. I don't feel right.

Something is very, very wrong.

"Finn?" I call and the panic in my voice is obvious, "Will? Anybody?"

Some small, shuffling sounds come from deep inside the forest. We see movement in the treeline which gets closer towards us. Our eyes meet with the boys and they're yelling at us to get out of the way.

"Run!" they all shout, "Hide!"

I can't see what's behind them, but none of us hesitate to get a look. Ebony pulls me away by my wrists. Her grip burns as she guides me behind some thick, dark trees. We crouch for a moment and watch the scene play out. A terrifying, huge beast bounds past us grunting and growling. I stare in horror as Finn draws it out into the clearing.

The beast's gaze is focused and dark as he fights. His fur is ragged like a wild bear and has a long, snout with a wet, black nose. His ears are big and flexed as he runs on his four paws towards Finn. His bright white canines overhang his lips, catching flickers of sunlight. A loud, echoing snarl forces the boys to stop the taunting and face the beast. They turn and get ready to fight. Will leads the attack with Finn following him closely behind. The boys work in unison like a pack of lions, copying the other to make sure the beast has no opportunity to fight back.

Sol is now keeping the beast entertained with punches whilst Finn and Will move to its side. They have the animal surrounded, splitting its focus in three. The creature gets agitated and swings a paw at them, striking Finn on the arm. I wince and stand up instinctively, my feet moving for me.

"Rose!" Ebony yells my name.

The beast suddenly looks at me with eyes like burnt orange marbles. I recognise them from somewhere before. His gaze is almost suffocating as he licks his lips and sneers. I try to look away, but an image of a man flashes in front of my eyes.

The hospital.

"Rose…" the beast snarls.

Shocked, I gulp and stare. Racing towards me is a very focused Finn. I hear him telling me to move but I can't. It's like my feet are trapped, keeping me there like a mouse in a sticky trap. The beast gets ready to pounce and I brace myself for impact…

A blood-curdling screech forces open my eyes. The beast whips around, whimpering. I realise one of the boys has pierced the thick, ratty tail with a piece of wood. Oozing, black, iridescent blood pours from the wound and soaks into the ground. I watch as the beast attempts to attack the group of boys but doesn't land one hit. His attention is split between the pain and the increasing attacks on his remaining limbs.

"Rose!"

Finn instantly appears, takes my hand and leads me to safety in the undergrowth of the forest. He's saying something to me and asking me questions, but my eyes won't leave the beast. What was that thing?

"Come on," Finn says, "Look at me."

We hear a groan from one of the boys and I want to see what has happened. Trying to do what's best, Finn immediately turns me away and tries to block my view. My focus falls on his bleeding, wounded arm. There's a gash between his wrist and his elbow which seems to be deep, revealing muscle and a sliver of bone. I go to touch it and see my hands trembling. The blood is nauseating as it pulses out from the wound. Finn notices and hides it behind him, telling me to breathe.

Suddenly, someone grabs me from behind and I scream into the hand that covers my mouth. Realising it's Ebony, I follow her as she takes me away and we run towards the parked cars to hide. Will and Sol manage to coax the beast back towards the tree line. There's something running down Will's brow, but he wipes it away. I realise it's blood and gag. I really didn't like blood.

"Don't look," Ebony says, pulling me into her side.

Gladly taking her offer, I bury myself in her embrace and pray for the fighting to stop. I press my fingers into my ears in hopes to drown out the sickening cracks of bones and mighty roars of the beast. My mind keeps lingering on the blood I'd seen. Nausea threatens so I try to fixate on something else. The image of the man I saw when the beast was approaching me, returns. He was more human in the hospital. Somehow, there had to be more to him than what we knew.

Minutes feel like an eternity as we wait. Ebony mumbles something about the beast being gone so I look up. Her pulse is steady as she rubs my arm and checks for any injuries. I tell her I'm fine and she sighs, relieved. Eventually, the boys return and beckon us out one by one. Amber goes first, then Ebony and then me. We walk watchfully towards the boys. They are panting heavily, exhausted. I grasp how much damage had been done and feel sick again.

Ebony quickly attends to Will's head, and he smiles, reminding her that he can take it. She puts her hand on him and slowly, the wound closes and vanishes without a scar. Ebony quickly moves to Sol who is being comforted by his sister.

"You're an idiot," Amber scolds him, but her smile betrays her, "I'm so glad you're okay."

"Same," Sol replies, pulling her into a hug.

Watching their interaction warms my heart and stills the anxiety within. Ebony gently takes Sol's arm and places his hand on her shoulder. She tells him to brace himself before twisting his elbow. I wince as Sol tries not to cry out.

"Rosebud!" Finn bursts through and wraps his arms around me, "What the on earth is wrong with you? Why didn't you run earlier?" he asks, clearly worried.

I shrug and his gaze softens as he sees that I'm still in shock.

"I'm sorry," he says gently, "I didn't mean to scare you. It's okay…"

Pangs of guilt radiate from his touch as my tears fall silently. I'm not sure why I'm crying, but I don't really know how else to process what I had just witnessed. It was so sudden, and I was really, *really* scared.

"Rose?" Ebony says, realising I'm crying. "What's wrong?" she asks Finn.

"I'm fine," I say, bursting out into strained laughter.

"What's so funny?" Ebony asks, confused.

"Nothing," I smile and wipe the tears away, "I'm just so tired of crying."

They both look at one another and Ebony strokes my arm.

"Well, it's okay if you do. We're here for you," she says.

"I know," I smile.

"Come on, let's go home before that thing comes back again…" Amber says, steering us away.

Nobody says anything. We follow Amber, pulling our gaze away from the forest. I wonder if the beast is still lurking, but I don't want to wait to find out. We each get into our chosen car and drive off, still unable to explain what just happened. The boys must have agreed to stick together because we trail Sol's car for most of the journey. Even when a small, white tourist car tries to cut between us, Finn is quick to overtake. He remains close to Sol all the way until we finally reach the Manor.

"So, who was that beast?" I ask, as we gather in the kitchen.

Everyone is here, except for the twins who must have gone to bed. This seems to stop anyone from raising their voices, but an alarmed Ava looks up and asks who I was talking about. By the state of the boys, she can see that something bad happened despite Ebony's attempts to heal. Eli seems concerned, but not unnerved like Jesse. However, I can tell Jesse is angry when he starts asking questions.

"What happened?" he asks; his stern, oak eyes searching for answers.

"Well, um…" Sol starts, but Will cuts in.

"We thought we heard something whilst we were changing and so we went to find out what it was," Will explains, "We had no idea it could have been him…"

His eyes flicker to Eli momentarily as if to gauge what he was thinking. Eli remained calm, listening quietly as he tends to Finn who is showing him the wound. Ebony had made a tourniquet and bandaged him up before we drove away to stop the bleeding.

"We broke his arm, so I don't think he'll be coming back anytime soon," Sol reassures his mother.

"Hurting them will only anger them more," Ava says firmly, placing a hand on her son. "You should know better than that."

"Ava's right," Eli says, "We shouldn't engage with them. It'll only make the consequences far more damaging."

My stomach twists and churns. I didn't like the sound of that.

"Rose, this is exactly what your friend was telling you about," Eli pauses, referring to Jasper, and continues, "Those who are after you aren't like what you know about the Gifted. The poor man that you encountered has been altered so that he is able to shapeshift."

Horrified, I remember how the beast spoke my name. My mind thinks back to the hospital incident where I met the man behind the beast. He was still human to me then, now it seemed impossible to ever see him as human again. Eli clears his throat and addresses everyone.

"I fear this only the beginning," he says, "We need to keep watch to make sure none of them make it to the house."

His confidence falters revealing troubled waters in his eyes. Everybody begins to mutter between themselves. The boys group together behind me and discuss a plan of action. I overhear them talk of nightly shifts to watch the house and possibly escorts for everybody when they leave Blakewood. In front of me, Ava's cool exterior is slowly unravelling as she asks Jesse what he plans to do to keep them safe. I feel for Jesse as he tries to reassure her. She's clearly distressed as she snaps at him.

"I will not calm down," Ava says, storming out of the room.

Jesse quickly follows her out into another room. Everybody seems anxious and there's nothing I can say that'll help. Realising this, Eli sees that I'm lost and beckons me over with a wave of his hand.

"This is not simply about you, Rose. This is far greater than you will understand." Eli says softly, "But don't be afraid. We will keep you safe."

"But I'm tired of not understanding…" I reply, looking around and soaking in the room's nervous buzz, "Why are they after me? That beast-thing almost killed one of the boys. What if someone else gets hurt because of me? Or what if they get me? What if-"

"My dear," Eli hushes me with a sombre chuckle, "We cannot worry about the future for we are still in the present." His smile wavers, "Teo is not a 'thing', Rose" he reminds me, "He is a young man, and we should still allow him that title. Despite what you saw, you shouldn't fear him. Teo and his sister are merely pawns in this and acting on what they believe to be true. Can you really blame someone if they do not know better?"

There's a quiet moment as I consider what Eli has said. It made sense to not blame someone for not knowing, but then again, how could he overlook the bloodshed? Surely, Teo and the rest of them were capable of so much more. Otherwise, why would everyone be getting ready to protect the Manor like a fortress?

Eli sighs heavily and seems deeply saddened, contemplating the events that have taken place. Maybe even things that I don't know about.

"You should rest, child," Eli says.

"Maybe," I shrug and turn, already looking to the door.

"Nobody is going to get you," Finn whispers after earwigging in on the end of our conversation, "Not Teo, not his sister, and certainly not Luke. I promise."

"Luke?" I repeat.

That name rings a bell. I recall my conversation with Will. I'm sure he said his brother was called Luke and yet, he appeared uncomfortable when I asked why he wasn't here anymore. Maybe this is why? Everybody looks at me. You could hear a pin drop if my heartbeat wasn't thumping in my head. I search for an explanation, but it's clear the secret is out. My gaze lands on Will. His guilty face is enough to give me the answer I was looking for.

Luke *was* his brother.

Luke was the one who wants me.

CHAPTER
Twelve

"Okay, so explain it to me again."

I pace back into the living room with a fresh glass of fruit juice. The nightly hours are rolling on as we discuss the new revelation. Eli is sat with Ebony, Finn and I, attempting to answer everything as clearly as possible. Except 'clear' seemed to be practically opaque.

"Luke wants you because your Gifting is different to any other Gifted being," Eli explains for the fifth time.

Sitting across from us, he leans forward with his hands clasped, rubbing his thumbs together. He seems distracted, yet the ocean in his eyes remains still.

"But why?"

They look at one another and Ebony places a hand on mine. Her words are earnest as she speaks tenderly, clearly trying not to upset me more.

"Because you can do more than others. You're a Pure Gifted, that means you're very much a wanted woman, but listen…" she pauses, "They won't get you, okay?"

"Sweetheart," a voice appears from the kitchen, "You can't worry about it now. You need to get some rest."

I'm not sure how long Ava has been there, but she seems weary. Sighing, I take their advice and they walk me upstairs. Ebony offers to stay in my room for the night and I take it. She smiles, calls it a sleepover and goes to grab her pyjamas, leaving me with Finn. His face is cast over with shadows and I can't tell what he's thinking.

"Are you okay?" I probe him.

Shrugging, he nods and tells me not to worry. I'm not accepting his response and punch him in the arm playfully.

"Come on, Shark-Finn," I smile as I use his nickname, "I know you. Something's wrong."

Breathing deeply, he looks up and places a hand on my shoulder. The cool air from his lips washes over me as he exhales and forces a smile.

"I just want you to know that you're safe," he says, "I want you to believe it."

Pulling him into a hug, I hold him tightly and tell him I know. It was unclear why Luke or anyone was after me, and I knew it was a battle I needed to face in the morning. Right now, Finn needed me as much as I needed him.

When Ebony returns, we each say goodnight and Finn heads downstairs to keep watch. Ebony and I go into my room to get ready for bed. There's not a lot to say as we both lay there. Ebony is asleep before me with her gentle, quiet snores giving away that she was dreaming. Silently, I lie awake beside her, still processing the day and piecing everything together.

At 3:00 am, I decided I needed to do something else other than stay in my bed worrying. Ebony is fast asleep, but she seems content, so I don't wake her. Swinging my feet over the edge of my bed, I stand up, stretch and wander to the door. I check to see if anyone is in the hallway to catch me in my pyjamas. The moon's silvery light casts light along the corridor giving me clear vision.

It's empty.

Before I leave my room, I grab my dressing gown, just to be safe. It would be just my luck to have one of the boys wake up and see me prancing around in my lacy shorts. Especially when I'm trying to be inconspicuous. I tie the dressing grown around my waist and tiptoe out of my room.

As I head towards the stairs, I noticed Eli's not-so-secret study door was slightly open. The lights were on, so I presumed Eli was still awake. Though I'm tempted to join him, I'm thirsty and decide to get a drink from downstairs. The house is quiet and eerie, making it quite creepy to wander alone. I don't hesitate to flick the lights on as soon as I get to the kitchen.

The yellowy light tingles in my eyes. I'm squinting the whole time as I fetch myself a hot chocolate. My eyes blur whilst I wait for the milk to heat up in the microwave. I lose myself in thought. Mum had always said that a hot drink helps you sleep. There were many times she would pop downstairs in the middle of the night. I would hear her if I'd woken up too. Sometimes I would join her, and we would have some of the best conversations.

"Rose…" a voice interrupts me.

Gasping, I turn around to see who it was. No one is there, but I could've sworn there was someone behind me. I scan the room nervously and find nothing.

Time to go back upstairs… I tell myself.

I'm in a rush to finish making my drink and I keep glancing over my shoulder to keep watch. Nothing appears. I run up the stairs and return to the safety of my room. Ebony is sleeping soundly with her face buried in the pillow. I watch her for a moment, seeing her peaceful and carefree seems to settle the fear that had risen. Each sip of hot chocolate makes me sleepy until I finish it. My dreams are filled with the memories of a little copper-brown haired girl with freckles and a beaming smile. Her comfort was found in a familiar, childhood house with a shiny, red-painted door.

EXHAUSTED, I DIDN'T WAKE UP UNTIL LATE THE NEXT MORNING. I WAS alone and started to call for Ebony in hopes she hadn't left yet. Relief flooded through me as I heard her reply from the en suite. The shower started and I lay there almost ready to fall asleep again. My dreams seemed to grow strange last night as the beast with marble eyes crept in and never left.

"Rose," a voice sings.

Gasping, I look up and see a hazy face staring back. I blink, rub my eyes and hope it goes away, but it doesn't. Jasper waits with a confident smirk across his face as I sit up defensively.

"Why are you here?" I ask, unnerved by his presence, "Is this for real?"

Shaking his head, he seems disappointed by my reaction and his shoulders lower. His focus changes as he leans on the wall, playing with a toothpick.

"It's a vision," he mutters before pausing, "He came for you again, didn't he?"

"Who?" I reply.

Waiting for him to respond, it dawns on me that Jasper had warned me about the beast. He tried to protect me.

"How did you know?"

"Rose, I know a lot of things you don't," he laughs tensely, pushing himself off the wall to face me again.

Maybe it was because of how heightened I had become after yesterday's experiences. Or maybe my emotions were getting to me because I hadn't slept properly. Either way, I wasn't in the mood for his cocky replies.

"Why are you here, Jasper?" I glare.

His brows furrow as he seems hurt by this. He brushes his fingers through his hair slowly, thoughtfully.

"How do I make you trust me?" he asks, meeting my gaze.

Shrugging, I don't have an answer. I didn't know *if* I could trust him. His shady responses and inability to answer a question directly made it hard to build a foundation of trust.

"What side are you on?" I sigh, "That's what I want to know. Because if you're with Luke then I don't think I can trust you."

"I'm on your side, Rose, that's all I've ever been," Jasper replies.

"What abo-"

"Rose?"

Ebony appears beside me. I blink and Jasper is gone.

Staring at the wall where I'd left him, I begin to feel slightly nauseous. Ebony's worried as she tries to get me to focus again, but my head is fuzzy. Her touch is warm and damp, and I realise she's got out of the shower and dressed in a t-shirt and shorts.

"You were talking to someone…" she says when I finally zone in on her.

"Yeah," I reply, trying to shake the vision off, "I saw Jasper. He… he warned me about yesterday. He knew Teo was coming."

"Okay, so…" Ebony says, sitting back, "What are you trying to say?"

"I think he's helping me," I exhale.

At first, Ebony goes quiet. I can see the thoughts ticking over in her mind on what this could mean and whether there was a possibility for it to be true. As she's about to open her mouth, someone knocks, and Finn's head appears behind the door. He looks tired, but he beams as he looks over us. He's dressed in black jeans, a grey t-shirt and a black bomber jacket when he walks in.

"How was the watch last night?" I ask anxiously.

"Silent," Finn replies, "Nothing to worry about." Finn seems confident, but his smile fades as he sees our expressions. "What's wrong?"

Looking to Ebony, she says to tell Finn about my vision of Jasper. She adds that I think that he's trying to help me. This leads to an uncomfortable and short discussion where they argue. Ebony thinks it's crazy and Finn appears to believe me. He seems curious, wondering if maybe Jasper could help more.

"No," Ebony snaps, "I think that is a ridiculous idea. We have no idea what this boy is capable of."

"But the possibility is worth exploring, Ebony," Finn sighs, "Why can't you see that?"

"Why can't you see that we have her safe, here, now," Ebony's voice breaks, "I will not let them take her. If Jasper is not with us, he's one of them. End of discussion."

"Okay, okay…" Finn says and curls his hand around the nape of her neck, rubbing it gently.

This is the first sign of affection I've seen between them, and it makes me feel weird. I don't like it and hope that I can say something to stop it.

"Okay, so what now?" I ask.

"Well," Finn says with a bright tone, "Right now, you have a lesson with Eli."

"Oh?" I frown, "He didn't mention anything yesterday."

"Things have changed," he replies, yawning.

Nodding, I catch the yawn and stand up to stretch. Finn gets up to leave and tells us both to hurry before disappearing out the door. Ebony doesn't take this very well, but she doesn't snap. Instead, she pulls her knees under her chin and wraps are arms around them. Her eyes are glazed over as she loses herself in bubbling fears.

"What is it?" I ask, rubbing her knee gently.

"Things are only going to get worse," she sighs, releasing her legs from her tight grasp, "You need to remember who the good guys are," Ebony says whilst standing up, "Yes, Jasper may be helping you, but you need to ask yourself why."

"I am," I assure her.

"Good."

Chewing my lip, anxiety simmers in my chest as I feel torn. Ebony's stubborn gaze is waiting for me to give in and admit that I believed Jasper. She thought it was stupid to trust him and nothing was going to change that. Maybe she was right.

"Okay," I shrug, "Well, I need to shower so that I can meet Eli."

Ebony nods in agreement and wraps her arms around me, telling me she only wants me to be safe. I know this and squeeze her back, reminding her that I love her. There's a little giggle as she tells me I stink before running away. The door closes as she tells me that we will talk later.

Silence falls and I realise I'm alone. Sudden fear comes crawling in on all fours hoping I will succumb to its will. I can't give the fear what it wants and push it away so that I can shower and find Eli. Once I'm done, I throw on some shorts and a pink t-shirt and sprint down the stairs. Ava is in the kitchen packing the rest of the breakfast away, singing to herself.

"I'm sorry I missed breakfast," I apologise.

Immediately, Ava turns around and waves my apology away. She reaches into the fridge and unwraps something. It's a pain au chocolat, especially for me. Thanking her, I take it and ask if she knows where Eli is.

"He's in the stables," she says, "Hang on, I'll get someone to take you," she smiles, waving to someone in the living room. "You can't be wandering the grounds alone my dear."

"Oh that's not neccess- "

From where I'm standing, I can't see who it is until their poised stature enters the room. He looks between me and Ava before asking what was going on. Ava fills him in to which he nods, muttering an 'ah' before turning to me.

"Come on then, little miss," he says.

Walking through the hallway, Will escorts me through the games room where we played ping pong on my first day. He pulls back a curtain which reveals French doors and opens them, allowing me to step out first. There's a slight decline as we walk further away from the Manor. Butterflies flutter between rows of technicolour flower beds. Giant daisies line the pathway and wood chips bend underneath our feet. It must have taken years to make this place as stunning as it was. I had never seen anything like it.

"So… Luke, hey?" Will asks eventually.

"He's your brother," I exhale.

"Yep, that he is."

Stopping, I turn to confront him. His calm collected gaze narrows in on me. A quizzical expression blooms across his face as I figure out a way to ask my next question.

"Why didn't anyone tell me?"

Shrugging, Will tells me that he didn't see how it would help. I understand his reasoning, but surely it was important to know who we were up against. Then again, the more I asked, the more it seemed like they didn't know.

"Eli knows more than I do, so you should ask him."

I nod and think about it. I had already tried to get answers and still, Eli had not been very forthcoming. It was getting a little infuriating, and that made me feel bad for saying it aloud.

"I know it seems confusing now, and I don't blame you," Will reassures me, "Eli can be tricky to understand because he knows everything has a time and a place."

"Do you think he knows why Luke wants me?"

"I don't know," Will admits.

Shortly after this, we approach some buildings surrounded by pine trees. I'm almost certain I hear some kind of squeal and frown at Will. He chuckles, telling me that it's where they keep their horses.

"Yes, Eli has horses," Will confirms, "We also have an area for training. Eli wants you to practice your Gifts, and maybe you'll even discover some new ones."

Shooting him a questioning look, I try to ask what he means when Eli approaches us from the barn. He thanks Will and lets him know that Solomon and Amber were looking for him. They mention switching shifts, but I stop listening. Instead, I find myself drawn to the wooden building and make my way to its door.

Leaving Eli and Will still talking, I enter the barn through the gated door and walk quietly through the stables. A few horses whiny as their sense my presence and peer out. Their loud breathing and watchful eyes wait for me to approach.

One dapple grey horse captures my attention and I whisper a greeting. The horse shakes his mane and dips his head as if he understands.

"That's Brin," Eli explains as he catches up with me, "He's a very strong and reliable horse. Once upon a time, he belonged to Luke."

"Oh," I reply, feeling uncomfortable.

Brin starts to bray and snort as Eli approaches him. He places his hand on Brin's nose and strokes it soothingly.

"You're a good boy, aren't you hmm?" Eli smiles.

Brin shakes his head and trots around his pen, breathing heavily. He looks back once before heading out into the paddock that is attached to the barn. Eli is staring off into the distance when I finally ask my question.

"Why are we here?"

"To learn," Eli says ambiguously.

Beckoning for me to follow, Eli walks to the next stable. I read the wooden name plaque. It's painted with flowers and a black border which says 'Noelle'. Eli unlatches the door and invites me into the stable. The shaded area is cool on our skin as we walk across the straw bedding. We approach a small blonde pony in the corner. She appears nervous when she realises that I'm entering her space and remains close to the wall. Eli crouches, clicking his tongue, and extends a hand to her. The little pony immediately trots up to him, snorting a greeting. I try to stroke her, but she gets spooked.

"Don't worry, she's always nervous around strangers," he chuckles, "This is Honey…" Eli pats her on the belly and she closes her eyes, appreciatively. "Honey's our little Shetland pony. She shares with Noelle sometimes," Eli explains.

Nodding, I watch Honey flick her ears back and forth. Closer now, I can see she's a beautiful honeycomb colour with a white marking down her nose.

Another horse trots into the stable and she's about the same height as me. Her mane is pure white much like her gleaming white coat. She bows her head as she enters, and Eli gets up to meet her. The white horse notices me and approaches with no fear in her big, black eyes. She brings her head close to mine and stares as though she were looking for something. I automatically reach out to stroke her. Her coat is warm as I feel her emotions tingle under my palms. The horse looks away and expels a sense of calm which takes over my entire body. I almost forget that Eli is standing beside us when he asks me a question.

"She's magnificent, isn't she?" Eli beams and scratches the horse's nose. She nuzzles him and he whispers something, making her whiny. "Rose, meet Noelle."

We watch in awe of the beautiful white mare as she stands proudly, shaking her mane. She points her nose in the air and whinnies contently.

"Come on," Eli smiles, then he addresses Noelle with a nod to me, "I need her for training."

Past the horses' stables is a door which Eli leads me through. We walk into a round, wooden room with a dome ceiling. Full-length mirrors are dotted around the walls whilst punchbags and other training equipment are placed in specific areas. Eli guides me to the centre of the room. There are two dark blue, rectangular padded mats on the floor with red and black boxing gloves abandoned on top.

"I thought you were going to teach me about my Gift?"

Feeling a bit disappointed, I hoped to have spent more time with the horses. A smile spreads on Eli's lips and he laughs gingerly. He picks up the gloves from the floor and hands them to me.

"I am, but I'm going to teach you to fight first," he replies.

Looking between Eli and the gloves, I wonder what he's going to ask me to do. I'm not hitting him, that's for sure. I refuse. No offence, but Eli was still an older gentleman. It would be a crime to hit a man of his age, surely…

"Not me," Eli chuckles again, reading my thoughts, "I want you to hit that."

Pointing to the tall, free-standing punch bag, Eli explains that we will be doing combat training. I turn and throw him a puzzled look; I had never hit anything in my life. Maybe once when I was in primary school but that was child's play. This was something else. Eli reassures me to trust him whilst I hesitantly slip my hands into each glove. He tightens the straps and asks if I'm ready. I nod.

Ready as I'll ever be.

IT'S BEEN A WEEK SINCE WE BEGAN TRAINING. SOCIAL SERVICES HAD called to ask how I was doing and said that they planned to visit soon. Everyone reassured me that it was nothing to worry about as they were used to visitors. Gradually, I started to feel settled and confident, not always second-guessing them. It was bizarre how time changed things. I had stopped asking questions and instead, learned to listen and engage as 'every day was a learning day'.

Now, I can punch in a straight line, high kick on cue and even dodge a few hits from the opposition. Finn and Ebony had come to sit in on some of my training and Eli used them as training opportunities. Although, yesterday, we found out that I have superhuman strength as well as speed. Something Eli had noticed before, but could tell by our response, it was a shock.

"I'm so sorry," I had apologised over and over again.

Ebony sat with her hand over her jaw, clearly trying to heal herself. She seemed to wince under the pain, and I placed a hand on her, trying to help heal her. Annoyingly, I still couldn't do it despite using every injury as an opportunity to try.

"Why is this so impossible?" I cry in frustration to Eli.

"Patience, my dear," he exhaled, joining us on the mats.

Gently, he moved Ebony's hand and placed his own over her face. She stopped grimacing almost immediately and relaxed under his reassuring healing touch. A thank you followed shortly after. We continued training today, but I had hit a metaphorical brick wall. As another injury had presented itself as an opportunity, Eli agreed I should try and help.

"Again," Eli instructs, "Try focusing on what you want her to do…"

Holding onto Myrtle, one of the palomino horses, I can feel her pain and it shocks like electricity through my fingertips. I let go and try again, telling her softly to trust me, promising that I will make her better. I'm able to cover her pain with a sense of calm which she responds well to. I return to her twisted hoof and sigh, trying to hold off the negative thoughts. Again, I close my eyes and imagine the hoof turning itself back into place. Something moves under my palms, and I exhale before peeking to see if it's worked.

"Ah!" I growl in frustration; it hasn't worked. "Why isn't this working?"

"Stop, stop, stop," Eli says calmly.

Agreeing to give up, I let go of Myrtle and she snorts at me, rubbing her nose against my cheek. I'm glad she's okay with me, but I'm annoyed at myself.

Why was healing so difficult?

Eli watches me thoughtfully and then sighs. I think he's disappointed.

"I'm sorry," I mumble, but Eli shakes his head.

"Don't apologise, my dear," he reassures me with a growing smile, "You are doing better than you think."

Eli nods at Myrtle and tells me to have a look. I frown and run my fingers over her hoof, but something's different. It feels smooth and painless, like how I had imagined it to be. I'm confused and tell Eli that I don't understand.

"You did it," he confirms.

The relief and shock are evident on my lips. I can't work out how I did it, but I'm staring at the evidence. I *did* do it.

Myrtle seems calmer and her emotions are bubbling with relief and joy. I stroke her again and thank her for being patient. She neighs softly and stands up again, wobbling momentarily as she takes the weight of her whole body.

"You can do this, Rose," Eli says, "You need to have more patience with yourself."

Standing up, I shrug and say, 'thank you'. He welcomes me into a warm embrace, and I close my eyes to take a deep breath. His firm, comforting hold is something I have become accustomed to. Like the rest of the family, he's affectionate towards me as though I were his own. I feel safe knowing I was becoming a part of his family.

"Right, let's get you back to the house," Eli sings with his arm resting lightly around me.

"Okay," I reply, picking up my bag.

As I walk with Eli, we talk about the attack last week. There's only been a small amount of movement in the grounds. Nothing that anyone has deemed alarming enough to share. Not that anyone was really telling me a lot. Eli insisted it was better to be on a need-to-know basis.

"Have you seen Jasper recently?" Eli asks.

I had been telling Eli about my more recent encounter and asked for his advice. He seemed unfazed by the interaction and offered his thoughts. His words were, 'if he's on our side, it'll become clear'. So, I took that, stored it, and left it alone.

"No," I shake my head before remembering, "I did dream about him, actually, but this time it was different."

"Oh?" Eli seems intrigued.

"Yeah," I laugh uncomfortably as I remember what happens, "We were at the lake at Ashmore. It was the middle of the night, like scarily quiet and dark. Jasper was running into the water, and he didn't see me, but I watched as he started to swim. It was peaceful and then he started struggling. It was like something was pulling him under..." I gulp as the images flash in front of my eyes, "It was as though I was over him and I could see him being pulled down. Bubbles escaped his lips and I..." I pause, touching my throat subconsciously, "I felt him... drowning."

Breathing heavily, I could still feel the lack of oxygen in my lungs. Ebony had been sleeping in my room so when I woke up, she assured me it was just a dream. I couldn't talk about it until now. I had tried to forget it, but the vivid image of his death wouldn't go away. It made me worried for him and I couldn't help wondering what it could mean.

"Interesting," Eli says after a brief moment, "Write it down in your book, like the rest of them. It's probably nothing, but it's best to keep a note, just in case."

Eli was referring to a small, leather notebook he had given me. This was because I had started having more frequently memorable dreams which Will insisted were important. Eli agreed that maybe it was part of my Gifting. Whatever it was, they insisted I wrote them down for safekeeping.

"I'm worried about him…" I admit; although I didn't trust him, I still cared.

"So am I," Eli agrees, "He has no idea what he's got himself into."

Someone interrupts, calling our names chaotically through the grounds. An alarmed Finn is running towards us, full pelt. He stops and pants, catching his breath before relaying his urgent message.

"We need you," he says, looking at Eli with uneasy eyes.

Our feet take us as fast as they can into the house where Finn leads us to the kitchen. Everyone is crowding around and whispering, and there's a strange atmosphere. I can feel the anxiety racing through the air and increasing with our adrenaline rush. Nobody moves until Eli enters, and they split.

His broad shoulders are hunched over as he tries to look up and I can't breathe. I'm certain it's not a vision anymore as everyone can see that he is there. He looks battered and bruised with one bloodshot, juniper eye. There's crimson liquid dripping from his lip, but he licks it away. He can't keep his head up for long as it seems too painful for him. His body weight is taken by Sol, Jesse and Amber who are forcefully holding him upright.

Who did this to him?

"Put him on the sofa," Eli says, waving everyone away, "He is hurt, and we need to heal him, quickly. Ebony?"

Eli looks for her in the room and she slips past me, rubbing her hands together. He beckons her over and she complies. They lay hands on him and begin to heal his wounds. Ebony seems stoic as she touches him, gently removing the bruises and cuts. Jasper thanks her repeatedly but she doesn't respond. He coughs up dark fluid when they try to touch his side. Eli replaces Ebony and tells her to wash off the blood on her hands. When Ebony moves, Jasper relaxes into the chair under Eli's healing touch. By the time Ebony is drying her hands on a towel, Jasper is almost healed.

"How did he end up here?" I ask Finn who is watching tensely.

"I don't know," he shrugs, "He just appears at the door, no explanation. He was bleeding and so we carried him in here. Ava insisted we couldn't leave him," he seems anxious, "It doesn't make sense…"

Straightening up, Eli turns around and addresses us. He asks us to leave him and Jasper to talk alone, which Jesse protests. His concern is not lost on us, we all feel the same. Can Jasper be trusted? Eli firmly reminds him that it is okay and that he needs to trust him. They nod, and Jesse reluctantly agrees to leave them to it.

We all filter out of the room and look around. Nobody knows what to do or say. His presence only brought back a flurry of mixed emotions. At this moment, I knew I didn't want anything bad to happen to Jasper. What I felt was, compassion, pity and fear; a nauseating blend. Glancing back, I try to catch up glimpse of them talking but Sol is in the way. I look around to see who is with us and suddenly it dawns on me. Someone is missing.

I grab Ebony and Finn's arms and spin them around.

"Where's Will?"

CHAPTER
Thirteen

Tensions were high as no one knew what to say. Everyone was now aware that Will was missing, but nobody understood why. They assumed Jasper was something to do with it. Or at least, they had their suspicions. Ava suggested we sat down for a meal and discussed what we do next. She has laden the table full of finger food so that we can help ourselves. Jesse's eyes kept flicking between his wife and Jasper. I couldn't help sneaking a look either.

"Do you think Luke took Will?" I whisper to Ebony.

"Probably," she tuts under her breath.

Ebony hasn't touched her food, instead, she's staring at it in a world of her own. I nudge her, forcing her to come back to reality. She seemed on edge since Jasper had arrived. I'm not sure if she felt something when she was healing him, but he had unnerved her.

"Are you okay?" I ask and she immediately starts shaking her head.

"No," she whispers, "When I touched him, he seemed off. Like, I couldn't read his emotions."

"At all?" I ask, "I mean... his were always in and out for me..." I say, remembering how confusing he was to read for myself, "Hasn't that happened before?"

"Never."

Shaking her head again, she picks up her fork and starts eating. She chews slowly, still thinking about Jasper's change. I continue eating as well and glance at the boy we're all thinking about. For a moment, he looks at me and we freeze as he pleads silently for me to smile. I look away and return to my food, forcing myself to swallow.

"I know we are all worried about Will," he says, "Amber and Sol have volunteered to go to Belwick. This a rescue, not a fight, after all."

Belwick was supposedly where Luke resided with his followers. I had heard the name only once before, but nobody really talked about it. Sol and Amber are already dressed and ready to go, nodding when their names are mentioned. They know that the remaining Gifted needed to stay here and keep me safe. Now we were down one man, this could be their opportunity to attack, and we had to be ready.

"Thank you," Eli says to them before addressing us, "Now, can we please make our guest feel welcome. He won't bite," his tone lightens, "Maybe you can tell us a little bit about yourself, Jasper."

Nervously, Jasper looks around the room and places his cutlery down. He finishes his mouthful and gulps loudly, quickly taking a sip of water to clear his throat. His eyes lock with mine as he starts introducing himself.

"Well," he says, "I'm Jasper. I went to college with Rose," his smile is meant for me, but I remain poker-faced, "… and Ebony and Finn. Hi guys!"

Jasper's laughter is very clearly forced. Nobody knows how to react which makes the situation even more painful. Jasper looks at Eli for reassurance. There's an exchange and then, Eli nods back, encouraging him to continue.

"Um," Jasper's tone is earnest, "I think you guys should know that I'll do everything in my power to get Will back."

Everyone nods, and a sense of understanding settles across the room. Though we don't trust him, his intentions are clear; he wants to help. He wouldn't have told us where Luke was if he was against us. The conversation moves along as Ava offers more food to Jasper. He thanks her, folding his napkin agitatedly, and excuses himself, saying his stomach was still aching. Ava seems sad to watch him leave as Eli tries to put her mind at ease.

"He'll be fine."

The conversation flows more freely as we finish eating. Ava stacks up the plates and offers pudding, but we're full to the brim. Nobody really wants something sweet and sickly. One after the other, everyone leaves the table until only Eli, Jesse and Ava remain. I turn back, offering to help with the washing up, but Ava refuses.

"At least you tried," Jesse mutters.

Running along, I catch up with Ebony and Finn. They're talking about their shifts and Ebony seems insistent on doing one tonight. Finn shakes his head, telling her no. He blames himself for Will's disappearance and insists he needs to stay awake. They start arguing, fuelled by lack of sleep and on their last nerves.

"Why don't you both do it together?" I suggest forcefully.

"No," they sigh in unison.

Confused, I look between them. Finn's face is creased with concern and frustration. He had dark, grey bags under his eyes which seemed to be getting more prominent by the day. It didn't take much to know this boy was drained. Ebony's tight-lipped smile told me she was infuriated because she was trying to help.

Unfortunately, Finn was riddled with guilt, so he wasn't going to back down.

"Well, what do you suggest?" I ask, crossing my arms across my chest.

Enough was enough.

Regardless of Jasper's presence or the fact that Will was missing, we couldn't start turning on each other. We were finally getting along.

"I'm going to go on my shift," Finn yawns, pushing his hair back and pointing at Ebony "And you're going to keep her safe."

I see Ebony in the corner of my eye about to snap when I put my foot down. He'll listen to me.

"No, Finn," I shake my head, "You can't. Let Ebony take the shift, or maybe one of the others. You need to sleep."

Finn exhales frustratedly and another yawn escapes. He wanted to do his duty and help, as did all of us, but being burnt out wasn't an option. Finn was on the edge, and he knew it deep down. There's a long pause as he fights his inner pride before giving in and surrendering. I take his hand, and reluctantly he follows me. I ask Ebony to explain Finn's situation to Eli and suggest that she takes his shift instead. She agrees and hurries off.

We climb up the stairs and Finn continues to mumble weak protests, but I ignore them. I walk him to his room and push open the door. His room is white and navy blue with a dark, oak four-poster bed in the middle. White, framed pictures of different leaves and fossils are dotted along the navy walls. Like mine, there's a door that leads to an en suite, and double doors which lead to a Juliet balcony. The chest of drawers and furniture is also made of dark oak.

"Come on," I say, ushering him in.

After pulling back the duvet, I lower Finn onto his bed. Automatically, he swings his legs up so he's lying down and rests his head on the pillows. I tuck him in and perch on the bed. I run my hands over the duvet across his chest, but he stops me, clutching my fingers.

"I don't need to sleep," he says, his weary eyes boring into mine, "I need to keep you safe."

With a knowing smile, I rest my chin on my hand which is holding his. He starts to play with my hair and breathes slowly, finally relaxing his whole body.

"And how can you do that when you're exhausted?" I reply.

Finn's expression breaks into a grin as he stares at me. We both sit in silent combat, and I know I've won this fight. He pulls my head onto his chest and continues stroking my hair rhythmically. A heavy breath forcefully flies from his mouth as he drifts in and out of sleep. I giggle and he starts stroking my hair again.

"What?" he asks.

"Nothing," I reply, "Go to sleep."

"Goodnight, Rosebud," he yawns.

"Goodnight, Shark-Finn," I whisper in return.

Finn rolls over onto his side when I get up to leave. I'm careful not to disturb him and tiptoe to the half-opened door. On my way out, I notice a photo of us on one of the tables and stop. I pick it up and study the familiar frame, recognising it from when we were little. We bought frames that said 'best friends' on them for each other as a gift. We'd promised to always fill it with photos of us as we grew up together. I remember my own picture frame that I kept on my desk at home. I hadn't changed the photo in years as it was our primary school dance picture. Now that the fire had claimed it, I guess it didn't matter anymore.

As I close the door, I stand in the hallway and sigh, suddenly saddened. Someone's footsteps are growing louder and so I look to see who it is. The swagger stops as he reads the evident hesitation on my face.

"Am I really that bad?"

"No," I reply, "I just don't understand why you're here."

"Ah," Jasper nods, "Makes sense."

There's a pause. I look at the floor, searching my mind for something to say. I didn't know anything about him. Even though we had been somewhat emotionally involved with one another, he felt like a stranger.

"They… they kicked me out," Jasper says.

My eyes flicker up, meeting his, and I tilt my head. I'm confused about why he's telling me this now.

"After I had visited you, they found out…" Jasper speaks slowly, almost as if it's a confession. "I tried to tell them that I hadn't, but they didn't buy it. They said I might as well be on your side. Then, they beat me and left me here," he shrugs, "I… I didn't have anywhere else to go."

It made sense, he *had* warned me of Teo's attack. Although, I did want to know why… *and for what?*

"Do you want to get a hot chocolate?" I ask.

Jasper's eyes sparkle with hope as he nods. He seems grateful, catching a glimmer of a smile on my lips. We walk down the stairs, side by side, and head into the kitchen. Nobody is around. I tell Jasper to take a seat and begin heating up some milk in the microwave. There's a weird sense of déjà vu which I will away. Jasper watches me silently as I make the hot chocolate.

"This looks great," he says once I hand it to him, "Thank you."

Sitting beside him, I take my own mug and continue stirring the chocolate in. We talk about how his conversation went with Eli. He seems unsure and confused, which I completely understand and assure him that Eli was a good person. He seems open to it and explains that he doesn't know what he's going to do about Luke. I try to ask about him, but it makes Jasper visibly uncomfortable.

Promptly, Jasper changes the subject and asks me how I've been and about my parents. I tell him about Mum and the fire, thankfully without crying. He seems genuinely shocked and apologises repeatedly.

"It's okay," I say, "I thought you knew."

"N-no, I didn't…" Jasper stammers, "How… what… I mean," he stumbles over his words, "I just can't believe it."

"Why?"

"I just thought that…"

Someone coughs loudly behind us. We look around to see Ebony standing at the doorway. Her arms are folded across her chest as she stalks in, keeping her eyes fixed on Jasper.

"What's going on?" she asks.

Watching Jasper fail to use words, I wave Ebony's concerns away and tell her we're catching up. I explain briefly what Jasper had said to me and watch as her disapproval becomes more evident.

"I thought you were on watch," I add, hoping to ease some tension.

"Eli and Jesse wanted me to stay with you tonight," she mutters, "Probably to keep you safe from… *unwanted visitors.*"

Ebony clearly is aiming her comment at Jasper. I try to get her attention, but she doesn't take her eyes off the poor boy. She sits beside me and leans an elbow on the marble surface and props her head up. Her eyes squint at Jasper whilst pursing her lips.

"So… Why are you here?" she asks pointedly, "For real, I mean."

Mortified, I turn to Ebony and tell her to stop. She shrugs and flicks her hair over her shoulder, ignoring me. She mutters something about him being dangerous and Jasper lowers his gaze.

"Ebony," I hiss.

"You can look at me like that all you want, Rose. I'm not going to leave you alone whilst he's around. Okay?" she replies sternly.

I exhale, banishing all the words I wish I could say to her. Ebony notices my frustration with her and has the audacity to tell me to calm down. I glare at her which catches her off guard.

"What?" she says defensively.

"You're being extremely mean, Eb," I snap.

"And you're being incredibly stupid," she claps back.

Seething, I remain glaring at her and bite back a scream. She shrugs unapologetically which is enough to tip me over the edge.

"You can be such a…"

"Such a what?" she jabs.

"Such a… a… a brat!"

Stunned, Ebony leans back. This hurt her because it was the one insult that Finn had used that truly got under her skin. I had always defended her, until now. Ebony gets up and storms out. I'm angry with her, but I instantly regret what I've said. She didn't deserve it. I had to apologise. The guilt in me forces me to follow and make amends.

"I'm sorry," I say to Jasper and chase after Ebony.

She's halfway up the stairs when I catch up to her. Her lip twitches and I can see her rigid eyebrows suggesting she's mad. I grab her hand, and it confirms her feelings towards me. She snatches it away and tells me to go back to Jasper. I try to apologise, and she tells me to forget it. She pushes me away. I tell her to stop, and she continues, so I yell.

"Just listen to me!" I shout. "Please!"

Ebony freezes, motionless. We hear the muffled cry of one of the twins and I realise all the commotion has woken them up. Ebony still won't look at me when I stand next to her. Instead, she stares ahead blankly.

"I'm sorry," I sigh, lowering my voice.

"I said it's fine," Ebony replies.

"Please can you try to get along with Jasper?" I sigh.

"No," she huffs.

"No?" I echo.

"No, Rose, why would I? He has openly admitted that he knows Luke and not only that, but he has also worked and most likely been working with Luke this whole time. You know what he's capable of. It's up to me to look after you, and that means questioning why the hell you two were cosying up in the kitchen."

"What… that's not what happened," I protest.

Ebony finally looks at me, enraged. "Then what was that?"

"Talking!" I shout. Bedroom doors are squeaking open, wondering what the shouting is all about. "We were talking because he told me what happened, and I wanted to make sure he was okay." I pause, glancing up at the pairs of watching eyes above us. "Because funnily enough, I'm not the only person who is caught up in this. He is, too."

"Is he, Rose?" she sighs, "Or is that what he wants you to believe?"

Shaking her head, she walks up the remainder of the stairs and is greeted by a very worried Lily-Grace and Cole. They look down at me confused and then notice someone else over my shoulder.

"I swear, I'm here to help you," he insists softly, "You have to believe me."

Ava appears behind the twins and wraps her arms around them. She walks them away but whispers something in Ebony's ear. They exchange a nod and Ebony says she's going to bed, apologising for raising her voice. As she walks away, I realise I shouldn't have pushed her before she was ready to talk.

"I'm sorry," Jasper says as he sits beside me on the steps, "I didn't mean to upset her, or you…"

"Please just tell me. Why *are* you here?" I ask again, joining him.

"I'm here because they didn't want me," he replies wearily, "They think I'm against them because I helped you."

His answer seems honest as he doesn't shy away from my gaze. I decide this is my opportunity to ask more questions. It seems like now he has realised what's at stake. If he was going to tell me the truth, it was going to be the whole truth and nothing but the truth.

"Do you think Luke took Will?"

For a brief minute, his eyes glaze over. He fiddles with his hands and breathes steadily, considering an answer.

"There's a good chance he did," he admits.

His face fills with worry and resentment, knowing that his admission would mean somehow betraying 'them'. Not that he had any reason to protect them anymore. They had almost left him for dead.

"It's okay," I reassure him, "I just want you to be honest, Jasper. That's all."

We sit quietly, staring at each other for a moment. He nods, brushes a strand of hair away from my face and tucks it behind my ear. I'm taken back to when we first met, and we were sitting in the stairwell. His smile was the same, yet the light behind his eyes had faded. Creases on his forehead were more prominent now, and there was a scar on his chin that wasn't there before.

"What's that?" I point to his chin.

Covering it, he explains that it came from a fight a couple of weeks ago. I frown. I was sure I could heal it. I'm already placing my hands on him when he grabs them tightly.

"It doesn't work like that for this," he sighs, "I can't fully explain it, but this scar isn't like an ordinary scar. No healer's power is going to be able to get rid of this," he scoffs, pointing.

"But I'm not a healer."

Jasper seems adamant so I decide to let it go. I mutter an apology and cross my arms over my chest.

"Don't be," he says, "Thank you, you've been more understanding than I expected. I'm sorry that they, Luke and the others, tried to hurt you."

Shrugging, I laugh out loud. There was nothing I could do at this point about Luke. It was unbelievable to me that in less than a couple of months, I was sitting here, nowhere near resembling the life I once had.

"Are you okay?"

I manage to pull myself together enough to catch my breath and reassure him. Jasper is still staring at me; his expression is a mixture of concern and amusement. The corners of his lips curl upward whilst his eyes are studying me with angst.

"I'm fine," I brush away his concern.

"Okay," Jasper replies, but his tone suggests he doesn't believe me.

"Who knew that Gifted people existed, hey?" I giggle again, tickling myself at the absurdity of the situation we found ourselves in. Then I remember something and it sobers me quickly. "Wait... your Gift... it's..."

Looking at his hands, I freeze as the reality of his power floods over me. Jasper's sheepish grin gives more evidence to my hypothesis that he had some explaining to do.

"Um, about that... it's not what you think..."

"What do you mean?"

My dreams are strange tonight. I'm walking on walls and ceilings until I come to a clearing. Running water and the rustling of leaves bring me to Ashmoore. The lake lies still before me. I look at my reflection and I'm wearing a white dress. My hair is wild, moving freely in the gentle breeze. The water remains still, even as I begin to step into it. It's not my choice, but I walk in deeper. It's cold on my skin and I shiver in the water. There's no ripples or no change as though I'm not even there.

Listening to the space around me, I realise how deep I am. There's no rustling of trees out here. I feel my heart beating faster to keep up with the cold. It's almost at my neck when I try to fight back. Forcing myself to stop, I search for someone or something to help me to the bank. My eyes flick up and there's a face watching me. They open their eyes and I'm met with a juniper stare.

"Rose?" Finn calls my name, waking me up.

Sunlight streams from the double doors. It burns my eyes and I close them again. Finn's muffled laughter increases as he crouches down beside the bed. I'm covering my face when the image of me drowning forces them open again. I sit upright and will the sickening feeling to go back to where it came from. It felt too real, and I could taste the murky water on my tongue.

"Are you okay?" Finn asks with concern.

"No," I reply, "I… I just had an awful dream."

"What happened?"

"I… I think I died," I whisper as though it was a secret.

Wrapping his arms around me, Finn pulls me into a hug and tells me not to worry. He kisses my forehead, reminding me that I will always be safe when he's around. I bury my head into his shoulder and yawn again, barely rested. His cotton shirt is warm under my cheek. I take a moment to enjoy the peace that overwhelms me and steadies my anxious heart.

"So, when's your next shift?" I mumble.

"Not today!" he beams as I lean back, checking to see if he was being serious, "Today, I'm in charge of looking after you."

Suspicious, I ask him why.

"Is this because of Ebony?"

Confused, Finn doesn't seem to know what I'm talking about. Hopefully, that means she didn't tell him. I hadn't seen her all night and she didn't sleep in my room like usual. I'm trying to ignore the guilt that rises and swallow it down.

"Hey!" Finn says. He places both hands on my shoulders and shakes me playfully. In a silly voice, he tells me to relax to make me laugh. "It'll be fun," he adds.

Excitement oozes from Finn as he tells me how he's planned the day already and wants me to dress in an outfit that makes me feel comfortable. We agree to meet in the kitchen at 8:30 am. My jaw drops; that's half an hour. I usher him out of the room hastily and slam the door shut. I'm in and out of the shower within minutes and slip on the purple dress with the white flowers on it that I had spotted when I first arrived. A dainty necklace is laid out on the chest of drawers with a note from Ebony. She left it for me as a present for when I arrived, but it riddles me with guilt as I hold it now. I'm almost ready when I glance at the necklace again. I make a quick decision to wear it and run out the door.

Skipping down the stairs, I fly past Eli and he sings a joyful 'good morning'. I return the greeting, turning around briefly to wave and then head to the kitchen. Jesse and Ava are getting breakfast when I sit down beside them and grab a bowl.

"Nope!" Finn grins as he walks me out of the room, "We are going somewhere else."

I frown at him; why was he being so mysterious? It was fun and it reminded me of how things used to be. Excitement flutters in my stomach as we laugh and walk to the car.

"Hop in," he says, unlocking the doors.

We drive with the radio on full blast whilst I try to guess where he's taking me. The windy roads are unfamiliar to me and I'm losing patience as my stomach growls. Finn laughs, not giving anything away and tells me it won't be much longer. Another turn and we're on a main road which gives the destination away.

"Annie's Diner!" I exclaim.

Finn and I order two sausage and bacon sandwiches and some orange juice. We add some hash browns to the order and then drive around to pay.

"Thank you," I say for the fifth time.

"Rosebud, it's fine. You don't have to thank me anymore."

We park up and eat our breakfast. The view is stunning as we look over the sea, watching the sunlight glimmer on the waves. It's another blue sky and the humidity is rising, bringing the promise of a hot summer's day.

For a while, we talk about Eli and the family at Blakewood. Finn tells me of how he came across Eli and what he had done for him. His eyes lit up when he spoke about Ava and Jesse; he was grateful to them for their kindness.

"They aren't like any other family you'll meet, Rose," he says with a sparkle in his eye, "I know it'll take time, but these people really do care about you."

I'm nodding as I consider all the things that they had done for me since I arrived. They had given me so much for the little I had to offer. If I was honest, I didn't think I deserved such generosity.

"I guess this is just strange for me," I admit quietly.

"Why?" he asks.

"It's only ever been Mum, Dad and me..." I say, tearing corners off a napkin, "Now that they've gone, I feel lost. Everyone at Blakewood is so sweet and kind, willing to protect me at all costs. I... I just don't understand why..."

My lip quivers. I knew I need to talk about it and get it out of my head as it had been on my mind since the beast incident. Now that Jasper had turned up, almost beaten to death, I knew the extreme lengths Luke was going to for me. I also knew that people were willing to put their life at risk to protect me. And for what? I couldn't bear the weight of that on my shoulders. It was too much. I wasn't worth that kind of sacrifice.

"Oh Rosebud," he sighs and squeezes me tightly into his side, "You have never seen the beautiful, incredible, talented person you are. This Gift you have needs to be protected, no matter what that means." Finn smiles as he wipes the tears from my cheeks. "Look, I will always protect you and keep you safe. Even if we were two ordinary people with ordinary lives."

"Really?"

Finn cuddles me again, resting his chin on my head as he tries to soothe me. His heart is beating steadily in his chest, so I listen intently.

"Really," he whispers.

For a split second, I find myself inhaling his familiar scent and battling the butterflies that are being triggered. I really didn't want to complicate our friendship with unnecessary emotions. Mum's voice is repeating in my mind, reminding me that we can't force someone to love us back. Sometimes we had to take what we had and enjoy it for what it was. The right person would come along, one day.

"Right, what's next?" I ask as Finn pulls away.

"You're going to love it," he grins.

We continue driving for another half hour through Corden's town centre. Finn takes us along many familiar routes before pulling over and putting the hazard lights on. He jumps out and tells me to wait there. After a few minutes, he returns with two beach towels, a pale, yellow bucket, and a peculiar-shaped spade.

"Guess where we're going?" he grins.

Giggling, I take the stuff from him and sit them on my lap. Our excitement builds as we get closer towards the sea. The roads become sandier and less defined, crunching under the weight of the wheels. A secret, beautiful beach comes into view and a stir of emotions swirls inside.

A Rún…

Once the car is parked, Finn asks me to take our towels, bucket and spade down to the beach. The sea is out so we have plenty of places to sit when Finn appears with some food in a bag. We start talking about where we would be in ten years' time and it's just like old times. I had always wanted to live in a big city and have an apartment where I could walk to work. My dream would be to become a journalist or writer. Finn had always wanted to pursue his sports. He loved basketball and football, but his favourite sport was swimming. He wanted to come a professional swimmer and maybe enter some big-time competitions.

"Hey, do you think we'll ever get the chance to do these things now?" I ask, taking him by surprise.

We're laid down on the blankets, staring into the sky. I feel Finn sit up and cast his shadow over me. I join him, studying his expression carefully.

"Maybe," he shrugs.

There's a long reflective pause. I have no idea what the future holds, but neither did Finn. We were all working it out, together.

"Come on," Finn grins "You're going in that water, even if I'm throwing you in there."

Laughing mischievously, he takes my hand and pulls me up. I don't argue as he leads me to the shore.

CHAPTER
Fourteen

"Come on," Finn says, gesturing to the house, "Let's see who's about, maybe we can watch a film before my shift?"

I'm still beaming from the day as I glance at the clock; it's 10:00 pm.

"You couldn't even watch a quarter of the film," I laugh and Finn shrugs.

We'd had the best day at the beach. Between swimming and checking out the rock pools, we had laughed so much that our sides hurt. Finn spotted a rare yellowish-grey starfish with black spots in one of the pools which we'd never seen before, so I took pictures. We talked about everything we could possibly think of throughout the day. I felt like we had finally reconnected after a whirlwind of craziness.

Halfway through the day, Finn encouraged us to reminisce about Mum whilst we made a small rock pile as a memorial for her. A Rún was a special place for our family and so it felt right to remember her there.

"I'm sure Ebony won't mind it if I'm a little bit late..." Finn says with a wink.

Locking his car doors, we switch on our recharged phones after their batteries had run out from being used all afternoon. I watch as it springs to life and missed call notifications flash across my screen. Most of them were from Ebony.

"Finn? Rose?" a voice appears, "Thank goodness you're back!"

We look and see Ava standing at the door, but she appears distressed. I glance at Finn and he mirrors my confused expression.

"What's going on?" I ask.

A sea of eyes greets us with solemn despair as we enter the foyer. I search for Eli and realise he's absent which is unlike him. Ebony is kneeling next to a figure lying on the carpet surrounded by bloodied towels and gauze. Sol and Amber are close by, looking worse for wear and watching anxiously. Quickly, Ava kneels beside Ebony and encourages her to keep trying.

"Who is that?" I ask.

"It's Will," Ebony sobs, hearing my voice, "We...I... I can't... he..."

Clearly traumatised, she is blinded by her tears as she attempts to heal him again. Moments pass as I watch in horror whilst Will doesn't move. My heart sinks like a rock. It hits me that someone's life was going to be lost because of me. It was one of my worst fears coming to life. I stare transfixed on Will's body, limp and twisted, clearly broken from his encounter with Luke.

Eli could fix this.

I become agitated as I wonder where Eli was. It was unlike him to be absent like this, especially when we needed him. All I knew is that Will couldn't die tonight; I would never forgive myself for it. If Eli wasn't here to do it, then I had to try. Determination swirls around in my chest as I place my hands over Ebony's. She seems confused but I'm not looking at her. A strong voice inside tells me to focus so I close my eyes and plead for Will to live.

"We're losing him," Ebony whispers after nothing happens.

Running my hands along Will's sides, I feel light movements under his ribcage. His lungs are fighting to keep going but the battle is almost lost. I draw up all my courage and might, telling myself not to give up this time. I demand his body to listen as the minutes drag out and command him to live.

"Breathe, Will, breathe!"

There's a sudden gasp for air. Will's body convulses as he takes a deep breath in. His eyes open momentarily, and he mutters something. I lean in to hear more clearly, but he slips out of consciousness before I can catch it. My hands check his pulse and find that he is breathing evenly. There's not a hint of strain on his lungs and so I can let go knowing he was going to be okay.

"Woah…" Lily-Grace says, watching me in amazement.

"Oh," I mumble, startled.

Everyone's expressions are stunned. Relief washes over their faces like a much-needed rain, allowing them to relax again. Eli appears from behind an awestruck Jasper and offers a helping hand.

"What just happened?" Jasper asks once I'm stood up.

"I healed him, I think," I say in disbelief.

"You did more than that, there was light and sparks and…"

"Well done," Eli pats me on the back, "You did it."

"I… I… I didn't know what else to do," I stutter. "Where were you?"

"I was exactly where I needed to be, Rose," Eli beams. "Well done."

Next to me, I see Jasper nodding still a picture of awe and wonder. He looks at my hands, at me and then at Eli. Chuckling, Eli tells us to get some rest. My head hurts from the comedown of adrenaline. I watch as Ebony and Finn help Will upstairs to his room whilst Jesse embraces his eldest children. I ask if I can help with anything else before I go, but Eli shakes his head.

"You have done more than enough tonight, my dear," he says proudly.

Jasper gently pulls on my arm, leading me to the staircase, telling everyone 'goodnight'. As we ascend, my eyes become heavy and glazed over. We pause at the top as Jasper is still watching me with amazement and I don't know why.

"You literally lit up the room. It was like magic radiated out from your body into Will."

Shaking my head, I assure Jasper that it was probably nothing like that. He laughs and reminds me that he was the one watching as I had my eyes closed. It was true, but why on earth would I glow when I healed Will? Eli had never mentioned it before. It must've been a mistake.

"Right, you," Finn's voice appears from the darkened corridor, "I think someone needs to sleep."

He approaches us and fist-bumps Jasper. We're both a little taken aback by it, but Finn doesn't say anything. Instead, he wraps his arm around my neck and guides me towards my room. Jasper watches us leave and I glance back to wave goodnight. He waves back and then saunters along towards his own room.

"Okay," Finn says excitedly, "We will talk more in the morning but what you did was honestly *awesome*… I'm so proud of you."

A yawn escapes and the smile remains on my lips. I was happy to know I was finally figuring out my Gift. If anything, it made me want to talk to Ebony and find out if she had experienced light and sparks when healing. I wasn't even sure if I believed Jasper and yet the only person who was going to know would be Ebony.

As Finn pushes open the door, I notice Ebony is sitting waiting for me. Finn excuses himself before I can ask him to stay. I exhale slowly, figuring out how I'm going to start the conversation. I'm hoping she wants to talk things out, but her body language is defensive.

"Hey," I begin, "I was going to…"

"Everyone thinks it would be safer for you if I slept in your room. I don't want to talk about it," she sighs, "It's just easier for me to protect you if I'm here."

My heart sinks. She doesn't even look at me and her voice is toneless. There's no emotion or warmth. I feel like a burden rather than her friend.

"I'm sorry for what I said yesterday," my voice croaks, "I know you were trying to look out for me."

"Okay," Ebony shrugs.

Wounded by her cold reply, I try to meet her gaze and find some understanding, but she won't look up. I close the bedroom door behind me and suggest we get changed. Ebony chooses to change in the bathroom, so I stay in the bedroom. Once I'm dressed, I open the French doors to let some air in. It's got a bit too hot in here.

A dark, shaded figure catches my eye and I squint to see who it is. My heart is pounding in my ears as I can't work out who's there. I turn to tell Ebony but she's still in the bathroom getting changed. The crescent moon is casting shadows over the grounds, so I wait for the person to move into the light. Keeping myself hidden, I watch them wander around the grounds. Then, the silver light catches his face, revealing their identity.

Finn.

He waves, giving me a quick thumbs up and tells me to go to bed.

You don't have to tell me twice.

Waving goodbye, I turn and walk back into my room. I crawl into bed and wait for Ebony. I wrack my brain and replay our argument from yesterday. There's no reason she should still be so angry with me. I'd apologised and I thought she had accepted it.

What changed?

I'm somewhat irritated by her. She was being unfair. Surely, she could look at me when I apologised to her.

It's been a while since Ebony disappeared into the bathroom and I know she's purposely taking her time. I eventually get bored of waiting and roll over, closing my eyes. A few moments later, I hear her open the bathroom door and the click as it shuts behind her. I open one eye and watch as she climbs into the bed, pulling the covers on with her back turned to me. I stare at her head, hoping she'll turn over, but she doesn't.

Even though I don't want to, I apologise again. There's a long gap until I realise, she isn't going to respond.

"Well," I sigh, "Goodnight."

"Darling?" she says, taking her sunglasses off.

I smile and embrace Mum. We're on the beach again; our safe place. I'd dreamt of her every day since Finn took us to the beach for our day out. It somehow made me feel closer to her. This time, Mum and I have our jeans rolled up to our ankles. I can smell the salty air as the waves splash along the sandy dunes. The sun is warm on our faces as a gentle breeze tries to cool our tender skin. Mum sits down on a rock next to me to talk.

"How are you doing?" she asks, and I shrug.

I didn't know how I was doing anymore. I just felt numb; like my emotions had given up on me after such a whirlwind of events over the recent weeks.

"I understand," she says.

Mum pulls me into an embrace and holds me in the safety of her chest. She strokes my hair like she used to, bringing tears to my eyes. I could almost trick myself into believing it was real.

"Darling, you have to be strong. I know it isn't easy but being strong is what's going to get you through this," Mum says and pulls back so she can look me in my tear-filled eyes. "Oh, Rose…" she wipes the tears away with her thumbs and her lip wobbles. "Please, don't cry. I know I'm not there anymore, but I am so proud of you. You have achieved so much already, don't give up now."

She says it so clearly, I wonder if it really is a dream. Her skin tingles under my fingertips as I search for her love, but there's nothing there. Of course, I knew how she felt from memory. I just wished I could feel that reassuring spark again.

"Mum," I sigh, "I miss you so much."

This time, Mum tears up and nods slowly.

"I know darling…" she wipes the escapee tears away and tries to smile, "I guess we have to make do with what we get, hey?"

"Will I ever see you again?" I ask and her lips curl.

"Whenever you need me, I'll always be there…" she answers with such assurance, but my heart still drops. "Darling, I can't promise to meet you here forever, but I will never truly be gone." She takes my hand and places it on my heart. "I will always be with you, in here."

So many tears fall between us. I stare into her chocolate brown eyes, hoping that somehow, I could change what was coming. We take a slow, deep breath to calm ourselves. Vanilla perfume tickles my nose and I sense her starting to fade.

"Mum?" I look up at her.

"I love you," Mum says, knowing her time was limited with me.

"I know," I nod, "I love you too…"

"Don't be afraid, Rose," she says as her voice grows fainter with every word, "I will always be with you."

"I won't," I reply with a lump in my throat.

I couldn't bare saying goodbye again. Remembering my question, I try to keep her with me for a few more moments.

"Mum?" I ask and she looks at me, barely a ghost in front of my eyes, "What's heaven like?"

With a knowing smile, she opens her mouth to answer but disappears before she can say her reply. Tears stream down my cheeks as I fight to get her back. My eyes search the beach for a glimmer of her curly, wild hair. I get up and wander the sandy dunes, hoping she'll appear again. Desperation overcomes me as I run the length of the beach, pleading for a few more minutes with her.

Nothing. She's gone.

"No!" I cry out, "No!"

Burying my head into my pillow, I sob until my stomach hurts. I don't think I'm quite awake as a cool, light touch tries to bring me out of my trance. I'm trembling and try to fight away the hand. I want to see my mum again. I want to feel her again. I couldn't keep saying goodbye.

My pillow is drenched as I plead to dream again.

"Rose…"

Ebony's concerned expression greets me when I come to. She's turned on one of the lamps and is sat up, clearly worried. Her hand is wrapped around mine as she rubs it slowly. There's a knock at the door and we both look to see who it is. A kind, familiar face appears, and I feel relieved when she enters.

"Rose?" Her light, grey eyes are full of confusion as she sits beside me. "Sweetie, what's happened?" Ava asks, putting her arms around me.

Ready to burst, I sob as she rubs my back and rocks me gently in a calming embrace. She must have heard me screaming and come straight to me because she's still in her nightgown. Her thick, grey hair tickles my face as she soothes me. Ava reminded me so much of Mum. It only made me want to cry more. Her gentleness and love were overwhelming as she touched my skin. Eventually, I find some way of breathing evenly again.

"Now my love," she says, "What happened?"

As I begin to explain my dream, Ava nods and listens quietly. I glance at Ebony who remains incredibly stoic.

"I miss her…" I admit, and more tears roll down my face.

"Oh sweetheart…" Ava pulls me into her, holding me tighter than before. "You're bound to miss her. I'm so sorry," she sighs, "I'm so, so sorry."

I feel Ebony joins the embrace and notice her sniff a couple of times. I know the cold façade has fallen and we pull away. Ebony sits up and wipes her eyes as I do the same. We both apologise to Ava for soaking her shoulder with our tears.

"Oh stop," Ava gently scolds us, "Sometimes it's right to grieve with one another," she says, looking at us both.

There's a small exchange of smiles between Ebony and me. We don't say anything, but there's an understanding that is shared. We both missed Mum.

"Your mother is right though," Ava continues thoughtfully, "She is always with you, whether you believe it or not. It's not the same as having her with you, like you and I are right now," she gestures to us, "But she is still with you and all your memories together are always there…"

"But what if I forget something?"

"Oh sweetheart," Ava shakes her head, "You can never forget those memories. She is someone you can and will never, ever forget. Ever!"

"I won't let you either," Ebony reassures me.

Placing my hand over hers, I feel her sadness and love flow through me like the steam of a hot drink. We had both lost sight of what the other was going through. Our mourning time wasn't over. We had allowed other things to get in the way of our friendship when all we needed right now was each other.

I notice the morning light shining behind the curtains, but I don't want to let it in. I feel like I haven't slept at all. My eyes are heavy as though I could fall asleep again and Ebony feels tired, too. Ava's reassuring touch is helping, but it's not enough to rejuvenate this weary head.

"Will you be okay if I leave you be?" she asks, noticing our exhaustion and I nod.

Yawning, we thank her and settle back into bed. Ava tucks us in, kisses our cheeks and shuffles to the door. She whispers a 'goodnight' and assures us that we don't have to get up until we're ready. I tell her how grateful I am before curling up to sleep. This time I don't dream of anything at all.

THERE'S A GENTLE, PERSISTENT KNOCK AT THE DOOR.

I've been hiding away in my room for quite a while. Ebony left to do her shift a short while ago. I'd slept for half an hour or so before getting up and taking a shower. It was much needed after such a long night of tossing and turning. The hot water was relaxing on my skin. I chose some comfy clothes as I didn't plan to leave my room. I'd been reluctant to go anywhere all morning; I couldn't help mulling over my dream of Mum.

The knock continues to get louder and more insistent.

"Come in!" I say, unable to ignore it any longer.

Preparing myself, I pull out a smile and manage to wear it before the person enters the room.

"Hello?" I call again, but there's no reply.

There's another knock so I get up, muttering irritably to myself, and open the door. I stop suddenly as I recognise the two faces staring at me.

Oh no...

"Miss O'Donnell?" a voice says brightly, "How lovely to see you!"

My eyes land on a brunette lady I had seen only a handful of times at the hospital. It was Ida from Social Services. Embarrassed and tongue-tied, I look to Eli who is standing behind Ida and hope he can chip in and save me. My cheeks are flushing red when Eli decides to change the focus.

"As you can see, we make sure Rose has her own room," Eli begins, "We try to make it as comfortable as possible for each young person we look after."

Eli and I exchange glances and I tilt my head, hoping he would explain what was going on. I knew she was coming, but did I have to hang about and talk? Was I meant to talk to her about my experience of living here? Did she know about Luke and everything that was going on? Surely, she doesn't. If she starts asking, I wouldn't know what to say.

"However," Eli says meaningfully, "I believe Rose is going to be rather busy today so it will most likely be just the two of us to talk about arrangements for the coming weeks."

"Oh?" Ida frowns.

I think we're both surprised by my sudden busy schedule. She raises her eyebrow at me, and I look to Eli again for understanding.

"Rose has some chores to do."

Eli nods confidently, but I stare blankly at him; what on earth was he on about?

"We have the young people do chores in and around the grounds," Eli begins to explain to Ida who appears very interested, and quite impressed. "A couple of them are out there now waiting for Rose to join them," Eli pauses and nods to the stairs, "Run along now, my dear. They will be waiting…"

Managing to mutter some kind of agreement, I grab my shoes and slip past both of them. I run down the stairs quickly. Once I've made it to the bottom, my stomach growls. I decide to grab something to eat before going to find whoever was waiting for me. I'm assuming they will have more answers.

Nobody is in the kitchen, so I freely take what I fancy and grab a bottled water. Footsteps are heading down the stairs so I dart across to the playroom. The sun is bright as I slip out the back door and squint to see who I could find. Guessing who was waiting for me was hopeless so I make an executive decision to walk towards the stables. It was the main post for anyone who was doing lookout duty. Hopefully, someone would still be there.

"Rosebud!" Finn's voice calls from behind, taking me by surprise.

I spin around to see him bouncing towards me with Ebony close behind.

"Eli said you would come eventually," he smiles before glancing over his shoulder.

"Good morning sleepyhead," Ebony teases.

There's a short pause as we look at each other. She seems warm towards me today and I hope that means we were okay. Maybe all the discomfort was over between us. At least that's what I had hoped for, life was too short. Mum was a reminder of that.

"I'm sorry," Ebony says, catching me off-guard "There's so much going on, and I don't want to fall out now."

Embracing her, I tell her I feel the same. We giggle and squeeze each other tightly before pulling away. Finn is looking less than impressed.

"Are you two finished?"

"Shut up," Ebony sasses him, "Just because she's showing me love, doesn't mean she doesn't love you."

"Yeah, true… but just remember that I knew her before you did," Finn retorts with a cheeky grin.

It looks like they're being cute and playful, but I can see this turning into a real argument soon.

"Yes, but I know her more than you do…" Ebony retorts.

Finn scoffs, but I know he's really wondering if it's true. I hurry to defuse the situation before it gets ugly.

"Now, now," I say light-heartedly, and they both soften their expressions, "You know I will never choose between you, so let's just agree that I love you both equally…" I look at them and then add as a joke, "But points will go to the one who can tell me why Eli sent me out here…"

"Well," they both talk over one another.

They stop and try again, repeatedly cutting the other off. Ebony uses her dominance to stare Finn into submission before explaining what was going on.

"Eli wanted us to continue your training," she says and points towards the barn.

"Oh goody," I sigh; that was *not* what I had hoped to do today. In fact, I was avoiding it.

"Come on grumpy," Finn teases, "After what you did yesterday, this will be easy."

"Okay…"

Looking between them, I see a wicked glint in their eye which makes me nervous. I ask them what's going on and Finn looks to Ebony who laughs and shrugs.

"You'll see…"

CHAPTER
Fifteen

pparently, Eli had decided I was ready to learn a new type of skill; the art of knife combat. Although these knives had a particular name, they were called the Mira blades. Each knife had a short, pointed, steel blade with a black, textured hilt. Small, silver rivets encircle the blade's handle to allow a good grip. Moving it between each hand, the blade catches the sunlight through a skylight. The reflection's glare is almost blinding as I start seeing dark spots.

"Don't do that," Ebony says, lowering my hand that's holding the Mira.

Somehow, Finn and Ebony manage to show me how to use it without getting into an argument. They combat with their own blades, demonstrating the ways in which to strike first. Finn tells me to fight smartly rather than rushing in quickly as waiting created opportunity. Ebony is quick and light on her feet, dancing around Finn. This forces him to focus on his positioning and his blade lowers. Ebony takes the opportunity, but it's a trap. Finn swings his arm up and over, cutting the air right in front of her nose. Gasping, she stops and her confidence crumbles.

"Gotcha," Finn beams.

"Lucky shot," Ebony tuts with squinted eyes.

Finn tells me to hold my blade up and begins to walk me slowly through the combat. It doesn't take long for me to learn all the handy little techniques for fighting and protection. The blade barely misses the skin as Finn jerks towards Ebony. She smiles and flutters her eyes before pushing back, knocking the Mira from his hand.

"Ha!"

Ebony laughs triumphantly as Finn falls to his knees in front of her. The blade bounces on the ground beside him and glints in the light. Spots appear again as I stare and it's slightly intoxicating.

"You feel the pull right?" Finn asks when he follows my gaze, "The blade protects you by drawing your opponent in. The glare should stun and distract long enough for you to make your move."

"Oh," I nod, now staring at the blade in my own hand, "Cool!"

We continue to practice our skills, using our Miras as well as hand-to-hand combat. Finn and Ebony team up on me and I try to fight them off, using all they had taught me. All my effort seems lost on them as they bring in new tricks and attacks, testing me. They repeat the training over and over again until there's sweat dripping down our faces. Finn calls time and we collapse, panting on the mats. They hand me a bottle of water and I down it in one go.

"Easy there, kiddo," Ebony teases.

Once we've recovered, I insist I go back to my room to have a thorough shower. Sweat was getting into every crevice, and I wanted to cool down properly. It was too hot to be working this hard. Finn agreed. He and Ebony were on watch again anyway, so they needed to go.

"Are you okay walking back on your own?" Ebony asks.

"Absolutely, I have this," I reply, "Thanks again."

Waving the Mira knife around, I realise I have nowhere to put it. Finn hands me a little, leather scabbard to keep it in and suggests I leave it somewhere safe in my room.

"Do you really trust me with this?" I ask.

"Maybe we should…" Ebony says pretending to take the knife back.

Rolling my eyes at her, I playfully snatch the knife from her and state how lucky she is that I can handle myself. This provokes sass from Ebony about her job as my protector before we both burst into cackles of laughter. I say goodbye to them and head back, remembering that Ida from Social Services is there. I nervously peer up the stairs and listen for Ida and Eli. Not a sound.

"They've gone sweetheart," a voice confirms.

Recognising the gentle tone, I follow the voice into the kitchen and see Ava sitting there, reading. She's wearing glasses on the end of her nose and peering down to read a book on a stand. There's a mug of steaming coffee between her hands that she raises to her lips for a sip. I realise she's looking at a recipe as I sit beside her. She instantly looks up, beaming.

"How are you, Rose?"

I wipe off the sweat on my brow and explain what I've been doing. Ava appears impressed as she takes another sip of coffee and removes her glasses. Intuitively she gets up and begins making me a drink and snack. I thank her as she places a glass of juice in front of me with some ice and a plate of biscuits. Sitting back down, Ava asks about how I slept after she came in last night. I tell her about the heaviness I've felt all morning, niggling in the back of my mind.

"You're mourning her," Ava says softly, "It will take time."

I nod and explain how the training had taken my mind off it. I also probe to see if she saw Social Services whilst I was with Finn and Ebony. She laughs at this and shakes her head, telling me that Eli had kept them in his office – apparently a second one to his not-so-secret study – for most of the day. They left shortly after lunchtime.

"Well, I'm going to take a shower because I *stank!*" I giggle, beaming.

"Okay, sweetie," Ava chuckles, "How about I make you something for when you get out?"

"Perfect!" I say, already leaving, "Thank you!"

"Well..." I sigh as we watch the sunset, "Isn't that beautiful..."

Deep pinks, reds and oranges paint the sky as the sun sinks behind the Great Hills of Corden. It's weird to see them from here, but it's becoming a regular view on duty. There's a faint neigh and we both look towards the barn. Another more distressing sound follows, and Finn tells me to wait where I am whilst he checks it out. I nod and keep an eye out for visual disturbances. I glance at Finn as he disappears into the building. There's a small wait until he reappears, popping his head over the fence.

"It was a pigeon..." he laughs, returning to me.

If anything, we've learned how wussy the horses are this evening. Finn says it's because they've been disturbed before, a couple of nights ago. It wasn't anything to worry about, but the horses had been tense ever since.

"Do you think Will's going wake up soon?" I ask.

My mind lingers on Will's current comatose state. He hadn't been conscious for the last few days. It was likely that he would wake up soon, but something about his injuries was making the healing process longer than expected. Eli had visited him every day to lay his healing hands and see if he could ease the pain, and so had Ebony and I. We all wanted him to wake up, but Eli more than anyone seemed disturbed by the prolonging of his recovery.

"Yeah," Finn says, "It won't be long, I'm sure."

"Really?" I ask, checking to see if he was being genuine.

Finn meets my gaze and smiles, "Of course, Will is strong. He is probably having too much fun not doing anything. When he's ready, I'm sure he'll awake."

We stand in a comfortable silence as we continue our watch. I had been asked to stay with Finn as Ava and Jesse had taken the family out for the evening. Ebony was resting, Eli was writing, and Jasper was... well I had no idea.

As I think of Jasper, I remember what he said about Luke and his hands the night he arrived at Blakewood. Something had gone wrong, though he didn't specify what, and it had taken his Gifts away. Apparently, it was some kind of chemical experimentation that Jasper didn't really want to be a part of. His eyes were sullen and desolate as he spoke about the painful experience. Every word seemed laced with anger at the betrayal of his friends.

If I were honest, I wanted to tell him how relieved I was that he couldn't hurt any of us, but that seemed a bit insensitive. Instead, I listened without interruption, and I knew he appreciated it. For a moment, it felt like nothing had changed between us and we could pick up where we left off.

"What're you thinking about?" Finn's voice draws me away from my thoughts.

"Oh nothing," I shrug.

"Come on," Finn begs, "You can't smile like that and then tell me it's nothing."

Somehow his comment forms fear in the pit of my stomach. I think I almost feel guilty that Jasper is making me happy, stirring up all kinds of feelings again. Ebony had repeatedly told me that he was not to be trusted, or at least was to be held at arm's length. It wasn't like I was letting him in as such, but his confident smile did linger in the back of my mind.

"You know what?" I say, "I think I'm going to head inside. I can ask Ebony to come out, she's already had a three-hour nap."

A confused Finn grabs my hand and scrutinizes my expression, trying to figure out what he had done wrong. The truth is, he hasn't. I was uncomfortable in my own skin. Torn between forcing away feelings that came naturally and feeding the ones I secretly enjoyed, there was a conflict of interest.

Jasper made me feel special and understood like I wasn't alone in my uncertainty anymore. The more we spoke, the more I realised that we weren't as different as I had once thought. I needed that reassurance in the chaos that surrounded us.

"You didn't say anything bad, Finn," I reassure him, "Honestly, I'm tired and could do with having some time out. I'm sorry…"

"Oh," Finn says, straightening up with a smile, "Clearly someone is a lightweight."

"Oi!" I protest.

Someone clears their throat loudly, forcing us to look around. Sol and Amber are approaching us with beaming faces. They clearly have found the serotonin boost they so badly needed. Colour had returned to their paling cheeks and their eyes finally twinkled again. They were ready for duty.

"Go on," Amber nods, "We've got this!"

Finn and I discuss the rest of the watch duties as we get back to the house. I'm not on watch until tomorrow and decide to take the opportunity to rest up. We go our separate ways as Finn states he's hungry again. Giggling, I tease him about not eating too much. I can still hear him laughing when I notice a hunched-over figure sitting on one of the steps on the staircase.

"They've used Melolin on Will," Jasper says quietly and points to his chin, "They used it on me and that's why it never fully healed."

"Who?"

"Luke…"

Sitting beside him, I place a hand on Jasper's arm to sense his emotions. There's not a lot I can pick up, so I try to read his face, looking for clues.

"Why didn't you say anything before?" I ask.

"I… I wasn't sure," Jasper replies, "I had hoped that maybe it wasn't true."

Finally, he looks at me and exhales for a long time. He begins to explain the strange, translucent liquid that has the ability to scar the Gifted. The more Jasper went on, the more I was concerned.

"Come with me," I say, "Maybe we can help."

To Jasper's surprise, I grab his hand and we march up the stairs to Will's room. We find Will laying peacefully in his bed with his head propped up slightly. Ava is titivating the room to make sure he was comfortable. She looks at us, her eyes noticing our interlocked hands, and then back to me. I drop Jasper's hand and ask how he's doing. Her head lowers as she tells me nothing has changed and that we can only keep trying. Agreeing, I say that I want to try again and explain Jasper's theory. This seems to worry Ava, but she doesn't stop me and says she'll come back later when we've finished.

"Let me know if anything changes," Ava says softly.

"We will," Jasper replies with a warm smile.

Clearing my mind, I focus on Will and his confident, mature nature as he walks through the halls of Blakewood. His strong presence is brought to life in my mind and I latch on, searching his body for signs of residual Melolin. There's an odd taste in my mouth, yet I find nothing. His body is completely clear of pain. I collapse into the chair frustrated by the agonising need to help him.

"You tried," Jasper says in a frail attempt to comfort me.

"It's not enough," I sigh, "Why can't I do it?"

"Maybe I'm wrong, Rose…"

Will's expression is peaceful, and the swelling had gone from around his eyes. Yet, his hands were curled in tight fists. I touch him again and feel a cold shock of fear scurry up my arm. It's unexpected and I let go, unable to control my reaction. I take a deep breath and place a hand on his, pushing soothing emotions out and denying the fear to touch my skin again. It works momentarily until Will gasps for air. He opens his eyes and I lean over him, hoping we can talk. Instead, he sinks back down and fades away, his coma overtaking him once more.

"I think we should go," Jasper says after a long pause.

Placing a hand on my shoulder, he rubs it gently and squeezes. I look up at him and then back to Will. It mattered that I tried. I wasn't ready to give up until it was certain that I had done everything I could. It was the least I owed him.

"Okay," Jasper nods, "Then I will stay."

"Actually," I turn to him, "I think I need to do this alone."

Jasper nods, understandingly, and walks out. I turn my focus to Will who is breathing steadily and watch his hands uncurl. I take hold of one and feel the fear again, but immediately I rebuke it. There was no place for fear here.

"Don't worry," I whisper to Will, "We are going to bring you back to us."

"Rose?"

A gentle, soothing voice pulls me from my sleep. I try to lift my head, but my neck is stiff and aching. There's giggling as I rub the soreness away.

"That's what happens when you fall asleep sitting up," the voice sasses softly, "How is he?"

Shrugging, I lay a hand on Will's and try to feel his emotions. They're calm, serene even, but there's no sign of him waking. I had tried all night and yet, nothing. It was hard not to feel disappointed with myself.

"Don't be stupid," Ebony scolds me, "You're doing everything you can."

"Yes but," I argue.

"Yes but? You need to rest too. You can try again tomorrow."

Though Ebony was right, I didn't want to leave. I wanted to keep trying as it increased my belief that something would change. I'd never truly thought I could do it until now. I couldn't understand why it wasn't changing anything.

Ebony grabs both my hands and pulls my reluctant self up from the chair. She links arms with me and walks us out of the room, insisting that I let it go. I shrug again and rest my head on her shoulder. She guides me to my room and points to the bed. I stifle a laugh and begrudgingly climb in, pretending to be extra dramatic. Ebony teases me again and tells me to hurry up or she will be forced to sit on me.

"Like that would do anything…" I murmur as sleep begins to seep in.

The door closes shortly after and the darkness behind my eyelids takes over.

Over the next couple of nights, odd dreams fill my sleep replacing the comforting ones of Mum. They all seem to be painted with a red, smoky sky and flashes of lightning. I can't hear a lot, but everyone I see appears to be trying to tell me something. As the dreams speed up, it gets more repetitive until one face finally overcomes them all, dispersing every shadow of darkness and feelings of impending doom. Sharp like a razor, his confident gaze pierces through with light that fills every crevice of my mind.

Jasper.

"Yes?" a voice interrupts the dream.

My eyes fly open, and I'm met with two juniper eyes. He seems almost as surprised as I am to see him peering around my door. My shock is replaced with a smile as relief floods through me when I realise it's not a dream anymore.

"You said my name…"

"I did?" I ask, feeling embarrassed.

Day by day, we had been getting closer and everyone was seeing it. The walls that had been put up were tumbling down as the boys began to banter with him and the girls tolerated his cheeky demeanour. He was settling in and proving his loyalty to Eli and to Blakewood, truly trying to show that he had changed. It had resolved the confusion in my heart and now I knew where it lay.

"You did," he says, but there's a teasing smirk on his lips. "So, this is the abode… hmmm…"

"Yeah? I thought you could see it in your visions."

Shaking his head, he shrugs and sighs before explaining the complexities of a vision. It seemed that when you vision, you can only see the person and not their surroundings. If you aren't well connected, then what you see can be reduced even more. However, if you have a strong connection, you can pretty much see and feel everything they do.

"So how do you ensure a strong connection?"

Jasper starts pacing as if to decide whether he should tell me. I'm not sure if it's making him uncomfortable or that he doesn't really know himself.

"Emotional connections are what the visions are based on," he pauses, "It can't just be anyone. Like for you and I- uh…"

Hesitating, Jasper decided not to continue the sentence he started. His eyes divert to something else as he continues pacing more rapidly.

"Oh, I see…" I mutter.

"Yep," Jasper says with a pop of his lips. "Any-who…"

He clicks his fingers together as though to fill the silence that has grown between us. His eyes are curiously searching the room, possibly for something to say.

"Are you okay?"

"Our rooms are identical. Except that balcony…" he says, standing up to open the French doors. "Wow!"

The cool, refreshing breeze is welcome on my dampened, sweaty skin. With all these intense dreams and the summer's humidity, I was probably losing more water than any normal human should.

"We should go for a walk," Jasper announces enthusiastically.

"We should?" I quiz.

"Yep, it would be good for you," he nods, "Plus, it's either that or more training."

Groaning, I throw my head into my duvet and shake it vigorously. There was nothing appealing about training. My body still ached, and the endless repetition was more than I could handle today.

"Okay, walk it is."

It's another scorching summer's day despite the yellow-tinged grey that hides the sun. Wildlife is thriving as bees hover over the technicolour flowerbeds collecting pollen. A swallow dives above our heads and chirps before disappearing into one of the gaps in the Manor's roof tiles.

"What a glorious day!" Jasper sings.

Glancing at the sky, I wonder if he's even noticed that rain was coming. Whatever had come over him, it was adorable, and I wanted to understand what had brought it on. His excitement was becoming infectious.

"What is with you today?" I probe, giggling.

We're nearing the barn and the horses' whinnies become more prominent. Amber and Sol are on duty and wave at us as Jasper tells Sol that they should spar later. They agree and we continue our walk. There had been no movement on the grounds for almost 48 hours which allowed us to believe that Luke may have given up. It seemed almost too good to be true.

"I don't know," Jasper says finally.

"It's kind of scary," I tease.

Pausing, Jasper stands by the barn door and thinks about what I've said. There's a bit of hurt in his eyes but it's willed away by another self-assured smile.

"I'm finally able to be alone with you," he says, tucking some loose hair behind my ear. "I feel like they finally accept me for me, you know?"

"Yeah," I agree, "I get it."

"I've missed you," Jasper whispers, drawing my attention back to him.

My cheeks warm as his words, bringing out the pink in them. I wonder if he knew that I felt the same as my eyes search his. I'm drawn to him; his lost boy persona and the unshakeable idea that we needed each other.

"Rose... I- "

Cut off by the rumbling of thunder close by, Jasper and I look up into the heavens before the rain pours down. Fast, large drop-lets pound our clothes and attempt to drench us, stinging our skin ever so slightly. Jasper grabs my hand and pulls me into the barn instinctively, laughing breathily.

"I was enjoying that," I joke.

Jasper gives me a look as though to say 'really' and then shakes his head. We listen to the raindrops clattering against the tin roof above us. It reminded me of times I went camping with my family and we would wait for the rain to pass by.

"I guess we're stuck here then," Jasper smirks, clearly pleased by this.

He saunters across the length of the barn, his hands on his hips before swivelling around. The word 'okay' repeats itself on his lips until an idea strikes. Focused eyes glow as they lock onto mine. His footsteps remain slow, intentional, as he reapproaches and holding out his hand.

"Um, yes?"

"Phone please," he replies.

"What for?" I ask, confused.

"Training..."

Frowning, I hand him my phone and can't hide my disappointment. Did he just trick me into doing even more training?

Gentle strums of a guitar crescendo into the open air of the barn. A male's voice begins to sing a low, soft melody and I find myself swaying subconsciously to the rhythm. I recognise the artist and realise what Jasper is doing once he places the phone on a stack of hay. I'm desperately trying to hide the smile as I pretend to not understand his intentions.

"Oh, come on, just take the damn hand," Jasper laughs.

"Fine," I feign a grumble, slapping our palms together.

With one firm pull, Jasper closes the space between us and starts to sway side to side. He twirls me around a few times, making me giggle, before leaning his head on mine. We dance quietly, both thinking about separate things as our hearts settle into a steady beat. Though I can't read Jasper's emotions clearly, I'm convinced there is a faint tingle of loving warmth radiating from his skin.

"So... this is training," I tease, pretending to be unimpressed.

"Yeah," Jasper agrees with a playful tone, "This is the best training you've been to so far, right?"

"I don't know," I shrug, "I've had better..."

Jasper's chest jolts as he chuckles, enjoying our flirtatious back and forth. The smile that spreads across my face is wider than my cheeks can handle. I'm staring into his eyes and wondering if there was any way he would understand. I know this is what I wanted so I don't hesitate as my lips find his.

Melting into our kiss, Jasper pulls me to his chest and cups my face in his hands. My fingers find their way to his waist and hold on, relieved that he doesn't push me away. The distant alarm bells in my head aren't enough to stop me when I know it feels this good. Ebony would be fuming if she saw this, in fact, everyone would. Yet, something about this moment was gratifying knowing I wanted it just as much as he did.

"Rose... I..."

Suddenly, Jasper stops and backs away. His distance makes it cold after the warmth that he had just given me. I'm mortified and desperately think of a way to salvage the situation whilst fighting the strong urge to cry. The embarrassment colours my cheeks red as the quiet grows more uncomfortable by the second. I don't understand what's happened, but Jasper won't look at me.

"I'm sorry..." I whisper.

"No, it's... it's not you, it's..." he exhales heavily, "It's complicated, you see. I just can't... with you. I'm sorry."

Maybe it was my way to counteract my embarrassment, but anger raged in my chest. After the way he looked at me, the way he danced and held me. What the heck was he playing at? I thought he wanted this. I thought he wanted me.

"I do..." Jasper says after I explode. "It's hard to put it into words. I don't think you'd like the answer."

"Try me," I challenge him.

Another empty space as I wait for an answer. Jasper is still staring at the wall behind me, unable to give me what I was searching for. I don't understand, but I know I'm not going to stand there and wait for him. This was humiliating enough as it is. I couldn't bear the tension as well as the heat. I turn to leave, ignoring the fact the rain hadn't stopped. Angrily, I push the barn door open and am greeted with a rush of cool air.

"Rose wait!" Jasper calls after me.

"No!" I shout.

There's no time for a response as I run through the grounds. Sol and Amber have been replaced by Ebony and Finn whilst we were in the barn. They are holding umbrellas and watching us with confusion. A look is exchanged before they come running to stop me in my tracks. They're barely able to get answers when Jasper arrives behind me.

"What did he do?" Ebony asks, already enraged by the tears streaming down my face.

"He didn't," I reply.

"I didn't do anything," Jasper repeats.

Rain trickles off my brow and blurs my vision. I angrily wipe it away with a soaked sleeve and sigh. Ebony glares at Jasper as she rubs my back, telling me it's okay. Her expression doesn't change when she asks me again what's happened. Behind us, Finn has put himself as a barrier between Jasper and me. He's asking him if he knew what was wrong and getting nowhere.

"Let's get you back to the house," Ebony insists with her arm already wrapped around my shoulders. "You can tell me when you're inside."

"Thank you," I whisper shakily.

"We need to talk, Rose," Jasper says, "Please?"

"No," Finn says firmly, pressing his palm into Jasper's chest, "She needs some space. Let her go, man."

"It's not like that," Jasper sighs, "Come on, look..."

Their voices fade away as Ebony guides me back to the Manor under the protection of her umbrella. Unfortunately, I was already dripping wet and shivering. When we get to my room, Ebony quickly grabs a towel to wrap around me. She uses another to rub my hair and remove some of the water. Thankfully, she doesn't ask questions. Once I'm settled in bed and she's perched beside me, her probing stare is urging me to confess.

"I did something stupid..." I say as my voice breaks, full of regret and hurt.

"Oh Rose," Ebony sighs, "Whatever it is, I'm sure I've done worse. Trust me."

Nervously, I lean back into my pillows wondering if I should tell her. I knew she would be upset with me, but right now I wanted to process what had happened. Ebony wasn't his biggest fan, but she said she would always be there no matter what. This had to come out one way or another.

"I..." I pause and take a deep breath in, "I sort of... kissed him."

It's as though Ebony is frozen still as she stares vacantly into my eyes. She blinks a couple of times whilst processing the disclosure and considers a helpful response. I'm almost certain the bubbling feeling on her palms is annoyance, but she chooses not to show it.

"Okay," she says, laughing nervously, "And wh-how did that happen?"

"I don't know," I whine repeatedly.

"I mean, who kissed who first?"

Ashamed, I'm almost too embarrassed to admit it was me. She was already giving me her infamous tight-lipped smile which meant only one thing; she wanted to shout at me for being so stupid. So would I, if I were to be completely honest. Did I want it? Yes. Should I have done it? No.

"Look," Ebony says softly, tucking me in, "It doesn't matter now. We will figure this out when I'm off my shift. Right now, I can only imagine what the conversation is between Finn and Jasper. You know he won't hesitate to beat the living daylights out of him..."

Her attempt to make me laugh falls flat as a pang of guilt appears when I think of them. It was true, Finn was incredibly protective over me. He liked Jasper and approved of him early on, but if he ever hurt me... well, all is fair in love and war, right? Jasper didn't stand a chance.

"See you later," I say to Ebony as she gets up to leave.

Telling me it's going to be okay she pauses before closing the door behind her. I settle into the bed and rest my head on the headboard. It was safe to say that I had well and truly humiliated myself today. I wished the world would swallow me up, but that would be too easy. Instead, I decide to read and be alone, hiding from everyone who would judge me.

A copy of an old, untitled book sits in the drawer beside me, untouched from the day I moved in. I had noticed it momentarily before checking out all the other drawers and cupboards. It seems to be a children's book, so I open it up and begin. Nestling down, I get comfortable, being drawn into the fantastical world of a girl called Anna. It had a familiarity to it that brought peace as I read through the pages. Unsurprisingly, it doesn't take long for me to drift off.

My dreams come alive as I sink deeper into my slumber. Flashes of light cast shadows on the figures in my mind. Something scratches my leg and I flinch. It feels real, but the heaviness in my head tells me I'm still sleeping. Wind cools my cheeks and I hear a white noise as I fall unexpectedly. It was as if someone had been carrying me and slipped. Something smells rich and earthy on my face as dewy moisture cushions my body.

Opening my eyes, I see soil and leaves on a grassy bed. They're soggy from the rain which explains why my clothes feel damp. I rub the dirt between my fingers, working out if it's still a dream. I try to call for help, but my voice is croaky and dry. Everything is blurred until a figure appears before me. His apologetic tone grows familiar and I freeze.

"What are you doing?"

"Please trust me," he begs.

Picking me up again, his voice is soothing as it sends me back to sleep. I try to fight it, but I realise he's using his power, rendering me weak. The reflection of his juniper eyes burns through the dreamy haze as I realise the betrayal was his.

Jasper.

Printed in Great Britain
by Amazon